Zoella ♡

Praise for the *New York Times* bestseller GIRL ONLINE

"Sugg's obvious understanding of the complexities and pit-falls of the online world, coupled with her sensitivity to adolescence, make for a compelling and satisfying coming-of-age tale in the digital age."

—*Booklist*

"*Girl Online* left us wishing adorkable, quirky Penny was our BFF (especially if the package included her amazing best friend Elliot!) because who doesn't love a sweet, adventure-filled NYC love story? No one, that's who! A must-read for fans of *Dash & Lily's Book of Dares*, *Invisibility*, and *Suite Scarlett*."

—*Justine Magazine*

"The charm of *Girl Online* is the message that growing up doesn't have to mean leaving childish stuff behind. The book is sugary as a frosted cupcake, but so is Zoella and six million YouTube subscribers love her that way."

—*The Telegraph*

"Fun, relatable, and in some places heart-wrenching, this has Sugg's name written all over it, and I am very much looking forward to the second book."

—*The Mile Long Bookshelf*

Books by Zoe Sugg

GIRL ONLINE

GIRL ONLINE: ON TOUR

Girl Online

ON TOUR

ZOE SUGG

Keywords

PRESS

—

ATRIA

NEW YORK   LONDON   TORONTO   SYDNEY   NEW DELHI

An Imprint of Simon & Schuster, Inc.
1230 Avenue of the Americas
New York, NY 10020

First Keywords Press/ Atria Books hardcover edition October 2015

Keywords Press / Atria Books and colophon are trademarks of Simon & Schuster, Inc.

For information about special discounts for bulk purchases, please contact Simon & Schuster Special Sales at 1-866-506-1949 or business@simonandschuster.com.

The Simon & Schuster Speakers Bureau can bring authors to your live event. For more information or to book an event contact the Simon & Schuster Speakers Bureau at 1-866-248-3049 or visit our website at www.simonspeakers.com.

Manufactured in the United States of America

10 9 8 7 6 5 4 3 2 1

Library of Congress Cataloging-in-Publication Data has been applied for.

ISBN 978-1-5011-0033-8
ISBN 978-1-5011-0035-2 (ebook)

For the people who make this possible
and cheer me on from the sidelines.
I am eternally grateful.

20 June

How to Survive a Long-distance Relationship When Your Boyfriend is a Super-hot Rock God

1. Download Skype, WhatsApp, Snapchat, and basically every communication app you can find. Stay up all night in your panda onesie, chatting with your boyfriend until your eyelids start twitching and you absolutely have to go to sleep.

2. Whenever you wake up and miss him, listen to *Autumn Girl* on repeat.

3. Set up an app on your phone that tells you the time wherever he is so that you don't accidentally wake him at 3 a.m. for a chat. (I've done this *maybe* ten times already!)

4. Buy a calendar and mark down the number of days until you see him again (which, by the way, is now only FIVE DAYS AWAY).

5. Somehow win the lottery so you can quit school and fly to wherever he is and you don't have to be apart for this long ever again.

6. Whatever you do, do NOT go online and watch videos of super-stunning pop star Leah Brown as she dips and twerks around said boyfriend in front of millions of screaming fans.

7. And do NOT search his name so you can see all the cool stuff he's doing while you're studying for your exams.

My lovely readers, even if one day I feel like I could publish this blog in a non-private way, I never will.

Because, I know—I'm not allowed to admit to feeling insecure and less than pretty and more-than-a-little jealous when my boyfriend is the sweetest guy in the world and has given me no reason to feel this way, right?

Tell me this feeling gets better. I don't know how I'm going to survive.

Girl Offline . . . never going online xxx

Chapter One

Five days later

It should officially be illegal for exam rooms to have a view of the sea.

How is it fair that we're stuck inside, fingers cramping from gripping a pen for two hours straight, while outside the light is dancing on the waves and it looks so bright and comforting? How am I supposed to remember who King Henry VIII's fourth wife was when the birds are singing and I swear I can hear the happy, jaunty tune of an ice-cream van nearby?

I shake my head, dispelling the vision of a deliciously soft ice-cream cone with a cheeky Flake sticking out of it, and instead try to summon up a direct link into my best friend Elliot's brain. He won't be having much trouble remembering any of these facts and figures in his history exam. I gave him the nickname Wiki, because his brain seems to contain as much knowledge as Wikipedia, whereas my revision notes disappear from my memory as fast as a Snapchat.

I sigh and try to concentrate on the exam question, but

the words swim in front of my eyes and I can't make sense of my own messy scrawl. I hope whoever has to mark it has better luck.

Choosing to take history for GCSE was never a good idea. At the time, I just picked based on what everyone else seemed to be doing. The only subject I knew I definitely had to take was photography. The truth is I have no idea what I want to be when I leave school.

"OK, everyone, pens down," says the examiner at the front of the room.

My mouth instantly goes dry. I don't know how long I've been daydreaming for, but I know that I haven't finished answering all the questions. These exams determine what subjects I'll take next year and I've already mucked it up. My palms feel slick with sweat, and I can't hear the birds outside singing anymore. All I can hear is the squawk of seagulls. It sounds like they're chanting "Fail, fail, fail" in my ear. My stomach turns, and I feel like I might be a bit sick.

"Penny, are you coming?" I look up, and my friend and classmate Kira is waiting by my desk. The examiner has already snatched my paper and I've barely noticed.

"Yeah, just a second." I grab my bag and slide out of my chair.

And then, as I stand up, a wave of relief takes over the nausea. No matter what the result, that's it: my final exam. I'm finished with school for the year!

I have a stupid grin on my face as I high-five Kira. I feel closer to my classmates—and especially the twins, Kira and Amara—than I have in my entire time at this school. They gathered round me in the aftermath of the drama at the beginning of the year—a solid wall of friendship against the breaking tidal wave of news. The media went into a frenzy when they found out I was dating rock star Noah Flynn, and then they discovered my blog; they unearthed private details of my life and labelled me a homewrecker, since Noah was supposedly in a relationship with mega pop star Leah Brown. It was the worst few days of my life, but my friends helped me to weather the storm. And, when it was all over, the drama had brought us together.

As we spill out into the hallway, Kira says, "Celebratory burgers at GBK? We're all going there before we head to the concert. You must be so excited to see Noah again."

A familiar flutter rises in my stomach. I'm excited—of course I am—but I'm nervous too. I haven't seen Noah since the Easter holidays, when he spent my sixteenth birthday with me. Now we're about to spend two weeks in each other's company. And even though that's the only thing I want— and the only thing I can think about—I can't help wondering whether it will be the same.

"I'll catch you at the restaurant," I say. "I just have to pick a few things up from Miss Mills's office and then head home to change."

Kira squeezes my arm. "Oh god, I have to figure out what to wear too!"

I smile weakly as she rushes off, but the elation of finishing my exams has given way to a new set of nerves. The will-my-boyfriend-still-like-me kind. I know I should feel more confident that Noah likes me just the way I am, but when your first boyfriend is currently one of the most famous new musicians on the planet, that's easier said than done.

The hallways are almost deserted and the only sound is the squeak of my Converse trainers on the linoleum floor. I can't believe this is my last catch-up with my photography teacher, Miss Mills. It feels like she's been there for me a lot this year—she's probably the only person I've really opened up to about what went on last Christmas and New Year, other than my parents. Even with Elliot I sometimes hold things back. Having a set of impartial ears was something I never wanted—but also never knew I needed.

It didn't help that I had a panic attack in the small cupboard Miss Mills converted into a makeshift darkroom. It was only a couple of weeks after the news "broke" online about Noah and me. Normally I find the darkroom soothing, but whether it was the fumes or the enclosed space—or the fact that the picture I was developing was of Noah's handsome face, a face that I wouldn't be seeing for ages—I almost passed out into the chemicals. Luckily it was after school, so no one had to see "Panicky Penny" in action all over again, and Miss Mills made me a cup of tea and fed me biscuits until I started talking and just couldn't stop.

She's helped me ever since, but I knew what would've helped the most: my blog. Blogging had always been so liberating. Even though I had set all future posts on *Girl Online* to private after posting my final blog, "From Fairytale to Horror Story," I couldn't ignore the familiar itch that I wanted to scratch—that urge to share my thoughts with the world. *Girl Online* had been my creative and emotional outlet for over a year, and I missed it—and the community of online readers I had come to call friends. I knew, if I had just reached out to them, my blog readers would have supported me through this, just as they supported me through the early stages of my anxiety.

But the only thing I could picture whenever I closed my eyes and dreamt of updating my blog was all the hateful people online, poised over their keyboards, waiting to tear me apart. Even though so many people were supportive and lovely to me, it only took one nasty comment to send me back into a dark spiral. I'd never felt so paralysed before, so unable to write. Normally words flowed out of my fingers like water, but everything I wrote seemed stilted and wrong. I put it all down in a journal instead, but it just didn't feel the same.

I'd tried to describe these feelings to Miss Mills. In that spiral, the people online become clowns in thick makeup—and when they smile their teeth are razor-sharp. They're like monsters, but instead of lurking in the dark they're right there for everyone to see. They're all my worst fears rolled into one. They're a million nightmares. They make me want to pack up all my things and move in with a remote tribe in the Amazon rainforest who think aeroplanes are evil spirits sent from the gods. Elliot told me about them. I bet they've never heard of Girl Online or Noah Flynn. I bet they don't know about Facebook. Or Twitter. Or viral videos that just don't ever seem to disappear.

Even if I lived only in Brighton, England, it would be OK. Most of my school has forgotten about my "scandal," the same way they've forgotten the name of last year's *X Factor* winner. My dad says that today's news is tomorrow's fish-and-chip paper. And he's right—the novelty of finding out about my blog, and even about Noah and me, has now worn thinner than the knees of my favourite jeans. But I don't live in a remote jungle or really even in Brighton, England. Instead, I am a citizen of Planet Internet, and right now it's the worst place in the entire world to be me— because, on the Internet, I worry that no one will ever forget.

At least one good thing has come from the Internet, though. Pegasus Girl and I swapped email addresses after she supported me, and she's gone from being *Girl Online*'s most faithful reader to one of my best friends—even though we haven't met in real life yet. After listening to me moan for the millionth time about wishing *Girl Online* still existed, she told me that I could change my blog settings so that only people I gave a password to could read what I wrote. Now she, Elliot, and Miss Mills are the only people who read my ramblings, but it's much better than nothing.

I can see Miss Mills through the warped glass in her classroom door, her light brown hair tumbling forward as she leans over her marking. I knock on the door frame and she looks up at me, smiling.

"Afternoon, Penny. Are you all done for the year, then?"

I nod. "Just finished my history exam."

"That's great! Come on in."

She waits until I've sat down in one of the hard plastic chairs. All around the room are my fellow students' photography projects, mounted on black foam board and ready for the summer exhibition. Against Miss Mills's wishes, I specifically asked not to put my work on display. I completed all the assignments but couldn't face showing my photographs to anyone else. Most of my class also put their portfolios online, but I stopped uploading mine after Christmas. I'm terrified someone will find it and use it to make fun of me. Instead, I've been compiling a paper portfolio and handing it in to Miss Mills each week. The physical act of creativity has been very therapeutic.

She pulls out my portfolio and hands it back to me. "Great job, as always, Penny," she says with a smile. "This is our last meeting for a while, isn't it? I wanted to talk to you about your last blog. You know, it does get better."

I shrug. Getting through each day seems to be just about all I can handle.

As if she's reading my thoughts, Miss Mills continues. "I think you can do far more than simply survive each day. You can thrive, Penny. You've been through a lot this past school year. I'm glad you've decided to continue with your A levels—especially in photography—but I don't think you should let your choices worry you too much. You're allowed to not know what you want to do yet."

I want to believe her, but it's hard. It feels like everyone has their lives all figured out, except me. It's not something Elliot can relate to. He knows he wants to study fashion design and he dreams of one day having his own label. I just found out that Kira wants to be a vet so she's taking biology and maths to make sure she can get into a good university. Amara is some kind of physics genius and has always wanted to be a scientist, so she is set. All I like to do is take pictures and write blog posts that I can only publish in secret to a select group of my closest friends. I don't think there's a career in that.

I know there's an ocean of possibility out there, but I'm

stuck on the shore, not prepared to dive in. "Didn't you always want to be a teacher?" I ask.

She laughs. "Not really. I kind of . . . fell into it. I wanted to be an archaeologist! Until I realized that archaeology isn't about Indiana Jones–style adventuring and too often involves categorizing tiny fragments of bone for hours on end. I spent a lot of time feeling lost."

"That's how I feel," I say. "Lost in my own life. And I don't know how to use a compass. Is there GPS for your life?"

Miss Mills laughs. "No matter what those *other* adults might tell you, I'll let you in on a little secret: you don't have to know now. You're only sixteen. Go ahead and enjoy yourself! Live your life. Turn that internal compass of yours upside down and backwards and in circles so it doesn't know which way is up. Like I said, I fell into teaching completely by accident, but now I wouldn't want to do any other job." She leans towards me and smiles. "So, are you looking forward to the concert tonight? It's all anyone in my other classes could talk about. Isn't Noah supporting The Sketch?"

I grin, glad for the change of subject. My heart lifts as I think of seeing Noah again. There's a point when Skype and texting just don't cut it, and that point is now. It's also going to be the first time I've ever seen him perform live onstage, in front of thousands of screaming girls. "Yes, he's the opening act. It's a huge deal for him."

"Sounds like it. Well, you take care of yourself over the summer. And don't forget about your prep for A-level photography." She gestures to my portfolio. "Are you sure you don't want to exhibit? You've got some amazing work in here, and it deserves to be recognized."

I shake my head. She sighs, but she knows it's a losing battle. "Well, all I can say is keep on writing your blog, Penny. It's your talent. You know how to connect with people, and I don't want you to lose that. Make that your summer assignment from me this year, alongside your photographs. I want a full report of your travels when you get back."

I smile, sliding the portfolio notebook into my bag. "Thanks for all your help this year, Miss Mills."

I think about our photography assignment for the summer. Miss Mills has asked us to look at "alternative perspectives": a challenge to see things from a different angle. I have no idea what I'm going to do, but I'm sure going on tour with Noah will offer up a million different opportunities.

"You're welcome, Penny."

I leave the classroom, and am back in the deserted hallways. I feel my heart beating inside my chest as I pick my pace up to a jog, and then a run. I burst through the doors that lead outside, throw my arms wide, and twirl on the front step of the school. I blush pink when I realize how cheesy that must look, but I have never been so ready for the school year to be over. Freedom has never felt so good.

25 June

Exams Are Officially Over!
(And How to Survive Them When
They Return)

Drum roll please . . . I've finished school for the year! Done! *Finito!*

It wasn't that bad. Repeat: it wasn't that bad. But I did have some help (big thanks to Wiki, my bestest pal!) coming up with some strategies for coping when it felt like all I was doing was studying . . . studying . . . and more studying!

If I don't write these strategies down now, I know I will have forgotten them when exam time comes round next year. For some reason, no matter how many times I have to sit exams, I always find them just as terror-inducing as before.

Five Ways to Survive Exams (from Someone Who HATES Exams)

1. Revise

OK, some might say that's an obvious one, but this year I drew up a calendar with each subject on it and gave myself a gold star sticker whenever I completed an hour's revision. It felt a bit like being back in primary school again, but actually seeing all the progress I was making (by way of a constellation of gold stars all over the calendar) made me feel loads more confident in my preparation.

2. Bribes

Not ones for your teachers or your examiner, but for yourself! Whenever I completed a full revision week (see Step 1) I went to Gusto Gelato and got myself a gelato burger as a reward. Nothing like using a sweet treat as motivation!

3. Do the hard questions first

Wiki's top tip! He says to focus on the questions that are worth the most marks first of all so you don't get stuck at the end and have to scribble down nonsense for your big essay.

4. Coffee

I don't even like coffee, but, according to my brother, it helps. I did try it, but every time I took a sip it made me cringe, and I ended up staying awake all night, plagued by anxious shivers. So maybe that's not such a good tip after all . . .

5. Dream of summer

Remember that there is life after exams! This is basically what got me through. The knowledge that, very soon, I'll be with Brooklyn Boy again . . .

Girl Offline . . . never going online xxx

✦ ✦ Chapter Two ✦ ✦

All the way home, my excitement levels have been growing—so much so that I practically waltz into the kitchen. It
seems like a pretty apt thing to do because Mum is dressed in
a full-blown *Strictly Come Dancing* glitter outfit, twirling as she
and Elliot dance a mean salsa across the black-and-white
tiles. Elliot's boyfriend, Alex, is sitting on a stool by the island,
shouting out scores in the flamboyant manner of Bruno
Tonioli. "Seven!"

Just an average afternoon at the Porters'.

"Penny darling, you're home!" Mum says, between steps.
"You never told me Elliot was such a good dancer."

"He's a man of many talents!"

They finish off with an elaborate dip—of Elliot, by Mum.

Alex and I break into spontaneous and enthusiastic
applause.

"Upstairs?" I say to Elliot and Alex. They nod in almost
perfect synchronization.

Seeing them sends a familiar pang through my heart. Elliot
and Alex are the perfect couple—and they don't have to

contend with my and Noah's long-distance woes. They're able to be together whenever they want, without having to worry about time zones or whether there's enough Wi-Fi to Skype properly. They're completely relaxed in each other's presence.

In fact, they spend so much time together that my family has even given them their own portmanteau nickname, like Brangelina or Kimye. They're Alexiot.

"Are Alexiot staying for dinner?" Mum calls to us before we disappear upstairs.

"No, we're going to grab burgers at GBK before the concert!" I shout back.

"We are?" Elliot asks, raising an eyebrow.

I cringe. "Kira invited us. Is that OK?"

Alexiot exchange a look but seem to come to an agreement. "No problem, Pennylicious," says Elliot. He reaches back and grabs Alex's hand, and I smile.

I remember the day they met, not long before Valentine's Day. Elliot had dragged me to a vintage-clothing store in an obscure part of the Brighton Lanes, even though we'd just been in there the day before and we both knew they weren't going to have anything different in stock. But then I'd seen a new guy slouched behind the counter. It took me a few seconds, but I recognized him.

"Oh my god, Penny, he is so cute!" Elliot had pulled me behind a rail of clothing and covered himself with an enormous feather boa.

"That's Alex Shepherd," I said. "He's in sixth form at our school." Of course I knew him, but mostly because Kira had a massive crush on him. I lowered my voice. "Are you sure he's gay?"

Elliot rolled his eyes at me. "You think I would bring you in here if I wasn't sure? We've been eye-flirting since he started working here two weeks ago."

"You eye-flirt with everyone," I said, elbowing him in the ribs.

"Not like this." He gave me an exaggerated wink that made me giggle.

"So why haven't you made a move yet?"

"I will. Just . . . give me time."

Kira would be devastated to find out Alex plays for the other team, but she'd get over it. He was a little more clean-cut than I would have imagined for Elliot, but he had a mischievous glint in his eye that would make anyone melt into a puddle. When I peeked back round the rail to look at him again, he was still staring at us, so I lifted my hand in a little wave.

"Penny, what are you doing?" Elliot's whisper rose in tone by at least an octave.

Then I grinned. "Speeding up time. Besides, I'm just being polite. He was looking this way. OK, he's coming over—be cool."

"He's doing *what*?" Elliot's face was white with panic, but he smoothed down his hair. "How do I look? I knew I shouldn't have worn the trilby today! I look too jaunty; I should've worn something cooler."

"Elliot, you're rambling." I'd never seen him act so flustered before. I pulled the boa down so that it didn't sit like a fluffy animal on top of his head. "And, besides, your trilby looks—" But before I could finish my sentence Alex had reached us.

"May I help you?" he asked, with a small smile. He didn't take his eyes off Elliot for an instant.

"Will you marry me?" Elliot said under his breath.

"What was that?" Alex frowned slightly.

"Oh, nothing . . . I was just wondering if you could help me find a scarf to go with my trilby?" It was like Elliot was a different person. All his nerves seemed to melt away in front of my eyes, and he was back to his normal, confident self.

"Of course. I have something that would go with your *Great Gatsby* vibe over here." Alex walked across to another rail in the store.

"Did you know F. Scott Fitzgerald's wife wouldn't marry him until he had a book deal?" said Elliot, following Alex.

"I didn't, but I did know that he was really bad at spelling," replied Alex, without missing a beat.

I watched as the two of them walked away, swapping facts about an author I had yet to read (and I hadn't seen the movie of the book either). It was like they'd known each other their whole lives. I knew then that I needed to leave Elliot to it. I didn't want to cramp his style.

But, in true Penny fashion, I backed up straight into a coat stand, knocking a pile of vintage fur coats and stoles onto the floor. I blushed bright red and started picking up furs and heavy coats, but it was all a tangled mess. Trust me to have ruined Elliot's moment.

Alex and Elliot were by my side in a flash. "I'll clear this up—don't worry," said Alex.

"I'll help," said Elliot. They both reached down and each picked up one end of the same long fur stole, pulling at it until their hands touched. I could almost feel the spark of electricity in the air. It was their *Lady and the Tramp* spaghetti-and-meatballs moment—a film I *had* seen, loads of times, as a kid. I mumbled some excuses and attempted to sneak out of the store once more, but this time neither of them noticed. They've been an item ever since. And I like to think that my clumsiness helped *just* a bit.

Now Alexiot have to help me answer the ultimate question: What do you wear to see your boyfriend in real life for the first time in two months? We rush up the stairs to the top floor, where my bedroom is. Alex takes the steps two at a time with his long legs. He's much taller than both Elliot and me.

"Uh, Penny—aren't you supposed to be leaving for the tour tomorrow?" Alex asks when he gets to the top of the stairs and stands in the doorway of my room.

"What do you mean?"

But I know exactly what he means. It's like there's been a tornado in my bedroom. Every item of clothing I've ever worn—every scarf, belt, and hat—is in a heap on my bed. Stacks of revision notes are piled high on my desk and there are scraps of cardboard discarded on the floor from where I put together my final photography portfolio.

The only place that's clear in my entire room is the window seat, where I've tacked up a cutting from a celeb magazine with a picture of Noah and me, his arm wrapped round my shoulders. The caption reads: *Noah Flynn and his girlfriend*. It's the first time I've been in a magazine and, even though my hair looks like a mess, I kept it as a memento. There's also a calendar that's nearly completely covered in gold stars, and today's date is circled in red.

Elliot tiptoes through the rubble. "Holy wow. Ocean Strong does not know how to pack."

"Ocean Strong" was the name Elliot and I had come up with for my alter ego, the one I channelled whenever I was feeling anxious, like how Beyoncé used to use "Sasha Fierce" as a protective presence onstage. Beyoncé doesn't need Sasha anymore, and one day I hope not to need Ocean Strong. But, for now, I cling to the name like a life jacket that will keep me afloat on the stormy seas of my anxiety.

I gesture to my bed. "Um, take a seat, I guess." I perch on top of a pile of jumpers on my dressing-table chair.

"I'm kind of worried that you're hiding Megan's dead body under here somewhere," says Elliot, wrinkling his nose.

I stick my tongue out at him. "As if."

Megan was my best friend when I first started school—but she changed, morphing into this high-maintenance, boy-crazy, selfie-obsessed girl that I no longer recognized. Last year she became jealous about my so-called relationship with Ollie—a guy I had a huge crush on before I met Noah. Nothing had happened between us, but even the hint of it seemed to be enough to drive Megan wild with jealousy. It was Ollie who found out about my then-anonymous blog and recognized Noah Flynn, and he told Megan. In turn, Megan put two and two together and told the media, exposing me to the press and the public.

Still, I got my own back when Elliot and I confronted Megan and Ollie in a café, ending up with our milkshakes being dumped over their heads. I haven't had much to do with Megan since Milkshakegate. News of the incident—still my single greatest moment of stand-up-for-myself bravery—spread around our school like wildfire.

But girls like Megan never stay uncool for long. It's as though her inner confidence always shines through and bad or embarrassing stuff slides off her like water off a duck's back. She even makes jokes about how ice cream is the key to her milky complexion. And now she's got an acceptance letter from the top drama school in London. She's back to being untouchable and on top of the world.

Even Ollie is leaving our school. His whole family decided to relocate to help his brother take his tennis to the next level. I feel bad for him. Even after what he did to me I don't believe he's a bad guy. And now he's trapped in his brother's shadow. My two "nemeses" gone like that. The only challenge I have left to overcome is myself.

Elliot claps his hands together. He's in full-blown Monica-from-*Friends* organizer mode now. "OK, where's your suitcase?"

"Uh, I think Alex is sitting on it."

Alex jumps up and shifts a pile of clothes from underneath him. The sides of my bright pink suitcase finally become visible underneath the wreckage of my belongings.

"How long are you going away, again?" Alex says, appraising the bulging nature of my suitcase.

"She's gone for fourteen days, three hours, and twenty-one minutes," says Elliot. "I'm going to count every second!"

"I think my parents are too," I say with a sheepish grin.

"Did it take them a lot of time to come around to the idea?" asks Alex.

"Oh, only the two months since Noah suggested it at Easter! To be honest I wasn't sure if I could do it either."

Going on tour with Noah was a huge deal. It was the first time I was really, properly, going to go away on my own. And, even though every detail had been raked over with a fine-toothed comb, I was still nervous about going.

"Of course you can. This is going to be an incredible experience and I am *so* jealous. Now, Penny, unzip and show us what you have."

I follow his instructions and cringe at the first thing in my case. Elliot reaches inside and pulls out the biggest woollen cardigan you've ever seen, with wide, comfy sleeves I can wrap round myself almost twice. It belongs to my mum, who wore it—as she says—*only* when she was pregnant, and not before or since.

Elliot takes it out and holds it in front of him. It hangs down past his knees. "You do know it's going to be the height of summer while you're on tour, right? Why do you need to bring an entire flock of sheep with you?"

I snatch it out of his hands. "It's my comfort sweater." I hug it to my face and breathe in the scent of my mum's signature perfume. It smells like home. "It's to help with my anxiety. Miss Mills said that if I was worried about being anxious and homesick on tour I should bring with me the one thing that will always make me feel safe. That will remind me of home. Packing my entire duvet didn't seem like the most practical option, so the second choice was this cardie."

He takes it from me, folding it up neatly and putting it back in my suitcase. "OK, you can have that one. But this you can't have!" He pulls out a baby-pink button-down with ruched fabric roses on the pockets. "You're going to be on *tour*, not heading to afternoon tea with your nan!"

"OK, that one can go." I laugh. "I'm no good at this!"

Elliot dramatically rubs his temples. "Sometimes I think you're a lost cause, Penny! We'll have to deal with this later. But back to business: What are you going to wear *tonight*?"

Now it's my turn to be dramatic. "I've literally tried on everything I own! I can't find a single thing. Do you think I can get away with just throwing a black tank top on with my jeans?"

Elliot pulls a disapproving face. "No way. That's not nearly dressy enough."

"How about this?" Alex holds up a black skater dress I forgot I owned. It's got a little daisy print on it in white and yellow. I bought it from ASOS one day while I was supposed to be revising with Kira and Amara but have never worn it.

"That is just perfect!" says Elliot. "My boyfriend, ladies and gentlemen: stylist extraordinaire."

Alex shrugs. "Hey, you work in retail long enough, you pick up a few pointers."

I take the dress from Alex's outstretched hands and nip into the bathroom. I change into the skater dress, and face myself in the mirror.

I can't believe I'm finally getting to see Noah in concert. It feels like I've been both waiting for and dreading this moment ever since he got the call that he was going to be supporting The Sketch on tour. I pull my long red hair out of its bun, and it falls in waves around my face. Mum has shown me a little trick with eyeliner, which I try now, flicking the line up past the outer corner of my eye. Instantly my eyes look more alluring and catlike. Maybe I can pull this off. My new tagline: *Girlfriend of Noah Flynn.*

I think I'm going mad as the first few beats of Noah's album start playing in my head, but when I open the bathroom door I realize that Elliot and Alex are playing "Elements," one of the eight songs on *Autumn Girl*. Each song Noah has written is better than the last—but the title track, "Autumn Girl," which was written for me, is still my favourite, of course.

Alexiot have linked hands, and Elliot leans his head on Alex's shoulder. They're just way too adorable and I don't want to intrude. But Elliot must hear me because he looks over his shoulder at me. His jaw drops. "You're *killing* it, Ocean Strong!"

"Why, thanks," I say, doing a little curtsey.

"All right, kids—let's blow this popsicle stand," says Elliot in a low drawl.

Both Alex and I look at him, frowning.

"What, don't you like my new Americanisms? I thought I'd practise before seeing Noah again. Now, accessories." He pushes a handful of bangles onto my wrist and puts a long, dangling necklace round my neck. He smiles at me. "You just need your Converse, and then you're ready."

I look in the full-length mirror.

"You look great, Pen. That outfit is perfect," says Elliot. "Leah Brown, you may be the hottest pop star on the planet but you've got nothing on my girl."

I allow myself to smile, and tell myself I look good. And I do. I feel confident. But I still pick up a jacket to go over top. Elliot grimaces.

"What?" I say. "It might be cold in the restaurant."

"Speaking of, we better get a move on!" Elliot looks down at his watch.

"Tom!" I yell down the stairs to my brother. "Will you drive us?"

I hear a grunt in response that I'm going to take as a "yes."

But, when we get outside, Alex doesn't join us in the car. He shoves his hands in his pockets. "Sorry, guys, I have to head home to do something first. I'll meet you at the concert, OK?"

Elliot's happy mood deflates, his shoulders slumping.

"Are you sure?" I say. "I know it must be really boring to have to hang out with a bunch of Year Elevens but most of them are all right."

"It's not that," he says. "I just have stuff to do."

"Oh, OK."

He leans over and gives Elliot a quick kiss, but Elliot's heart isn't in it. Then, once Alex is gone, he shrugs his shoulders and is instantly back to his normal self. "Let's go!"

A few minutes later, we pull up in front of GBK, courtesy of chauffeur Tom. Elliot jumps out of the car, but just as I'm about to follow him Tom reaches over and grabs my arm. "If you get into trouble, or need any help, call me straightaway, got it, Pen-pen?"

I pull him into a hug, which he accepts with stiff shoulders. But I know he loves me really.

On a Friday night, Brighton is packed with commuters returning from work in London and revellers heading for a night out. There's a boy who looks younger than me playing guitar on the pavement. He sings softly, but he has an amazing voice. No one else stops to look—not even Elliot, who is so wrapped up in his own world he could walk past the

London Symphony Orchestra and not notice—but I find myself lingering. I'm rooted to the spot by the boy's beautiful music.

"May I take a picture?" I ask him when he strums a final chord.

"Sure," he says. I snap a few shots, and then take a pound out of my purse and put it in his guitar case. He grins gratefully at me and I make a dash for the restaurant as the heavens open and it starts to pour with rain. Typical British summer.

Inside, everyone is waiting. Elliot rushes up to me and pulls me to a stop. "Don't freak out," he says.

"What do you mean?" I frown. But then he steps to one side.

Megan is standing behind him.

And she's wearing the exact same dress as me.

Chapter Three

I wrap my jacket even tighter round my body, covering my dress. Megan smiles serenely, looking surprisingly cool about it, but that's probably because I've already turned tomato red with embarrassment. I almost turn round and walk out of the restaurant right there and then, but Elliot grabs my hand and gives it a squeeze.

"Oh my god, Penny, we're wearing identical dresses!" Megan says, tossing her long chestnut hair. "Did you find this on ASOS too? Better make sure Noah doesn't see me first or else he might get confused and give *me* the backstage pass." She gives me an exaggerated wink that turns my stomach. I can't help thinking she looks way better in the dress than I do.

"Grow up, Megan. It's just a dress—not a brain transplant to make you a nicer person," snaps Elliot.

Kira is sitting at the table behind Megan. She gives me an apologetic smile and a shrug. A sharp pain jabs my heart as I wonder if Kira told Megan about the dress I ordered. But then I tell myself not to be so paranoid.

"Glad you could make it, Penny!" says Kira. "Is Noah going to join us?"

I can sense everyone turn to look at me, even from the other tables. I laugh nervously. "Oh, I don't think so. Noah is too busy prepping for the show. I'll meet him after."

Elliot pulls me through the restaurant and into a booth as far away from them as we can be without seeming rude. It feels like my entire school and half of Elliot's is coming to watch the concert. Of course they are all excited to see Noah Flynn, but the main band, The Sketch, are *massive* at the moment. They're a group of four boys from the US who exploded onto the scene last year with their song "There's Only One." They've already done gigs in Manchester and Birmingham, but this is the first one that Noah is joining. He's then heading off with The Sketch to Europe, and I get to go with him.

My stomach flutters with nervous but excited butterflies.

I slide into the booth and Elliot sits down opposite me. "Ugh, I can't believe we have to be in the same room as Mega-Nasty," says Elliot. "Why did you agree to meet everyone here again?"

"Kira invited me and I couldn't think of a way out of it. They're all coming to the concert so it made sense for us to go together. Besides, it's the Brighton Centre. It's so big that hopefully we won't even see them," I say.

"Did you know the Brighton Centre can seat four and a half thousand people, and was the last venue Bing Crosby performed in before he died?"

"Is that the guy who sang 'White Christmas'? How do you know all this stuff, Wiki?" I say with a laugh.

"I know everything, Miss Penny P. You know that. At least we'll be sitting in the VIP box," says Elliot, flashing his ticket and grinning. "First class, here we come!" He bum-dances on the bench. "Wow, if we're this excited, how is Noah feeling?"

"Oh, Noah never gets nervous!" Though, as I'm saying it, I don't know if it's true. I've never seen him perform properly before—not in front of an audience this big. "I know he's super excited. This is his chance to really make it big in Europe."

"Yeah, there's no way people won't know his name after he's played with The Sketch. Even someone like you would know who he was!"

I smile, but Elliot's words have disconcerted me. It's strange to think that only six months ago I had no idea who Noah Flynn was, and now everyone is about to know him. I almost lost myself to the media storm before. Will I be able to hold on to Noah throughout the whirlwind that's to come?

"Have you met the rest of his band?" Elliot asks.

I shake my head. "Not yet, but I know he's got some of his best friends with him."

"I really wish I could come with you," says Elliot, his eyes downcast.

"I wish you could come too! But you're going to have an amazing time at *CHIC*," I remind him. Elliot's been looking forward to his internship since he found out at the start of the year that he got it.

"Did you know *CHIC* was started in 1895?"

I reach over the table and put my hand over Elliot's. I know when he's spouting facts out of nerves rather than for fun. "You're going to be brilliant," I say, reassuring him.

The waitress comes by and asks for our order, but I feel so nervous I can't bear to eat. I bury my face in my menu and we ask for a few more minutes, but almost instantly I wish that she'd stayed. Behind her is the person I dread.

"Hey, Penny."

I lower my menu slowly. "Uh, hi, Megan."

Elliot is throwing daggers at her with his eyes, but Megan ignores him. Instead, she focuses on me. "I'm sorry we're wearing the same dress—do you want me to change? I can run home before the concert."

Now *this* is a side of Megan that I'm not expecting: the sweet, friendly side. For a moment I get a glimpse of the girl I used to know. But I find it hard to separate that girl from the one who tried to destroy my life earlier this year—like two photographs overlaid on top of each other, a real-life double exposure. I still don't know which one is the real Megan.

"No, it's OK. It's kind of funny, actually," I say.

She smiles at me, and it seems genuine. "So, I was wondering . . ." she says, and suddenly her smile has become sharklike—all teeth—and it's clear she's got an ulterior motive for coming over. "Do you think you could get me, Kira, and Amara backstage later? I would absolutely *die* if I got to meet The Sketch."

I frown. Elliot tuts out loud and rolls his eyes. "Oh, I don't know . . . I'd have to ask Noah," I say.

"Well, why don't you?"

"What do you mean?"

She raises an eyebrow. "Why don't you text him and ask? You *do* have your boyfriend's number, don't you?"

"Penny doesn't have to do any favours for you," says Elliot.

"I wasn't asking *you*, Elliot," she snaps back. "I'm asking my *friend*."

"Um, OK . . ." I start to take my phone out of my pocket, but Elliot stops me with a glare. I take several deep breaths and then I look back up at Megan. "I'll ask Noah later, but I can't make any promises," I tell her. My phone remains firmly out of sight.

Megan hesitates. When she sees that I'm not going to change my mind, she shrugs, trying to act as if it's not a big deal. "Well, thanks—hopefully see you later, Penny." She flounces off, still smiling at me. But the way she snapped at Elliot makes me realize that she hasn't changed at all.

Now I do get my phone out of my pocket, and I read my latest text conversation with Noah.

> Can't wait to see you tonight! N

> Me neither! It's been way too long xxxx

Almost as if Noah knows I'm reading his texts, a new message from him pops up on my phone.

> How are you getting to the concert?

I quickly type in a reply.

> I'm walking to the Brighton Centre with Elliot and some friends from school xxxx

> No you're not. N

I frown at his message.

"What's up?" asks Elliot, spotting my confused expression.

I show him the screen. "What does he mean, 'No you're not'? How else does he expect me to get to the concert?"

Elliot shrugs, but then his mouth forms an O of surprise. His eyes widen as he stares past me towards the front of the restaurant.

"What is it?" I ask.

Even before I've finished asking the question, shrieks and squeals of delight surround us. I hear Kira scream, "NOAH FLYNN!" and I sit up straight in my seat and spin round.

There he is: my boyfriend, Noah Flynn. Rock god extraordinaire. He's wearing his trademark black T-shirt, ripped jeans, and a big smile. Seeing him makes the rest of the world—the restaurant, my schoolmates, even Elliot—just melt away. Like a camera pulling focus, suddenly the rest of the world looks blurry while he stands out, clear and sharp.

He spots me and grins even wider. He saunters over to the

booth, ignoring the squeals and slack-jawed stares of the girls at the other tables, grabs both of my hands, and pulls me up from the bench. "Penny Porter, do you mind if I steal you away?"

"Not at all!" I say, wanting nothing more than to disappear with him. But then I quickly remember and turn back to Elliot. "Wait, do you mind?"

Elliot laughs. "Go ahead, Pennylicious! I don't really want a burger anyway—I'm thinking about going vegan." He lowers his voice. "I'll go find Alex. I've been apart from him for about half an hour and already I think I might die." He steps out of the booth too, and Noah gives him a big hug.

"Elliot, my man! Good to see you."

"Good to see you too, Noah! You're going to kill it tonight." Elliot turns to me. "Don't forget me when you're off with the rich and famous, OK, Penny?"

"Never! I'll see you at the concert." I grin, then grab Noah's outstretched hand. Followed by the gawping looks of all my friends, we walk out of the restaurant and over to a waiting car. It's concert time.

Chapter Four

Standing by the passenger door of the nondescript black car, holding a big black umbrella, is a big, burly man with a bald head so shiny I'm almost certain I can touch up my makeup in it.

"This is Larry," Noah says. "He might look intimidating, but actually he sings along to Whitney Houston songs in his spare time and would choose a bubble bath over a shower most days." Noah gives his bodyguard a friendly punch in the arm as we pass him to get in. "Isn't that right, Larry?"

"You got me, sir," he says. "And you must be Penny?" He gives me a friendly wink and I instantly feel at ease. I know why Noah wanted to reassure me about him—he looks like the sort of man you might see standing at the doors of a night-club on a Friday night, keeping everyone in order. From what Noah just said, though, perhaps he'd most likely be found *inside* the club—at the karaoke machine, dancing around with a pink cocktail in hand—than outside it, pulling fights apart.

I'm imagining him belting out "I Will Always Love You" as I reply: "Hello! Yes, nice to meet you, Whitney." I hold out my hand, but my face flushes red as I realize what I've just called him. This was not the introduction to Noah's entourage that I had pictured! What ever happened to sophistication, intelligence, or even normal words? Straightaway I stammer out an apology, trying to rescue the situation, but Noah steps in.

"You're definitely not the first to call him that, Pen," Noah says, laughing.

Larry gives me a wink and a smirk. "Well, from now on, Penny, you can call me Whitney. Just don't go expecting any sing-along sessions, unless you're willing to join in." Larry hops into the driver's seat while I nervously laugh along with him.

Although the drive to the Brighton Centre isn't very long, it feels good to finally be with Noah. He slides over into the middle seat to sit beside me, his arm wrapped round my shoulders.

"It feels so good to have you next to me!" he says, squeezing me close. "How did your exams go?"

I shudder. "Don't ask," I say. "But they're over now. I can't believe it's time already!"

I lean into his chest and feel his heart beating; I can't help but think this is *way* better than Skype. I stare up at his chiselled jaw, messy dark hair, and deep brown eyes. How did I get so lucky? I'm normally the unlucky girl who's always caught in the rain without an umbrella, who never has her number drawn in the school raffle, and who always loses at Monopoly. Maybe life has been storing up all my wins just for this: so I can be with Noah.

"Are you excited for tonight?" He squeezes my hand and I realize I've been staring at him in awe, like a complete weirdo.

"Oh . . . Yes! I can't believe it. You're opening for a band so big that even I've heard of them!" Noah's face goes a bit white, and I realize I must not be helping his nerves. "You're going to be amazing, I know it. Are you nervous?"

"I'd be lying if I said no, but I'm mostly just pumped. This has been my dream since I was twelve, and now I get to do it all, and with the best girlfriend on the planet." He lifts my hand to his mouth and kisses it, and I blush a deep red. "I guess my only wish is that my parents were here to see it, you know?" Noah turns to look out of the rain-streaked window as we pass the seafront, dark and grey under the thick clouds, and I feel a deep pang of sadness for him.

His parents died in a tragic skiing accident only a few years ago, and I knew the pain was still fresh for Noah. He and his younger sister, Bella, went to live with their grandmother, the wonderful Sadie Lee, but I knew there would always be a hole in his heart big enough to hold the ocean, a hole that only his music could help to fill.

"They are incredibly proud of you, Noah, I'm sure of it." I squeeze his hand back and he turns to look at me with a smile. "How are Sadie Lee and Bella?" I ask.

"Oh, they're great. Bella's starting first grade this September, and G-ma has her hands full with her catering business. G-ma also gave me a box of chocolate-chip cookies for you that should have *just* survived the flight over—but you'll have to eat them quick! I've got them in my dressing room."

"She's so sweet!" I feel like drooling at simply the thought of Sadie Lee's cookies—they are seriously the best I've ever tasted—then I quickly lift my hand to my mouth in case I actually *am* drooling. That's just what Noah needs to see: his girlfriend as a drooling, unsexy mess. But Noah laughs. Then he reaches up and cups my chin, pulling me forward gently, and we kiss for the first time in three months. Oh my gosh, I have missed this boy so much that it almost kills me.

"I've really missed you, my gorgeous, goofy autumn girl," he says, as if he's reading my mind.

"I'm pretty sure I've missed you more. In fact, I'm willing to bet on it."

"You don't strike me as a betting girl, Penny. I mean, three hours at those 2p machines you told me about is pushing it . . ." He raises his eyebrows and winks at me, then leans back in his seat and gives me an appreciative look up and down. "I really love that dress on you, by the way."

"Thanks, I really like those dimples on you . . ."

"Well, you're going to be seeing these dimples a lot more while we're away on tour together. I'm so happy that you decided to do this with me, Pen. It's going to be the greatest adventure."

"Well, adventures are my favourite . . . once we get past the flying part!" I laugh, although it doesn't quite cover up the nerves I feel at the thought of all the planes we'll have to take on the tour. Noah recognizes this in my eyes almost immediately.

"I promise you that I will look after you. We're going to have the best time."

His reassuring words bring a smile to my face. I can't believe I was so worried that things wouldn't be the same between us. In fact, I have a feeling things are going to be even better than before. "Hey, Larry—are we close?" Noah asks, craning his neck to see out of the front windscreen, the fast-moving wipers and thick drops of rain doing their best to obscure the view.

"Just round the corner," Larry replies.

"Can we drive past the front? I want to see the turnout."

"Sure thing, boss."

Noah grins at me, his eyes sparkling with a hint of mischief. It's a look I recognize from when we first met—and the end result was that he showed me all his favourite New York places. I don't know what he's up to, but I'm intrigued.

The road outside the Brighton Centre is packed with people already queuing to enter, and Larry has to slow to a crawl to drive past. The crowd must be at least ten people deep, some in colourful macs, others huddling together under umbrellas to avoid getting completely drenched. All of a sudden I feel a wave of anxiety come over me at the intensity of what I am seeing. My boyfriend is Noah Flynn. All these people are going to be watching him sing onstage, and if they don't already know who he is they will after tonight. Some of them are even holding handmade banners that say: MARRY ME, NOAH; WE LOVE YOU, NOAH; and LET ME BE YOUR SUMMER GIRL.

Then I relax. I don't mind that someone wants to be his "summer girl" (after all, I'm quite happy in the knowledge I'm his all-seasons girl now). I think about how lovely it is that he has so many supporters when he is the opening act for such a huge band. Most of these girls will only know him because of YouTube, and each one will have played a part in making him as successful as he is. Of course, there are a lot of people who are only there to see The Sketch—it helps that all four members look as though they have stepped out of a poster for Abercrombie & Fitch. I feel a huge sense of pride for Noah and this crazy journey he is about to embark on, and I do a little wiggle of happiness at the thought that I will be by his side along the way.

Noah clicks open his seat belt and I stare at him in alarm. "What are you doing?" I ask.

"I'm going to go out and say hello!"

"But it's pouring outside!" I say, stating the obvious.

"I don't care! I could probably do with a shower any-way . . . and guess what!" He holds out his hand. "You're coming with me."

"What?" I say, my eyes opening wide.

"I want everyone to see us together, and I want you to experience this with me. Be back in a second, Larry."

The car pulls to a stop, and Noah leaps out, dragging me behind him. I hesitate at the door, but then I see Noah's beaming smile and it gives me strength. I grab my bag, pull my camera from it, and jump out of the car.

My ears are pummelled with the shrill sound of fans screaming his name, and they wave frantically as he walks towards them.

There is something really magical about watching Noah chatting away with his fans. His face lights up, and he just doesn't care that he is getting wet and his hair is getting messier and curlier by the second. He's in his element.

I hear someone shout, "Penny! Look, there's Penny. It's Girl Online!" I glance over at two girls who are waving at me, and I wave back with a smile. This feels very strange, and there is a massive part of me that wants to run back into the safety of the car. Instead, I take a calming breath and start to photograph Noah as he hugs and high-fives some of the people in the queue. My camera feels like a shield. *You can do this, Penny*, I think to myself. I move backwards, and the two girls who waved at me are now right next to me.

"Are you excited to see Noah play in front of so many people?" one of them asks.

I nod vigorously. "I'm so excited. It's so crazy!"

"We absolutely loved your blog, by the way! You should start it up again soon," the other girl chips in.

"Oh, I'm not sure. I do miss it, though." I smile at them warmly.

"What's it like to be with Noah Flynn?" the first girl asks.

"It's like a dream," I say honestly. Noah catches my eye and gestures back towards the car. "It was so nice to meet you both," I say, as Noah takes my hand and we hop back into the car. I wave to the girls one last time, then turn to Noah. He has this Cheshire-cat grin on his face. I can only imagine what he must be feeling at this point.

"Are you feeling OK?" Noah says, his face frowning in concern.

"That was . . . amazing!" I say, and I wrap my arms round him. We laugh as my camera bumps against his chest, and we're forced to separate.

"Wait, I want to remember this moment," I say to Noah. I pull him close and turn the camera on my phone round to snap a selfie of the two of us together. Looking at the faces on the screen, all I see are two ridiculously happy, shining people, and my heart fills with so much warmth I feel like I'm about to explode. The best thing is, this feeling is going to last all summer long.

Chapter Five

When we finally get out of the car, Noah's manager, Dean, is outside, tapping his foot and staring pointedly at his watch. His hair is slick with gel and although he's wearing a suit he's left the top buttons of his shirt undone to make him look more casual. Noah calls this his effort to be "down with the kids." I'm instantly reminded of my old drama teacher, who we nicknamed "Call-Me-Jeff" because he wanted all his students to think he was cool; at least Dean has an awesome job.

"Hi, Dean!" I say. It's nice to see a familiar face. I met Dean over the Easter holidays, when Noah first brought up the possibility of me joining him on tour.

"Penny! Lovely to see you." He kisses me on both cheeks and I'm hit with a strong waft of aftershave. "Come on, you two lovebirds. I can't believe you've been hanging around out front! Don't you know the security nightmare you've caused?"

Noah doesn't apologize, and shrugs. "Have you noticed it's pouring with rain outside? I wanted to say hi to all those people out there who are being forced to wait."

I feel like I'm walking on air after meeting everyone, and I'm sure Noah does too. I don't even care that I probably look a bedraggled mess. Noah, of course, just looks even better.

Dean rolls his eyes, but he doesn't look mad—he knows it's all part of Noah's charm. Dean was the one who first discovered Noah on YouTube and signed him to Sony. Since then, he's almost been like a surrogate dad, helping Noah to handle all the challenges that come with being an overnight Internet sensation. It was Dean who got him on the tour with The Sketch, convincing people that Noah was ready—even if Noah wasn't so sure himself.

Dean had also been part of Noah's plan to convince my parents it would be all right to let me go away with him. Dean had spent a whole afternoon at our house, reassuring Mum and Dad that a rock tour with Noah and The Sketch was not going to be the crazy alcohol-and-drug-fuelled environment that gets depicted in Hollywood movies and TV shows.

"What with smartphones, social media, and paparazzi nowadays, we can't take *any* risks with our talent," Dean had said. It felt strange to hear Noah being described as "talent." "The moment they step out of line, someone will capture it on film and it will go viral, so it's my job to make sure it never comes to that."

That afternoon feels so long ago, and now everything is actually happening. I can hardly believe it.

Dean snaps me back to reality. "Noah, you're onstage in an hour—we have no time to mess around!"

"I spent all afternoon here rehearsing. I think I'm allowed to take a break."

"Well, it probably would have been good for you to *tell* me where you were going rather than leaving me running around like a headless chicken!"

Noah winks at me. It's typical for him to run off without telling his management team where he's going. I stifle a giggle.

It's far less glamorous backstage than I thought it would be. In my head, I had imagined a lot of leather furniture and big mirrors with naked bulbs surrounding them, or maybe somewhere really industrial, with exposed metal pipes and lots of speakers everywhere. Instead, we are ushered through a series of narrow hallways towards a door with a piece of paper tacked on the front that reads: NOAH FLYNN. Inside is a small, beige-painted room with a couple of grey sofas round a coffee table. Just that on its own would look really boring, but it's made much livelier by the sheer mess that's dotted all around. There are lots of instruments stacked in the corner, suitcases open and spilling their contents onto the floor, and several leather jackets laid across the back of the sofa. On the walls are photographs of famous people who have performed at the Brighton Centre, from Bing Crosby (who I now know all about, thanks to Elliot) to more modern bands like The Vamps, The Wanted, and even One Direction. I wonder if Noah's picture will end up there one day too.

"Are The Sketch in a room like this too?" I ask.

Noah shakes his head. "No, they get the fancier dressing rooms."

"Well, that makes sense. Will I get to meet them?"

Now he laughs. "Heck, I haven't even met them yet! I'm

just the support act, remember? Their management keeps them on an even tighter leash than Dean does me. I'd be surprised if we see them at all this tour, unless you're really lucky. Wait, you're not hoping to upgrade your rock-star boy-friend, are you?"

I punch him lightly on the shoulder and stick out my tongue. I quickly get over any disappointment at not meet-ing The Sketch as soon as I spot the array of treats laid out on the coffee table. There's a HUGE bowl full of Reese's Peanut Butter Cups, Jolly Ranchers, several bottles of neon-yellow Lucozade . . . and Cadbury Mini Eggs.

"Wait, Noah, how did you get these?"

"What do you mean?"

"It's the summer—these mini eggs are only around at Easter! I guess that's your big diva request," I say with a grin.

"I'll have to trust your chocolate expertise on that fact," says Noah. He reaches down, grabs a mini egg, and pops it in his mouth. He pulls a box out from underneath the table, and when he opens it the room fills with the aroma of chocolate-chip cookies. "But, seeing as Sadie Lee made me *promise* to give these to her favourite Brit and not eat them all by myself, mini eggs are the next best thing!"

"Nothing beats Sadie Lee's cookies!" I say, grabbing one. They're still soft on the inside. Even though I could eat the whole batch, I offer one to Noah and then to Dean, who has followed us in.

"Hey, who wants some beer?"

I look up from the box of cookies and there's a guy lean-ing in the doorway, a long, grungy fringe covering most of his forehead. He's wearing a black T-shirt like Noah, but unlike Noah he has a lot more tattoos running down his arms. In one of his hands, he grips the necks of two beers. Instantly I feel goose bumps prickle the back of my neck, though I can't explain why.

"Not for me, man," says Noah. "Blake, meet my girlfriend, Penny. Penny, this is Blake—he's one of my best friends from back home and the drummer in my band."

Blake barely looks at me—or, if he does, I can't tell because his hair obscures his eyes too much. I do hear a small grunt of acknowledgement from him, I think.

"Hey," I say. My voice squeaks and now I do see Blake's expression change—his lip curls up into a sneer. My heart sinks. I wanted to make a good impression on Noah's friends. Now I just feel awkward and a little pathetic. For the first time, I feel out of place.

The other two members of Noah's band pile in behind Blake—they are both carrying beers too, but they're much friendlier and smilier than Blake. Noah introduces them as they come in: the bassist, Mark, and a keyboard player named Ryan. Mark and Ryan sit on the chair opposite me and Noah, but Blake strides in and plonks himself down next to Noah so that I get squished between him and the arm of the sofa. He passes one of the beers over to Noah.

Noah takes it, but, rather than taking a swig, he puts it down on the coffee table.

"This is England, dude. You're legal," urges Blake, after taking a large gulp himself.

Noah shrugs. "I said I'm cool."

Blake looks about to push the issue, but Dean claps his hands together and the band looks up at him together. "OK, guys, this is your first big gig together, and you sounded great in rehearsal. Just repeat what you've been doing and you'll smash it. I don't think I have to explain how important this is for Noah, for all you guys. This could be a real game changer. No pain, no gain. Now, it's only ten minutes until lights up so, all of you, get out and get ready. This is your time to shine."

"Is he always like this?" I whisper to Noah.

"What, always speaking in clichés before we go onstage? Yep, that pretty much sums up Dean." Noah looks at his manager. "Can I get a minute alone?"

"*One* minute," Dean says, narrowing his eyes at the two of us so we know he means business. "All right, everybody out."

"Everyone except Penny."

Dean nods, but Blake lets out a loud grunt. Every move he makes seems heavy with reluctance, but eventually he shuffles out of the door after Dean.

Once we're alone Noah turns to me, and his body seems like it's overflowing with nervous energy. Then I realize he's not excited. He looks really worried.

"Penny, I don't know if I can go onstage."

✶ ·❈hapter Six✶ ·

Those are the last words I expected to come out of Noah's mouth. His trademark dimples are gone, his jaw tight. His face is drained of colour, and he's biting his fingernails. I've never seen him like this before. He stands and paces up and down the dressing room, running his hands through his shaggy brown hair.

I get up and race over to him. To stop his nervous pacing, I take both of his hands in mine. He stands still, but I can feel his hands shaking. Our foreheads touch and we breathe together for a couple of moments. Then I lift my hands to his face. "You're *amazing*. Of course you can do this. You're Noah Flynn. You can do anything."

He leans down and kisses me. It's a different kind of kiss to the one in the car. He presses his lips to mine and they feel fuelled by a desperate kind of energy, as if he's hoping our kiss will transport us to a different world, one where he doesn't have to worry about performing in front of a crowd of 4,500 screaming fans.

When we finally break apart, he says, "Penny, I really, *really* don't know if I can do this." His voice is so quiet I can barely hear him.

There's a pounding on the dressing-room door. "Your minute's up, Noah!" says Dean, who sounds slightly on the verge of panic—but not in the same way as Noah.

Noah slumps down onto the sofa, burying his head in his hands.

Seeing him like this makes my heart ache. I want to reach out and wrap him in something warm and comforting, like my mum's old sweater, but he can't exactly walk out onstage wrapped in a blanket (although, thinking about it, he might start a new fashion trend if he did). That's when inspiration strikes me. Maybe that's what he needs: his comfort object.

I cast my eyes around, and they land on the one thing that I know always makes him feel at home: his old guitar. The one he brought from Brooklyn. The one with the message from his parents on the back:

Stay true, M & D x

I pick it up and walk over to him. "Here. Take this."

"My guitar? How's that going to help?"

"Just do it," I say, more firmly.

He sighs, taking the guitar from my hands and lifting the strap over his head. As soon as it's nestled in his arms, he strums a chord. Music fills the room, and it feels like we're transported back to the basement of Sadie Lee's house in New York, just the two of us in our own world. Instantly I see the tension leak from his shoulders.

"You should take it onstage with you," I say.

"What do you mean?" He stares down at the guitar.

"That's the guitar you wrote your songs on, right? Take it with you and play the first few chords with that guitar. Then, during the buildup, you can switch to your stage guitar."

The room is silent for a few moments, and I wonder if I've suggested something really stupid. But then his face lights up. "Penny, you're a genius." He jumps to his feet and kisses me again.

"Careful of the guitar!" I laugh.

"Come on. Let's get out there before Dean has a heart attack," he says, slinging the instrument over his shoulder.

He holds his hand out to me, and I take it. Then, with his other hand, he opens the door.

Dean is leaning up against the wall outside, his head in his hands. He looks up as we emerge. "Oh, thank the Lord. Are you ready?"

"Yep, Dean, I'm coming."

"Good. You worried me for a moment." Dean starts striding through the backstage area. Noah and I hurry after him, dodging wires taped to the ground with thick black electrical tape and people wearing headsets who are frantically running around. I crane my neck to look up; the set for The Sketch is suspended above us. They're using giant screens that they'll bring down to the stage during their first act. Noah told me that they've hired live illustrators to draw onstage while the band performs, and the pictures will be shown on-screen. I almost trip on one of the wires, but Noah's hand tightens round my own, steadying me.

Dean looks over his shoulder. "What are you carrying?" he asks Noah.

"It's my guitar. I'm going to use it for the first part of the song—sing it a cappella—and then Blake can come in with the drum intro and I'll switch to the main-stage guitar."

Dean stops us all in our tracks and turns to face Noah, cocking his head to one side. Then he nods. "That sounds great. Not what we rehearsed, but, hey—it will be like a throwback to how you used to sound on YouTube. Let me go tell the rest of the guys and the crew. You never make my life easy, Noah."

"And yet you wouldn't have it any other way." Noah grins.

Before we know it, we're in the wings of the stage. I can feel the pulse of the audience, everyone waiting with bated breath for Noah to appear.

He turns to me, his dark eyes sparkling. I can see now that his nerves have gone—replaced by sheer adrenaline and excitement. "Thank you, Penny. I don't know what I'd do without you."

I smile. "See you after the show," I whisper.

Then the entire stage goes dark and even the audience is quiet. You could hear a pin drop. The anticipation for Noah's performance is so thick, I don't know how he can bear it.

Noah takes a deep breath, then walks out onto the stage in near-complete darkness. I can just about make out his silhouette as I watch from the wings. He adjusts the microphone in its stand, shuffling his feet until he feels comfortable. Then he places his hands on the guitar and strums his first note. The sound reverberates around the theatre.

The spotlight snaps on, he sings the first few bars of "Elements," and the screaming cheers from the 4,500-strong audience rise into a roar.

And that's when I realize that I'm crying.

Chapter Seven

"Hey, Penny, you might want to go to your seat to watch the rest of Noah's performance," says Dean from behind me.

"Oh . . . what?" Dean's voice snaps me from my spell; watching Noah out onstage is mesmerizing. Reluctantly I tear my eyes away from him. "I guess so. How do I get there from here?" I'm supposed to watch the rest of the show in the VIP area, where Elliot and Alex are too.

"Just follow this hallway and you'll come to a staircase. Go down it and out the door, then you'll be in the main stalls. You should be able to find your way around to the VIP sections up on the next level from there." Dean is wearing a headset and he appears to be distracted by something someone has said in his ear, because his face loses some of its colour and he looks wound up like a clockwork toy.

"OK, thanks. I've got it," I say with more confidence than I feel. Dean takes off and I try to follow his instructions quickly so I remember them. I know that Noah's set isn't that long, and I don't want to miss a moment.

I break into a jog, carefully picking my way through the

maze of the backstage area, and fly through the door that leads into the stalls. Just like that, I'm launched out into the crowd. Down here, it's so much louder than backstage. There are booming speakers, and girls (the crowd is pretty much all girls) are screaming and leaning across the barriers that separate them from Noah. They reach out, their arms waving, desperate for a piece of him. Like this, they stop being individuals and seem to merge into one entity, filled with rabid excitement. There was a specific announcement before the show not to throw presents up onstage, but I can already see girls are tossing teddy bears and flowers—and even a bra—at Noah's feet.

The adrenaline buzz of excitement rings through me, but it's edged with the extra-sharp teeth of nerves. The security staff move me along, not allowing me to linger by the entrance to the backstage area, and I'm thrown even deeper into the crowd. I look up at the balcony and try to find Elliot. Luckily, he's easy to spot, since he's right at the front by the railing with Alex. They're listening to "Elements" with their eyes locked together, arms wrapped round each other's shoulders. It's such a sweet—and rare—moment that my heart lifts.

They kiss, and I take out my phone and snap a picture of them, gutted that I left my proper camera in the dressing room. Even though it comes out dark, it still looks really atmospheric, and I can't wait to show Elliot later. He'll love it—he's wanted a picture of the two of them together for ages. Whenever I try to take a picture of them, Alex turns all shy. He isn't out to all his friends and family yet, so he shies away from any public displays of affection. Elliot has been really patient with him, and knows from his own experiences that he needs to let Alex take his time, but it's still a challenge that they both have to deal with.

Someone bumps into me, knocking my phone out of my hand. "Hey!" I shout and turn round, but the girl who knocked me doesn't even notice—she's too busy singing along to Noah's lyrics and jumping up and down. I look down for my phone and spot it underneath her feet.

I make a dive for it, but it just gets kicked further along the sticky floor.

"Oh, sorry about that!" the girl shouts, finally noticing me.

"No problem," I say, but the words catch in my throat. I need to get my phone. I lean down and try to follow its path, but every time I think I see it again it is moved further away.

I wince as someone steps on my fingers, and that split second is enough to make me lose sight of my phone. I swear my heart stops beating for a moment. Then I see it again—in a small clearing of feet. I drop down to the ground, grabbing for it. But, once again, it's kicked out of my reach. Through the sea of legs, I see a hand reach down and pick up my phone.

"Hey, that's mine!" I shout. Desperation sets in, and I crawl on my hands and knees, pushing through the crowd and nearly getting trampled.

"What are you doing?!"

"What the hell?!"

I ignore the complaints as I push past a forest of bare legs and ripped denim, but it's no use. My phone is gone.

I stand up before I get crushed, frantically searching the crowd for the phone thief. Every face looks the same: wide-eyed and staring at my boyfriend up onstage. I'm the only one whose eyes are *not* on Noah. Another person shoves my shoulder, launching me into the person behind me, who yells at me. Luckily the crowd drowns her words out, but I know they aren't friendly. "I'm sorry," I try to say, but I suddenly feel so enclosed. There's no space for me to move, let alone breathe.

I see the bright red EXIT sign above everyone's heads and I try to make a beeline for it. I feel like I'm swimming against a strong tide, caught in a current that is threatening to drag me under. I can hear Noah talking to the crowd between songs but it feels like a million miles away.

Then I feel a tap on my shoulder. "Hey, aren't you that girl with the blog? Noah's girlfriend?" asks a girl with her bright blonde hair tied to one side in an awesome fishtail braid.

"Uhh . . ."

"Oh my god, guys, it's Noah's girlfriend!" Fishtail Braid gathers all her friends round.

"Who, the blog girl?"

"Where?"

"Can you give this to Noah for me?"

Before I know it, the girl and all her friends are surrounding me. Other people in the crowd are noticing me, or maybe they're just using the commotion to try to get even closer to Noah onstage.

"I need to get out of here," I say, but it comes out as barely a whisper. All of a sudden this has turned into my worst nightmare. It feels like there are a million hands pressing down on me, all wanting to pull me in a different direction. My breath turns shallow inside my chest. I can't see where to go—every path through the crowd looks the same, leading deeper into all the faces staring at me. I can't even hear Noah's voice anymore over the screaming inside my head.

"Penny? Is that you?" asks a female voice.

I don't know who it is, but I can only answer in a whimper. The girl grabs my hand and starts to pull me through the crowd. "Come with me. This way." I feel stupid entrusting myself to her—all I can see is a cascade of long, dark brown hair—but, as she barges a path through the crowd, that feeling is quickly replaced by gratitude.

Chapter Eight

At last we break through the hordes of screaming girls and out into the wide hallway outside the stalls. I take a huge gulp of air, placing my hands on my knees. When I've finally managed to clear the fuzz from my mind, I look up. To my surprise, it's Megan.

She looks genuinely worried about me. "Hey, are you OK? You looked pretty overwhelmed in there." She puts her hand on my back.

I smile weakly. "I just couldn't deal with the crowd. It was too much. I lost my phone, and then all the people were pressing down on me . . ."

"Were you crying? Your makeup is streaked."

I'd forgotten that I'd cried at hearing Noah's singing, and I wipe my hands across my cheeks. That moment backstage seems like a lifetime ago now compared to the panic attack I just experienced. When I'm struck by anxiety, it's like everything else is pushed into the background and all my mind can focus on is *panic, panic, panic*. Nothing else matters. Even if my logical brain tells me that the exit is only a few steps away, my body just won't listen. It's like the two are separated from each other by the beast of anxiety. "Oh no, it's not from that—these were happy tears."

Megan smiles. "Do you want me to walk with you back to your seat?"

"Sure. It's upstairs . . . but—oh, I don't even know exactly where it is." That's when I realize that I don't have my ticket with me. I must have left it in Noah's dressing room—along with my camera, jacket, purse, and backstage pass. As I explain everything to Megan I can feel myself getting frustrated. I can't believe my excitement led me to make such a silly mistake.

"Don't worry about that." Megan strolls straight up to the nearest security guard, flicking her chestnut hair. "This is Penny Porter—she's Noah Flynn's girlfriend. She left her ticket backstage and she needs to get back to his dressing room."

The security guard gives us both a sceptical look. "Yeah right, and I'm Prince Harry."

"Sir, please," I say. "I just came out of the stage door in the front . . ."

"Look, girls, why don't you go back to the concert and enjoy it like everybody else. No more of these silly games."

"It's not a game," says Megan. She manages to keep her calm exterior, even though I feel like I'm about to break down. "Look, sir, if you'll find someone from Noah's entourage they will recognize her and explain."

He folds his arms across his chest. He's not going to budge one bit. "If you don't return to the concert now, I'm going to escort you from the premises."

"This is outrageous!" says Megan. "When Noah finds out about this, you're going to be fired!"

I drag her away from the security guard before he can put her in handcuffs, or whatever it is that scary-looking security guards do. I can feel him still glaring at us as we talk in the hallway. "I appreciate you sticking up for me but I—I think I want to go."

"Are you sure?" Megan puts a comforting arm round me. "You can just come back with me into the stalls?"

I shake my head. "Noah will find me if I'm at home."

"OK," she says, understanding. We may have fallen out recently, but she still knows a lot about me. "I'll come with you, make sure you get home safe."

"Really? You don't have to do that. I can just . . ." I was going to say "call Tom," but that's not an option either as I've lost my phone and I don't have his new number memorized. "It's not that far to walk. And, besides, you'll miss The Sketch and I know you were really excited about seeing them."

Megan links her arm into mine. "I think you need me more than I need to see The Sketch right now. Plus, I could use some fresh air. The crowd was crazy."

Megan being so nice to me still makes me feel uneasy, but I can't hear any hint of bad intention in her voice. We walk together towards the exit.

As soon as we get outside, we discover that the rain has reduced to a drizzle. As the Brighton sea breeze whips through my hair, I feel it sweep some of my panic away. My chest still feels tight and my palms are sweaty, but Megan is clinging on to my arm like she's afraid I could blow away at any moment. I couldn't be more thankful to her.

"Do you want to grab some candy floss from the pier?" she asks. "The sugar might help."

I smile and nod. "Sounds good."

We stroll beneath the bright lights of the pier entrance, and I can see the waves crashing under us through the gaps in the wooden planks. We pick the stall with the brightest selection of candy floss and share a big white-and-pink swirl. I pick a large, fluffy section and put it in my mouth, letting the sugar dissolve in fizzes and pops over my tongue.

"Mmm, this is lovely," I say. I lower my eyes. "Thanks for what you did back there. You rescued me—I don't know what I would've done."

Megan smiles, her hair flapping around her head in the breeze. She pushes it back off her face and sweeps it up into a loose bun on top of her head. It looks effortlessly cool. "It's no problem at all. Do you want to use my phone to call your provider and tell them your phone's been stolen?"

I nod. "Thanks. Luckily it's got a password on it, and I hardly have any minutes left on my contract so they won't be able to make a ton of calls or anything. I really hope the person who picked it up hands it in. I love that phone." *And everything on it*, I think. Pictures of Noah and me. Text conversations. Even the case was special. Noah had stolen it off me one night and doodled all across the back in black Sharpie. It was my favourite case ever.

When I finish, I hand the phone back to Megan. "All done," I say.

"Oh, good." She sighs. "Look, Penny—I've been meaning to talk to you for some time, but there hasn't been a convenient moment."

"What do you mean?"

"I really want to say that I'm sorry. For everything that happened earlier this year. It . . . wasn't me. I'm sorry for telling everyone about *Girl Online*. I feel so dumb, because I actually used to enjoy all your posts and I was just jealous that you were going out with a pop star. It seemed like you had everything. Ollie, then Noah and the crazy, wonderful trip to New York City—my dream place to live in the whole world—plus you're this amazingly talented photographer and writer. Everyone is always saying how brilliant you are and what a great career you're going to have . . . All I had was a terrible glue-stick commercial and a dream of being a movie star. I shouldn't have taken it out on you the way I did."

If my mouth wasn't full of candy floss, it would have dropped open. I swallow the sugary goodness, but find I'm still speechless.

"Can you forgive me?" she continues, when I don't say anything.

"I—I had no idea you felt like that. It always seems like *you* are the one who has everything. Megan, you're so pretty and popular, and you're a great actress—you got a place at that famous drama school! But I was really hurt after what happened . . ."

"I know." She casts her eyes down to the ground. "It was wrong of me. I don't know what happened to us, Penny. We used to be such good friends."

"I guess we just grew apart."

"Well, if there's any hope for us to still be friends, I'd like that . . ."

We stare at each other for a moment, and eventually

Megan smiles. It's so full of warmth that I can't help it: I nod. "I'd like that too," I say. Then I smirk, and look down at our matching dresses. "Hey, we must look like twins walking around in the same outfit."

She laughs warmly. "Yeah, well, you can't buy good taste, right? Come on." She takes my arm again. "Everyone will be worried about where you are. Let's get you home."

Chapter Nine

When we arrive back at my house, all the curtains are closed
and the hallway is dark. I'm confused. Did my parents go out
for the evening? Then I hear voices from the living room and
realize they must be watching a film. I gesture for Megan to
follow me in. The living-room door creaks as I push it open.

"Mum?" I say tentatively.

What I don't expect is for her to leap off the sofa when she
hears my voice. "Goodness, Penny!" she says, clutching her
chest. "You frightened me! Your father put on one of those
awful horror films that he knows I can't stand." She throws
him an evil glare, but Dad just laughs it off. He knows as well
as I do that my mum loves a good scare—it's all in the name
of drama, after all!

Then she genuinely does frown as she looks at me. "But
what are you doing home so early? We weren't expecting you
for hours yet." She looks at Megan, and I can tell she's trying
not to blurt out another question as to why Megan is here
with me after everything that happened with *Girl Online*.

I can't help it—I break down into shaky tears as I describe

my panic attack and the sense of claustrophobia in the crowd, and eventually Megan takes over, filling in the gaps where I don't remember. When she's finished, Dad flicks on the lights and potters off to make a cup of tea. Before I know it, I'm feeling much better, and a new feeling starts to dominate my nervous system. It's no longer anxiety; it's guilt. Even though I had no phone, no wallet, and no way of leaving him a note or getting a message to him, I still know that Noah will go crazy with worry when he finds out I left without telling him.

"I'm just going to nip upstairs and let Noah know I've come home," I say.

Mum nods, then she smiles at Megan. "How are your parents, sweetheart? It's so nice to see you again . . ." Leaving Mum to catch up with Megan, I run up the stairs, taking them two at a time.

As soon as I've written a direct message to Noah (he's far more likely to check Twitter than his email), I also take a moment to open up my blog. Megan's apparent change of heart has been playing on my mind, and I know who I want to tell.

25 June

Can You Forgive and Forget?

I know it's my second post today, but it feels like the longest day ever! So much has happened.

Do you remember a while back when I wrote about drifting apart from a friend? And then that "friend" turned out to be the very person who sold me out to the media? (I know—who needs enemies when you have friends like that, right?)

Well, she actually apologized.

Can you believe it? I never thought I would see the day.

She helped me out when I thought no one would, and was really nice to me. And, even though I kept looking for an ulterior motive, she didn't seem to have one.

She was just nice.

She was my old friend again.

It felt good to have her there to talk to. Is that weird? Is it even possible to forgive something so big? Can I ever forget what she did to me?

She even said she had been jealous of me. How can that be right? I guess we don't always know what other people are thinking, even if they seem to have everything figured out.

Wiki, I know you will hate this when you find out.

But I think I want to forgive her. I can't throw away that many years of friendship so easily . . .

Anyway, I will keep you posted.

Girl Offline . . . never going online xxx

I change out of my dress and into my most comfortable onesie, then head back downstairs. Mum and Dad switch the film back on, so Megan and I curl up on the sofa to watch as well.

It's not very long until there's a frantic knock on the door. Dad goes to open it and Noah runs into the room.

"Penny, thank god!" Noah's face is as white as a sheet. Seeing him wrenches the knot in my stomach. He rushes over and gives me a hug. "What the heck happened? I came out after my set to find you, and Elliot said he hadn't seen you at all. When I saw all your stuff in the dressing room, I was so worried about you. I called you about a bajillion times . . ."

"I'm so sorry, Noah. I can't believe I missed your set. I was so excited it just completely went out of my head to even check that I had my ticket with me. Then someone in the crowd knocked my phone out of my hand and it all became way too much for me. Thankfully Megan was there to help me out."

"I wish it could have been me. If I'd known what was going on . . ."

"You would have leapt off the stage?" I say, laughing. "There was nothing you could do. Besides, it's OK now." He hands me back everything I left backstage and I smile gratefully. Now it's only my phone that is missing.

"Hey, Noah." I look up at the unfamiliar voice and I'm surprised to see Blake standing there. "Now that you've found her, I'm going to get back to the hotel."

"Sure, man, thanks for helping me out. Can you let Dean know everything's OK? And get him to check with security to see if anyone's handed in Penny's phone. It's got a pink case with *PP* doodled in black Sharpie on the back," Noah says.

"Uh, Penny, I'd better go too." Megan stands up from her seat and gives me a little wave, but I can tell her attention is all on Blake, despite this being the first time she's met Noah. Slouched against the doorway, Blake strikes an edgier, grungier vibe than Noah, and possesses that rock-star confidence that can only come from being onstage in front of a huge, screaming audience. Megan casually takes her hair out of her bun, shaking it out around her shoulders, and I can see Blake stand up and take notice too. "Thanks for the tea, Dahlia."

"Of course, Megan," says my mum. "Thank you for being there for Penny today. It's nice to see the two of you together again."

"My pleasure. Any time. See you later, Penny." Megan flashes me a wide smile, tossing her hair and rolling her shoulders back to showcase her outfit—my dress somehow looks completely different on her. At least I know the world hasn't completely turned upside down; this is the Megan I'm used to.

"Megan . . . thanks. A lot," I say. "I'll see you around."

She nods and disappears down the hall towards the front door. Blake follows a step behind.

"What are *you* doing here?" comes a high-pitched voice from the hallway. I cringe as I realize Elliot must have come into the house just as Megan was leaving. Talk about bad timing.

"I was helping out my *friend*, which is more than I can say for you."

I let out a noise that is somewhere between strangled cat and deranged weasel, then jump up and run into the hallway. A battle between Megan and Elliot is not what I need right now.

"Elliot," I say, and I give him a look I hope says, *It's OK. Megan might have redeemed herself but I'm not sure yet.* Can a single look convey that entire message? I'm not too sure.

He seems to get it though, in the way that only best friends can.

"See you later, Megan," he says through gritted teeth.

"Bye," she says, before finally leaving, followed closely by Blake.

"Don't let the door hit your giant head on the way out!" he shouts at the closed door. He looks up and takes in my appearance, which I imagine can be summed up in one word: disaster. I've changed into my favourite onesie, my hair is a bedraggled mess, and my eyes are still swollen from crying.

We all regroup in the living room. "Princess Penny, what happened?" asks Elliot.

I decide to tell him the condensed version of the story—I can always fill in the details later, in private, and he'll also read the blog I wrote. It's not just my feelings that I have to consider right now—I'm also aware of the look on my mum's face, the frown that deepens every time she hears me talk about how panicky I got. I'm not used to seeing her look so worried. Normally she's carefree and breezy, taking every concern in her stride.

But now I can feel my chance to go on tour with Noah slipping through my fingers. If she thinks I can't handle it . . .

Dad pours more tea into my mug—a Disney one with Piglet, my favourite character, on the front. I hug the mug to my chest, feeling its warmth spread through my body. I lean into Noah's arms. He's holding me so tightly I don't think he ever wants to let me go.

Elliot sits down on the floor, and my parents both take chairs opposite. I feel like we're about to go into full-blown interrogation mode. Mum and Dad exchange a long look, before turning to Noah and me. "I think this is exactly what we were afraid of," says Dad, his voice grave.

Mum nods. "Your dad's right, Penny. There's no way we can let you go to Europe now."

Chapter Ten

"Mum, what? No!" I say, my jaw almost hitting the floor.

"Not if this is how it's going to be, Noah," continues Mum, and she sounds angrier than I expected. "It's not going to be possible for Penny to just walk home from a concert in Berlin or Paris! You promised she would be taken care of—if this is how it works in Brighton, how will she cope in Europe?"

"It was my first time backstage, Mum; I promise I'll be more prepared next time . . . "

Mum shoots me a look that makes me snap my mouth shut. I'm going to have to work a lot harder to prove to them that I'm ready for this; I certainly haven't proved it today.

Noah removes his arm from round me and leans towards my parents. "I promise this will never happen again. Penny won't have to go out into the crowds by herself at the concerts in Europe—it was only because she was going to sit with her friends this time that she even had a separate ticket. And I promise every single person on my security team and The Sketch's will know her face and will always look out for her. She's already met Larry, my bodyguard, and I'll make sure he doesn't let her out of his sight."

"Larry's really nice," I say.

"And you see this?" He grabs my hand, holding it tightly in his. "I'm not going to let go of this hand."

"Well, you can let go when you go to the bathroom," I say, a small smile playing on my lips.

Noah roars with laughter. "Yeah, except for that! You know what I mean. I'm going to be there for Penny," he says, returning to his serious expression. "She's my girl, and I will look after her."

"I still don't know if this is a good idea," says Mum, biting her lip. "This is just the beginning, honey. Are you sure you still want to do this?"

"I'm sure," I say. "I still want to go. Tonight was scary, but I made a mistake. It won't happen again."

"It can't be as bad as that school trip to Amsterdam when your class thought the air-raid warnings were going off and all ran screaming through Vondelpark," says Elliot. He's right—Mr. Beaconsfield had told us all to hide under park benches, which we did until a nice Dutch couple came past and explained that the siren was a normal thing that happened on the first Monday of every month at exactly noon. On Noah's tour, there will be far more people looking after me. And I have to conquer my fears at some point.

"Mum, Dad, please. I'll be fine." I give them a reassuring smile, but I'm not sure how convincing it is with my still-puffy eyes. "Hopefully I can have Tom's old phone and get a new SIM card before we go to the airport. That way I can still call you whenever I need to."

There's a tense moment of silence. Mum and Dad look at each other.

"OK. You can still go," says Mum.

I jump up and hug my parents. "I won't let you down," I say.

"You never have, Penny. We just worry about you," explains Dad.

"And now I'm worried that you're not going to be packed on time!" adds Mum. "Don't think I haven't seen the state of your room."

"I'll manage it!" I say.

Elliot smiles. "Good. Now that's sorted, I'm heading home—I need to get my beauty sleep. Alex is forcing me to use the season ticket my dad gave me to watch *rugby* tomorrow. Can you imagine? The things you do for love. At least the rugby men are *fit*. If only Alex would meet my dad, they'd probably get along—" Elliot snaps his mouth shut, as if he's not sure what he's just said. I raise an eyebrow but Elliot gives me a *Don't ask me* gaze. He turns to Noah. "The concert was awesome," he says. "You stole the show. The Sketch had nothing on you!"

Noah pulls him into a bear hug, squishing Elliot so tight his trilby almost comes off. "I wish you could come with us too, Elliot!"

"And cramp Princess Penny's style? No way."

"Another time then."

"For sure." Elliot turns to me. "I can't believe you leave so early tomorrow! I'm not going to get to see you for ages! I'm going to miss you so much." Now it's time for him to give *me* a huge hug.

"I'm going to miss you too!"

"You have to promise to write to me every day."

"And text!"

"And call!"

"Come on, you two, it's not like Penny's off on a mission to Mars. She *will* be back in a couple of weeks," says Mum.

"A *lot* can happen in a couple of weeks," says Elliot. "You're going to have to tell me everything. *Every*thing. Especially about Paris. I want to know all about Paris."

"Of course! And you have to keep me updated on every minute of your internship!" We finally release each other and I walk Elliot into the hallway. He skips out of our house and round to his house next door. He blows me a kiss before I shut the door.

"I'd better go too, Penny," says Noah from behind me. They're words I don't want to hear.

"But you just got here," I say, squeezing Noah tight.

"I know, but soon we'll have two weeks together. I have to head back to the hotel to get everything ready for Berlin tomorrow. I'm so psyched. I'll be back before you know it— five a.m. Bright and early." He reaches up and pushes a stray strand of hair off my face, tucking it behind my ear. "Are you sure you're OK? I promise you nothing like that will ever happen again."

"I know." I stand up on my tiptoes and kiss him gently on the lips. "I can't wait. It's going to be perfect."

"It really will be. We can have a Magical Mystery Day in every stop! Except it'll be a mission to find the best baked goods in whichever country we're in. Germany! Italy!"

"France! I want to eat all the macarons in the world. They're my favourite. Is that a promise?"

"It's a deal."

His warm, dark eyes are staring straight into mine. "I love you, Penny. Just never scare me like that again."

"I won't," I say, and I mean it. Tomorrow we're going to Europe and I'm not going to let *anything* ruin our big trip.

Chapter Eleven

Back in my room, I finish throwing as many clothes as will fit into my suitcase and zip it up tight. As long as I have my camera, laptop, Mum's cardigan, and a change of underwear, everything else is just extra.

The rain has started again, battering the windows. I grab my laptop and settle down on my window seat. I imagine every raindrop is a piece of my anxiety running down the glass, onto the street, and eventually out into the sea. I don't need to hold on to any of it.

I see an unread comment from Pegasus Girl on my latest blog post. I rush to open it.

Hey, GO!

So nice to hear from you! How did the concert go?

I know EXACTLY how you feel about your friend. I'm going through kind of the same thing over here. A friend really wronged me, and I just don't know if I can ever forgive her. But I think you have to offer people second chances. Even if you never become the best friends you once were, because now you're older, wiser, and won't make the same mistake twice, it's better to have a friend than an enemy. Plus, you don't need that kind of negativity in your life! Accept the apology, but also accept that you won't be the friends you once were.

PG xx

I quickly type a reply.

Thanks for your advice. How can I describe the concert? It was kind of a disaster. I had a panic attack in the audience and had to leave before BB had even finished his set.

But the one good thing that came out of it was that it gave my friend the chance to apologize. I'm not sure that I can ever trust her again, but it feels like a weight has lifted now that I don't have to look over my shoulder at every turn, wondering what she's going to do next.

I'm about to go to sleep, because tomorrow . . . I'm getting on a plane to Berlin! I'm nervous and excited all at once. I'm still using Wiki's tips on how to combat anxiety. Ocean Strong is going to be on board! I'm also taking my mum's favourite cardie with me to wrap up in.

I'll keep you up to date on everything that happens!

GO xx

I'm just about to log off when an email pops up on my screen. I wonder if it's a notification saying Pegasus Girl has replied super quickly. I hate leaving an email unanswered, so I open it . . . but the email address isn't one that I recognize.

From: TheRealTruth
To: Penny Porter
Subject: Enjoy it while it lasts . . .

ATTACHMENT: image_1051.jpg

The email itself is blank, but I can see a small thumbnail of the image and immediately my stomach turns in on itself. I feel like I'm going to be sick. I double-click on the attachment and up pops a photograph of Noah and me.

My mind begins to race. Is this a paparazzi shot? Or one of Noah's crazy fans?

But then I realize it's the selfie that I took earlier in the car. The one on my phone.

**⋆Chapter Twelve*⋆*

My heart beats faster inside my chest and my pulse quickens, but I take a big, deep breath. I am not going to let some phone thief bully me into panicking about this. I know exactly who I can turn to in this situation. I gather my laptop in my arms and run down the flight of stairs that lead from my cosy attic room and knock frantically on Tom's door.

"Yeah?" I'm surprised he can hear me knock over the thrumming bass of his favourite dubstep music, but he's very attuned to any disturbance of his privacy.

"It's me." I push open the door and see my brother at his computer. He spends so much of his time there that I'm surprised there isn't a permanent indent in his desk chair.

"Everything OK, Pen-pen?" He takes off his head-phones.

I bring my laptop over to him and show him the picture. "This was taken from my phone—the one that was stolen at the concert. Look at the subject line. I think someone wants to use it against me?"

Tom's body language shifts from relaxed to tense, like he's gearing up for a fight. "OK, first of all, have you called your provider? They can shut down the phone remotely."

I nod. "Yeah, I did that about ten minutes after I lost it. But I haven't done anything else . . . I guess I was still holding out hope that someone would find it and hand it in."

He grabs his phone and starts dialling a number. "Right, well, at least that's something. Is there anything that's really compromising on your phone? If they've got this photograph, they might have downloaded others from your phone already, or got your contacts list. Didn't you have a password?"

"I had a password but . . . it was Noah's birthday." I cringe at how obvious that sounds, now that I say it out loud. "If someone had recognized it was my phone, that wouldn't be too hard to guess. There are a few texts, and most of my conversations with Noah are on WhatsApp."

"Let's go through and change all your passwords—we can do that remotely, and set it so that your phone wipes if it's connected to the Internet. Then you'd better let Noah know that someone might have got hold of his number."

The thought of that makes me feel anxious all over again, but Tom reminds me that it's just a phone number, and not passport details or a full-blown medical history. "Pen-pen, it was an accident. Noah will understand. He cares more about you than a stupid mobile number."

After an hour sitting on the edge of Tom's bed, I've managed to shut down the phone, wipe it clean, and change all my passwords. I feel so much better knowing that I've done as much as possible, and that there's nothing more TheRealTruth—whoever they are—can do to hurt me. I don't want to be a victim anymore to people who think they can abuse my privacy and my emotions. I remind myself that they don't know anything about me and Noah, and how solid our relationship is after everything we've been through. I'm stronger than I was last year, and I want to remain that way.

I stand up and hug Tom from behind as he taps away at his computer, changing the last of my log-in details. "Thanks, bro. I love you."

He pats my arms. "I'm proud of you for not freaking out, Penny." He spins round in his chair. "And be careful in Europe. If anything happens, I'll be on the first plane out."

"I know." As I leave, I take a deep breath and finally feel like I am actually going. And I can't wait.

When Noah picks me up the next morning, my adrenaline is still running high from the previous night. I tell him all about TheRealTruth and he doesn't even flinch. Instead, he grabs my hand.

"Remember what I said, Autumn Girl. I'm here for you. Sounds like you and Tom got things sorted, but if anything else from this creep comes up we'll face it together. You and me against the world, all right?"

"All right," I say, and my heart lifts as I realize that whoever is trying to . . . blackmail me? Scare me? Trigger my anxiety? Whatever it is they're trying to do, I won't have to face it alone. If anything, our chat about TheRealTruth ends up being a welcome distraction from the short plane journey because, before I know it, we've landed and Noah is taking my hand and escorting me through the airport, into the car park, and up to the tour bus.

It is just as I had imagined: a great big black bus, with huge, tinted windows. It's super shiny and swish. Noah's face is lit up with excitement and he squeezes my hand so tight I feel my bones crush together.

"This is really happening, Pen! Look at this absolute beauty." He skips ahead and stands in front of it, attempting to take a tour-bus selfie—but of course he only manages to get his face and a tiny bit of black behind him.

"Let me take it, you doofus." I snatch the phone from his hand and take a much better shot with his arms outstretched and the bus behind him.

Larry pops his head out of the door and waves us in. "Oh, good. You're here!" he says. As we step inside, I realize how much of a boys' paradise this is. There are several mini fridges, games consoles, and TV screens everywhere. The rest of Noah's band starts filing in and, surprisingly, I don't feel claustrophobic. It's a lot roomier than I could ever have expected. There are two sofa areas, a small kitchen, a shower with a toilet, and at the back of the bus there are a few caravan-style beds in case anyone feels the need for a quick snooze.

I feel a hand slide behind my back and a husky voice in my ear.

"Wanna play?" I turn to see Blake gesturing towards the Xbox.

"Oh, I'm not very good really!" I say modestly, although secretly I'm an absolute whiz at *Sonic the Hedgehog* and *Mario Kart*. Having an older brother means that the majority of the time I've spent bonding with him has been over lengthy gaming sessions. A lot of my fondest memories with

Tom are of the days and weeks we used to spend trying to complete various games together, snacking on handfuls of cereal and leaving the room only for the occasional toilet break.

What is he doing right now? That's not hard—he's probably on his computer, playing *Halo*. I bet Mum is cleaning the kitchen, wearing her dusting shoes, flapping around with a feather duster and singing along to eighties classics. My dad, on the other hand, is probably playing solitaire on his computer, or pretending to do the crossword in the paper. He never does them properly; he just tries to think of the most immature words he can to fill the spaces, then leaves the crossword out for my mum to find on one of her cleaning sprees. She will usually laugh uncontrollably and they'll end up smooching like teenagers in a heap on the sofa. I shudder and quickly snap out of my daydreaming.

"That's not true, Penny!" Noah laughs. "I seem to remember you kicking my butt at *Mario Kart* last time I saw you!"

"Aha! I knew it," snaps Blake. "No excuses!" He shoves a controller into my hand and stretches out in a chair in front of a TV, placing a bottle of beer on the table and burping out of the side of his mouth.

"You're on," I say, sitting down beside Blake and putting on my best smirk as he starts a game of *Forza Motorsport*. I can't say car racing is my forte, but I'll give my best shot.

"Prepare to lose," he chimes back, with a strange smile on his face. He takes a sip of his beer, holding eye contact with me until I feel uncomfortable and turn towards the screen and select my car. Blake stretches out with one leg up on the table, burping and swearing at his racing car. I might actually beat him! I can hear the rest of the guys laughing behind us, and Noah is improvising an entire song about bratwurst.

"Hey, so your friend Megan is something else," Blake says without taking his eyes off the screen.

"What?" I'm so shocked I almost drop the controller, and my on-screen vehicle crashes dramatically into a concrete barrier.

Blake zooms past me and pumps both fists up in the air when he crosses the finish line. "Oh yeah! I knew this little girlie couldn't beat me. Better luck next time."

I don't care about the car—but I do care about this new piece of information. "So, you and Megan talked then?"

Blake winks at me. "Why, you jealous?"

"Leave her alone, dude," says Noah.

I look over at Blake, who is frowning in concentration at the screen. He's a really strange character; I have no friends like him, no one to compare him to. He is so different from Noah that I find it hard to think of them being close friends for so long. Noah is caring, gentle, and funny, while Blake seems very unaware of other people and somewhat cold. I can't place my finger on it, but something about him makes me feel uneasy. One thing I know for sure is that Noah wouldn't be drinking beer at two in the afternoon while swearing profusely at an animated car.

I want to know more about Blake and Megan, but I don't know how to ask. As the bus starts to crawl forward Blake throws his arms up in the air again.

"We're OFF!" he yells, and my thoughts of Megan are lost in the infectious cheers of excitement that ripple across the bus.

Chapter Thirteen

Larry emerges from the front of the bus, a large German flag draped on his shoulders.

"All right, you party animals, we should arrive in the city within forty minutes. Use this bus as your base. A lot of the crew will be staying here, but I want you to feel as though you can come here for some peace, or a game against me on the Xbox. That includes you, Penny!" He gives me a little wink. "It'll be hotels for the night in each city and then the travelling will continue in the bus or by plane to each country and city that we go to."

"How much are we paying you to be our tour guide?" Noah shouts, and everyone else laughs.

"Nothing, you silly fool." Larry throws the flag in Noah's direction and he wraps it round himself. It's nice seeing Noah in his element, laughing and joking with his friends and being so excited. It's a whole other level of attractive, and I honestly just want to smooch him right then and there.

"That's another forty minutes of me whipping your butt at racing then," Blake says.

"I guess so," I say, almost sighing. I take out the replacement phone that Tom has given me (his older, less cool one, which he doesn't mind me losing or breaking) and I text Elliot.

> Landed in Berlin and now stuck playing car games with Noah's drummer, Blake, who smells like BO masked in aftershave and stale cigarette smoke. Did I mention he's already on his third beer of the day and it's 2 pm?! Please remind me why this is a great idea xx

I immediately get a reply from Elliot.

> Princess P. Most impressed that you even managed to step onto the tour bus in the first place, but totally unimpressed that you are being made to play garbage on a screen in such a beautiful city. Please don't come back to England with game skills and a lack of sightseeing knowledge. It would break my encyclopaedic heart. Think of the photos, the adventure, and the history. If that fails, think of the food. THE FOOD, PENNY! Magical Mystery Day in each city is going to be absolutely amazing. You can visit the Berlin Wall, the Brandenburg Gate, the Reichstag Building. And OMG have you seen the Fernsehturm yet? x

Elliot, I believe you're forgetting that all I've seen so far are the dark windows of a tour bus and the side of Blake's head. I also don't know what the Fernsehturm is because I am not a walking encyclopaedia. MMD is the one thing I really am very excited about. It will be so romantic getting to explore each city with Noah. Hand in hand, strolling along sampling some of the finest international . . . cake xx

Beeindruckend, impressionnant, impresionante, fantastico! x

Elliot, in English please xx

Awesome. It all means awesome, Pen. You might need that for a few of the stops you're going to make. PS The Fernsehturm is a television tower and the tallest structure in Germany at 368m tall.

If I wasn't enjoying an extravagant lunch at
Browns courtesy of Alex right now I would be
smashing my head on the table. Didn't you
research some of the places you were going
before you left? I do love you, Penny, but you need
to broaden your knowledge of epic-ness. That's
the first thing I'm doing with you when you get
back. Let me know how it goes. My first day at the
internship is tomorrow. WISH ME LUCK. All the
love, your favourite gay x

I smile down at my phone and go to reply when Blake takes
it out of my hand and places it on the table in front of us.

"How am I supposed to beat you if you're not even playing? Put that away."

"Rude!" I say, picking it back up and putting it in my pocket.

"It's not rude. That's just how you've chosen to feel." He
smiles and hands the controller back to me.

Noah stands up and stretches, throwing his arms high
above his head and yawning dramatically. "I'm beat after last
night and the early start. I'm gonna grab a quick nap in the
back. Penny, is that cool?"

"Of course," I say. Even as I say the words, I stare up at
Noah, trying to communicate *Please don't leave me alone with
your creepy friend* with my eyes, but he isn't as good at decoding
my secret messages as Elliot is. He just smiles and heads into
the back of the bus.

In an attempt to enjoy the next half an hour, I ask Blake a few questions about the tour, Noah, the drums . . . anything I can think of. His answers consist mostly of grunts and mumbles, but altogether it about amounts to a conversation. It's not overly stimulating and not very enjoyable, but it makes the journey go a little faster and, since he's not concentrating so hard on racing, I actually manage to beat him a few times (much to his horror).

"So, you've been with Noah how long now?" he asks.

"Oh . . . a bit over six months? It's gone so quickly."

"Yeah, that sounds like a lifetime! You know, this tour is a big thing for Noah. It's his dream come true."

Even though I'm not sure how to take the "lifetime" comment, I'm shocked that we are actually having a nice conversation. It worked! I softened Blake the grump. Playing car games was totally worth it to realize I had the wrong impression of him and he just needed to wind down. I'd always hoped I'd get on well with Noah's friends and finally it's happening.

I smile. "I know. I kind of wish I'd known him before he achieved his dream. I bet he never thought it would take off how it has. His music is amazing, though. He's a great songwriter. I mean, I don't know a lot about songwriting or the music industry but—"

"See, that's the thing, Penny," Blake interrupts. "You *don't* know anything about the music industry at all." His tone changes. My throat feels suddenly tight and my face starts getting hot. Blake is still looking at the screen and racing his car round the track. "I'm sure you're great, Penny. Noah obviously thinks so. I'm just not sure he thought about the consequences of having a girlfriend as his career kicks off."

He puts down his controller and pulls out a packet of tobacco, then puts a filter in his mouth as he rolls a cigarette. I watch him and feel the horror of what he's just said creep over me like a rash. I stay silent, waiting for him to say something, anything that would redeem him and this conversation.

"The tour's going to be fun, though. Nights out in different cities, getting drunk, lots of girls," he says through pursed lips as he continues to roll the cigarette.

"I'm not sure what you're trying to say, Blake." I stare at him out of the corner of my eye, but try to remain cool.

"'Blake' sounds funny when English chicks say it." He puts the newly rolled cigarette behind his ear and gets up from the sofa to grab another beer from the mini fridge. When he sits back down, he's so close his leg brushes against mine. "I'm just saying . . . in the dream of being on tour, there's *one* thing on this bus that none of us ever wanted."

I'm stunned into silence. I want to come up with something witty to say, but my whole mouth feels numb, like it's been frozen solid. Mark, the bassist, comes over and picks up the controller from where it's dropped out of my hands. "Mind if I take over?"

"Go for it," I manage to say. I get up and walk towards the back of the bus. At the last moment before I enter the area with the beds I look back over my shoulder at Blake. He's engrossed in the screen.

I put my hand on the door frame to steady myself. It's only now that I notice how much I'm shaking, but it starts to pass, and I smile as I remember that there is a cure very nearby.

Chapter Fourteen

Noah rolls over and blinks his eyes at the light as I come in through the curtains.

"Hey, my girl."

"Oh, hey. Did I wake you?" I sit down on the edge of his bunk.

"Nah, couldn't sleep after all. It's all too exciting."

I nod, biting my lip. He sits up and covers my hand with his. "Are you OK? You look a bit pale."

I shake my head. "Well . . ." I want to tell him about what Blake said, but I also want Noah to think I can get on with his friends. I'm also hyperaware that Blake is his best friend, and I don't want to force him to have to choose sides between us. "How far back do you and Blake go?"

"Blake and me? He's one of my oldest friends. We practically grew up together. My parents bought me my first guitar the same year his parents gave him a drum kit. I used to go over to his basement and we would jam. Our first band was called . . ." He hesitates.

"Aw, come on, tell me!" I say, nudging him.

"OK . . . it was called The Wizard Boys. We were kind of obsessed with Harry Potter back then." He cringes, but it's adorable.

I laugh. "That's the greatest!"

"Yeah, Blake even used to pretend his drumsticks were wands and our lyrics were spells!"

"Are you serious?" Somehow I can't square the image of the grungy guy outside with that of a sweet young boy rocking out in his basement and inventing magic spells.

"You might not have heard of the song 'House Elves Just Want Some Love,' but it was destined to be a big hit!" He laughs, but then his tone turns more serious. "When things really started happening for me—like Dean finding me on YouTube and signing me up to his management company, all that stuff—Blake and I sort of had a falling-out. He started hanging out with a different crowd and we had some major arguments. It's one of the reasons why I completely retreated last year. Shut off from the world. I was ready to quit, throw in the towel. If I was going to lose my closest friends because of all this"—he gestures around the tour bus—"it wasn't going to be worth it. And then I met you. My Inciting Incident." He kisses my hand. "You showed me it was possible for me to have it all. You gave me the courage to repair things with Blake. Inviting him on tour is the best thing ever—next to you being here, of course. He's a bit of a joker, but he's been there for me from the beginning. And I know you two will get along great once you get to know him."

My face burns—from the compliment but also because I can't believe I was about to slag off Noah's best friend to him. I had no idea how much history they had. If Blake is a joker, he's probably just messing with me. I need to learn not to take so much to heart if I'm going to hang out with the band.

"Hey, I was going to wait until we got to the hotel, but I want to give this to you." He reaches underneath the bed, where his travel bag is, and pulls out a box wrapped in gold paper. "For you. Go on—open it," he says when I stare at the gold box.

I open it slowly at first, then I rip off the paper. It's a brand-new smartphone. One of the fancy ones that I would never have been able to afford on my own. "Oh wow, Noah . . ."

"I wanted you to have a new, better phone since your other one was stolen at my concert. You can't be happy with that old dinosaur Tom gave you. Plus, this one has an amazing camera."

He's right—I'm not happy with Tom's old phone—but I also just want *my* old phone, with Noah's doodles all over it, back. This fancy new phone can't compare to that one, but it does help. I stare at it in awe. "You shouldn't have! This is . . . this is too much."

"It's not too much, Penny, I promise. What's the point of being a rock star if I can't splurge on you every now and then?"

"Maybe because I can't splash out back?" I say.

"Don't think that way." He kisses me on the cheek. "You're my official anxiety monitor, remember? That's got to be worth *thousands*. Come on—should we go back out and join the fray?" He edges to the front of the bunk, his hand outstretched.

"Sure," I say. Noah's given me more confidence. Maybe I do just have to give Blake a chance. If Noah likes him so much, he can't be that bad.

When we emerge from the back of the bus, it's to hoots and cheers. Noah puts both his hands up in defeat. "OK, OK, guys, settle down." I feel my face flush red—why do boys have such dirty minds? I wish there was another girl around to help offset some of the testosterone.

Blake is back by the beer fridge. "You want one, man?" He offers a bottle to Noah, who looks at me, then back at Blake.

"It's early, dude. How many of these have you already had? You smell like it's three a.m. and you've just left a bar."

"Geez, Noah, lighten up a bit. This is supposed to be fun! You're starting to sound like Dean."

Noah takes the beer bottle and cracks it open using the corner of the table.

"Cheers to us!" Blake clinks his bottle on Noah's and smiles at me.

"Do you want a Coke, Penny?" Noah offers me a can from the fridge.

"Yeah, thanks." I glance out of the window and am treated to the sight of a giant gate with massive pillars and four horses on the top. It's huge and majestic and just what I expected from Berlin. I let out a little squeal of excitement. "Wow, look at that! Is that the Brandenburg Gate?"

As the others turn to look out of the window, I lower my voice so that only Noah can hear. "I'm so excited for Magical Mystery Day!"

"Me too," says Noah, squeezing my hand.

"Elliot texted me earlier with a long list of amazing places we need to check out. There's a structure that's over three hundred and fifty metres tall and—"

Blake interrupts me with a snigger. "A what now? Magical what?" He looks at Noah and me.

I feel a wave of embarrassment as I think about how childish it must sound to Blake. But Noah jumps right in to defend us.

"Lay off, man . . . You wouldn't know romance if it bit you in the ass!"

In typical boy style, Blake threatens to moon us, and instantly the tension is released.

Luckily, Larry shouts from the front of the bus that we've arrived—just before Blake's pants can come down. Perfect timing. Dean claps his hands together and everyone's attention focuses on him. "Guys, I have some amazing news!" His eyes are sparkling like he's won the lottery. "You'll never guess who's going to be joining The Sketch onstage tonight." He pauses for a moment, letting the anticipation build. "Leah Brown! It's a total secret for now, but the crowd will be absolutely buzzing! How awesome is that, guys?"

Everyone around me is jumping and high-fiving—this is a huge coup for the tour, and will raise the publicity levels through the roof. But, when I wished for another girl to be here, Noah's not-really-ex-girlfriend was *not* who I meant. If I think Blake is making this tour difficult, I'm almost certain the arrival of Leah Brown means it's about to get a whole lot worse.

Chapter Fifteen

The venue in Berlin feels twice as big as the Brighton Centre, and our footsteps echo across the stage as Noah prepares to do his soundcheck. There are people all around us, but having driven straight from the airport to the hotel to the concert hall in the tour bus, I don't feel like I've seen anything of the city yet. We could be anywhere. The only indication this is Germany is the bright red signs saying AUSGANG instead of EXIT.

I walk right up to the front of the stage, staring out at the sea of empty seats that will soon be filled with screaming fans. Even though the place is empty, I still get a little shiver down my spine.

At least I won't have to be out in the crowd this time. I have my backstage pass hanging round my neck and I look so attached to it that Noah joked I might take it to bed with me. I just might. I don't want to risk another incident like what happened in Brighton. I won't have any friends here who will be looking out for me.

I lift up my camera and take a picture of the empty stalls.

I have a vision that I can layer images of the crowd on top of the empty seats and make some kind of statement on the nature of the relationship between performance and audience. Miss Mills would like that for my alternative-perspectives project. *Is it still a performance if no one is there to listen?* I wonder.

I step back from the front of the stage, edging towards the shadows. Noah is standing in a pool of light in the middle of the stage, dressed in a maroon Harvard hoodie and black jeans, singing the first few bars of "Elements." I snap a picture of that too: the performer before the performance, the many hours of rehearsal and hard work that the fans almost never get to see. This is turning out to be perfect for my A-levels project.

I'm lost in the image of Noah losing himself in his music, until Blake smashes the cymbals on his drum kit behind me, making me jump. I stumble backwards, tripping over a bundle of cords on the floor. I'm so concerned with preserving my camera that I don't reach out to break my fall and I crash against a stack of speakers. The smallest speaker at the top wobbles precariously from the force of my impact.

Please don't fall, please don't fall, I pray to the gods of clumsiness.

They don't listen.

The speaker drops to the ground with a sickening crack, pieces flying across the stage. I'm slumped on the floor, my shoulder throbbing, but my camera is in one piece—a tiny silver lining, at least.

"Penny! Oh my god, are you OK?" Noah runs over to me.

I stand up quickly, brushing myself off. I try to avoid wincing, which turns my smile into a weird grimace. "I'm fine, seriously, Noah—you better keep on rehearsing. I—I can pay for the speaker."

"No, don't worry about that. Blake, what the hell, man?"

Blake looks over at me and shrugs. "Hey, it's not my problem if your girlfriend is a klutz."

"He's right—I'm a klutz," I stammer.

Noah frowns. "Well, you're *my* klutz and I don't want you to get hurt. Those speakers are seriously heavy."

I nod and, to hide the bright red blush of shame that has risen in my cheeks, I drop back to the floor and start to pick up the broken pieces of the speaker that have shattered across the stage. I'm never going to go on a stage again. Stages and I are officially cursed.

"Steve will help clear this up." Noah gestures over to one of the roadies, who's already at hand with a dustpan and brush. I vaguely recognize him from the quick-fire round of introductions when we first entered the venue. Noah knows the name of every member of the crew, even if he's only met them once; it's yet another thing that makes him so special. "We can get a new speaker here, right?"

"No problem," says Steve. "We can switch one out from the back."

"See? All good. Just ignore Blake and I'll come meet you after I've rehearsed."

"Sounds good," I say. I'm still frustrated. *Why do I have to be such a liability?* Backstage is hopefully much safer.

I pull my phone out of my pocket and text Elliot.

> One day in Berlin and I'm already a disaster

He texts back almost straightaway.

> What happened?

> Let's just say I'm not meant to be onstage

> Don't tell me there was an incident with the unicorn pants again?

> NO. Worse. I probably broke hundreds of pounds' worth of equipment

> I'm sure The Sketch can afford it. Seen anyone else famous yet?

I'm about to text back *No*, but all of a sudden that's not true anymore.

Leah Brown walks into the backstage area, her hair pulled into a ponytail, her face makeup free. In fact, the only thing that marks her as an internationally super-famous pop star is the fact that about a dozen people are trailing after her, struggling to keep up with her long-legged strides. Leah looks down at the tablet one of her minions is holding.

"Ugh, I hate that. Weren't there any better pictures than that one? Tell Frankie P. we might need to do another shoot if that's the best he can come up with."

I want a hole to open up and swallow me. If I look away she might not notice me, but I can't stop staring at her. Even before she gets all her hair and makeup done, she's beautiful, like a magnet that draws all eyes her way. I think this is what people mean when they say someone has star quality, the X factor. Her presence changes the air, makes everything feel more electric.

Elliot would call it a certain je ne sais quoi.

Megan would be jealous.

Ollie would be drooling.

I get the shivers.

I don't understand how Noah could have been in a "fake" relationship with this girl. How could any straight guy spend time in her presence and not fall in love with her?

Even though I'm making a fool out of myself by staring like a lunatic, Leah and her posse walk straight past me without stopping—with the exception of the girl who's been told to contact Frankie P. She grabs one of the other girls and I can hear her mutter, "Tell François-Pierre Nouveau that he has to redo this shoot? How am I supposed to do that?" Her face is white with panic and the ends of her sentences rise into a high-pitched squeal. I've heard of François-Pierre Nouveau—he's one of the most famous photographers in the world. I can't believe I'm in the presence of someone who has had a photo shoot with François-Pierre—or, rather, someone who is *rejecting* the work of François-Pierre and calls him *Frankie P.*

"You'll have to figure it out," the other girl says. "This is LB's *album* cover we're talking about. If she's not happy . . ."

"I'm going to die. I'm officially going to die."

This time they see me staring and they both shoot me dark looks. I keep moving, stammering an apology.

"Penny?"

I turn round reluctantly. Leah is standing with one hand on her hip, and the rest of her group is looking at me like I've grown another head. I nod, and swallow hard. "Hi, Leah."

She walks towards me, and it feels more like a predator approaching prey than someone coming over to say hello.

"So *you're* Penny Porter."

I don't really know how to respond to that, so I just nod again.

"You were the one that gave me so much trouble last year," she says, her drawn-out LA accent touched with a hint of her Southern roots. She looks me up and down, and I feel her entire group judging my outfit. I haven't exactly made an effort today. I'm dressed to ride in a tour bus, so I'm in my comfy jeans and a zip-up sweater. I fold my arms protectively across my chest but stand tall.

"Well, I guess I owe you a thanks for the song inspiration. Sweet camera. See you around," she says with a little wave, before turning back to her group.

Leah had used the media storm that exploded around her fake breakup with Noah to launch her latest number-one internationally bestselling single "Bad Boy." Leah writes a lot of her own music, and this one had been primed and ready in case of any eventuality—in this case, using her breakup with Noah to her advantage. I'm sure there were songs about how deeply in love they were too, in case things had continued to be smooth sailing.

As she walks away, I feel like I could faint with relief. I need to speak to Elliot. Stat.

Chapter Sixteen

From: Elliot Wentworth
To: Penny Porter
Subject: THE ELLIOT REPORT

Dear Pennylicious, aka Ocean Strong,

You've been gone ONE DAY and already I'm in a conundrum. Just HOW am I going to suffer through the next two weeks without you? Things have gone from bad to worse in this seaside town. I didn't tell you over text, but my dad is back. He's insisting on taking me to dinner. Something his therapist told him to do so he can "come to terms" with my "sexuality." He's staying in the house with Mum's permission, but they keep having these mega blow-up arguments whenever they're in the same room together. There's been more emotion in this house over the past day than I've seen in sixteen years.

Anyway, Mum's decided she doesn't want to see him. She hasn't even come home this evening—instead, she's putting in even more hours at work. Sometimes I wonder if she doesn't even want to see me either? Ugh, why is family drama so hard? I think I preferred it when my parents just ignored me and let me get on with life.

Speaking of life, my internship with *CHIC* magazine started EARLY! They wanted me in today, even though it's a Friday— ARGH. But it was so amazing. I got to work with a stylist and she actually complimented my blazer—you know the one I sewed those crazy buttons on? OK, so it's a lot of getting coffee and detangling about a million necklaces from an unholy knot but it's REAL FASHION WORK.

But enough about me and my monotonous life. How are things with you?

What's your hotel like?

Have you seen the Berlin Wall yet?

Did you eat any currywurst?

And most importantly . . . DID YOU MEET LEAH BROWN?

Miss you to the maximum, Penny P.

Elliot xx

From: Penny Porter
To: Elliot Wentworth
Subject: RE: THE ELLIOT REPORT

Dearest most dear of dear Elliots,

I did! I met Leah!

She was in the middle of rejecting images by François-Pierre Nouveau. CAN YOU IMAGINE? It's like telling Vincent van Gogh, "Yeah, your painting is all right, but just not good enough for my walls."

She's even more intimidating in person.

How am I supposed to compete with that? But, weirdly, she was kind of fine with me just now. I'm sure it's an act in front of Noah, though.

And no, I haven't seen anything of Berlin. But Noah and I are going on our Magical Mystery Day tomorrow so I will tell you ALL ABOUT IT.

That sucks about your dad. Majorly. But brilliant about the internship. I knew you would rock it! And OF COURSE they're going to love your style—you're Elliot! You're the most fashionable guy in Brighton!

But are you sure you can't hop on a last-minute flight to Berlin and come out and join me?

P xxx

From: Elliot Wentworth
To: Penny Porter
Subject: RE: Re: THE ELLIOT REPORT

Dear Pennylicious,

I wish.

Elliot x

PS Actually, Vincent van Gogh did get turned down many times. He only sold one painting in his entire lifetime and didn't become super famous until after he died.

From: Penny Porter
To: Elliot Wentworth
Subject: RE: Re: Re: THE ELLIOT REPORT

Dear Wiki,

All right, know-it-all.

Penny x

Chapter Seventeen

There's no doubt about it: my boyfriend *rocks*—and it seems like he's got just as many fans in Germany as he does in the UK. There's as much screaming for him here as there was in Brighton. I don't know why I'm so surprised, but it feels like the levels of Noah's fame keep rising higher and higher, while I'm feeling more and more left behind. He awes me with his talent. He's only two years older than me, and already he's accomplished so much.

I remind myself that Noah is not *normal*. I have loads of time to work out exactly what I want to do. Being "Noah's girlfriend" is only one part of my future.

The time between the soundcheck and the actual concert is jam-packed with pre-show interviews and photographs, a string of journalists entering Noah's dressing room one after the other. I sit discreetly in the corner, occasionally snapping a photograph but mostly just listening. Noah's a pro at interviews, but I suppose you would be after answering the same questions again and again. It's a wonder that not a single journalist asks him anything really interesting. Maybe it's the domineering presence of Dean behind him, arms folded, always ready to interfere in case the line of questioning dances too closely to delicate subjects, like his parents—or, for that matter, me.

A couple of the journalists recognize me, and, because he knows it makes me nervous, Noah is careful not to reveal too much about our relationship.

The closest one of the interviewers gets to an interesting answer is when she asks a question about Leah Brown. "So, Noah," a pretty brunette with a hugely popular German music blog asks, "what's it like being in such close quarters with Leah Brown after last year's . . . controversy?"

Noah smiles sweetly. "Leah and I are good friends, and I respect her musical talent. After all, I think she got her own back with 'Bad Boy.'" He winks, applying his natural charm to the situation.

"And Penny doesn't mind?" the blogger continues, unde-terred.

Dean moves to interrupt, but Noah shrugs and answers, with a slight shake of his head to let Dean know to stand down. "Of course not. Penny has nothing to worry about."

His words fill me with a warmth that spreads from my tiptoes to my forehead. I only hope that the blogger will print the statement as is, rather than twisting his words. Either way, the important thing is that he said them, and I heard. If only Blake were here—that would keep him quiet.

Dean claps his hands together. "OK, thanks, Ruby—that's it for this interview. It's showtime!" The room is already a hive of activity, but it seems to pick up tempo at Dean's announcement.

My stomach clenches in a twist of nerves, but Noah is straight by my side and grabs my hand. He promised this time was going to be different, and already it feels like it is. "Do you have your new phone?" he asks.

"Yeah, hang on." I dig it out of my pocket. He takes it from me and quickly dials a number. After a few rings, the screen lights up with the faces of two of my favourite people in the entire world: Sadie Lee and Bella.

"PRINCESS PENNY!" Bella bounces up and down on the screen, sitting so close her eyes bulge in the camera.

My jaw almost drops when I see her—I can't believe how much she's grown already. She looks more like a young lady than the bouncing four-year-old I saw at Christmas. "Bella! When did you get so big?" I say, unable to keep the astonishment from my voice. "Hi, Sadie Lee!" I can hear Sadie Lee's warm laugh in the background as she gently pulls Bella away from the screen.

"Now, honey, Noah and Penny can see us much better when we're sitting down nicely," she says in her slow Southern drawl. Then she turns her twinkling brown eyes—the Flynn family trait—on me. "How is Berlin, my two shining stars?"

"I'm just about to hit the stage, G-ma!" says Noah.

"That's great, Noah!" But then Sadie Lee's eyes fill with concern. "Penny, I heard about what happened in Brighton. Are you being looked after now?"

My cheeks turn pink and I nod vigorously. Noah pulls me tight towards him with his free hand, the other one still holding the phone at arm's length. "Penny's going to sit just on the side of the stage and stream my set for you, so I'll know all my favourite girls are watching."

Sadie Lee laughs. "Why, Noah, I don't think I've been called a girl for at least thirty years!"

He winks. "You know what I mean." He looks up as Dean calls his name. He passes the phone to me, blows Sadie Lee and Bella a kiss, and kisses me on the cheek for real, then runs out to join the rest of his band.

I'm left holding the phone and, for a moment, I'm flustered. But then I stare straight into the friendly gazes of Sadie Lee and Bella and I remember that I have a job to do.

"Did you bring Princess Autumn with you?" asks Bella.

"Princess Autumn had to stay at my house, Bells—I didn't want to bring her on tour in case she got lost!"

Bella nods sagely. "Oh, good. I don't think she would like being on tour. It's too busy for the princess."

"I know what you mean," I say with a bigger sigh than I intend.

Bella smiles and disappears off to find one of her toys to show me. Sadie Lee's eyebrows have risen so high that I feel the need to explain: "I just don't want to be a burden on Noah and Dean and everyone else . . ."

Sadie Lee slowly shakes her head. "Now you listen to me, honey. I know something very important that you might not realize: Noah needs you there as much as you need him. I promise you that. I'm glad you're there looking after him— not the other way around."

"But Dean—"

"Oh, don't worry about him, darling. Dean is there to work for you *both*, and if he isn't doing his job he's going to have me to answer to."

"Thanks, Sadie Lee." I hear the roar of the crowd and I

leap to my feet. I feel a surge of excitement and am so excited to have the chance to press the reset button on my experience of Noah's set. "Here we go, ladies!" I say to the screen.

I jog to the side of the stage, where Noah is waiting, jumping from foot to foot, pumping himself up. When he sees me, his face lights up with a huge smile, and I make sure the camera on the phone is pointed straight at him so Sadie Lee and Bella have a great view.

"OK, I've had my friend Jake place these boxes here so you can sit and see from the wings." He lifts me up onto the boxes just as the lights dim, ready for his onstage appearance.

"Good luck," I whisper in his ear, and he waves to Sadie Lee and Bella on the phone. Then, the confident, rock-god-tastic boy I know takes a deep breath and walks out onto the stage.

★ ★ Chapter Eighteen ★ ★

I'm grateful that I have the distraction of making sure Sadie Lee and Bella see the whole show, because any nerves I might have had completely disappear. I realize that I know all the words to every song in Noah's set by heart, but it's incredible to hear the audience joining in on the big choruses.

"Hey, guys," he says to the crowd, after forty-five minutes of energetic performance. "This is my last song." He's forced to pause for a moment while the crowd boos and complains, but he just chuckles into the microphone. "Some of you might not know this, but this is my favourite song on the whole album. This song makes me the luckiest guy in the world. Because the girl who inspired it is sitting just over there."

He turns and looks at me. He's sweaty, red-faced, and his hair is wet and dishevelled, but he's still incredibly gorgeous—and everyone else melts away as he locks eyes with me. It's only when I hear chants of "Autumn Girl! Autumn Girl!" that I realize the crowd out there knows me too. It's so bizarre.

"Now, she's a little bit shy, so she's going to stay out of sight for now, but, Penny, baby, this one is for you."

He strums the first few chords of "Autumn Girl" and I'm taken straight back to the time I first heard it, on my bed, listening to the recording that he made me. I want to tell Sadie Lee how amazing this is, when I realize that in all the emotion I've let the phone drift down; Sadie Lee and Bella are now facing the black box I'm sitting on. Not a good view at all! I whip the phone back up so it's pointing at Noah and whisper an apology to them both.

Noah finishes the song to thunderous applause, then he jogs offstage and straight into my arms. We head back to the dressing room arm in arm, the noise from the crowd following us like a wave of love and support.

"You were incredible!" I say. "The best. I'm so proud of you."

"That was excellent!" He can't wipe the grin off his face, and I know my expression mirrors his.

If only TheRealTruth could see us now, they'd know their threats were pointless. Maybe there is something to this rock-star life after all.

"G-ma, Bella, what did you think?"

On the screen, Sadie Lee is wiping tears from her cheeks. "Noah, I have no words. You light up that stage."

"Thanks, G-ma. You're the best."

"You kids go have fun now. It's going to take me at least another hour to get this one to calm down after that." Bella is running around on the screen, singing Noah's songs at the top of her lungs.

"Goodnight!" Noah and I both say in sync, waving to the phone. I go to turn it off, and the battery flashes red.

"Oh no, I need a charger . . ."

I scan the room, desperate for a glimpse of my lost cable. But, instead, the rest of Noah's band literally bounces into the room, and even Blake has a huge smile on his face. He smiles at me and I smile back. Maybe I did misjudge him.

"That was *awesome*," Blake says to me as he passes. "Are you coming back to the hotel with us, Penny?"

"No, man. I have something planned for us," says Noah, interrupting. He drops off his guitar with one of the technicians and sheds his leather jacket, then begins rooting through his duffel bag.

"Oh, cool." With a couple of bounding leaps, Blake jumps on Ryan's back, one fist pumping in the air. I laugh, watching them.

"Where are we going?" I raise one eyebrow at Noah.

He tosses a red beanie my way, then pulls a grey beanie down over his own hair. "I thought it would go well with your hair."

"If you insist," I say, putting on the hat.

"Now these." He passes me a pair of glasses. They're just frames, really—they don't even have any glass in them. Noah puts on a pair too, but they go a bit crooked.

I reach up and straighten them on his face. I smile. If this is meant to be some sort of disguise, it's not going to work. "You still look gorgeous—you can't hide that!" I say to him.

"We don't need a total disguise, just something to throw people off a little. Besides, where we're going, no one will expect it to be me, so I need to play to that." He pulls at my hand, and I follow him.

"But where *are* we going?"

"Why, we're going to watch the world's hottest boy band, of course."

My face drains of colour, and I stop moving. He turns round as my hand slips out of his. "Penny? What's wrong?"

I swallow and close my eyes. I can't believe he's asking me this. "Do you mean out there?" I say, really hoping that's not what he means.

"Well, sure. You didn't get to see their show last time— you left before you could. They're amazing. Plus"—he takes a step forward and gathers my hand up in his—"I'll be there with you this time. The whole time."

He must be able to read the dubious look on my face, because all of a sudden he gets down on one knee and says, "I swear to you, Penny Porter, I won't leave your side for a single moment!"

"Stop that!" I shriek, convinced that someone is going to take a photo of him and think that he's proposing—now that *would* be another scandal. "OK, I'll go with you," I say, and I can feel a blush rising up my neck, prickling the skin on my cheeks.

He grins and stands up. "Good. And, if you don't enjoy it at any time, just tell me."

"Oh, what about my camera?" I ask.

"Take it—you might capture something cool from the audience." He gives my hand a squeeze and pulls me out through a side door, down a few hallways, and out into the crowd.

✶ Chapter Nineteen ✶

I can feel my heart beating in my throat as the darkness of the audience surrounds us. It's also quiet, even though there are thousands of people all around us—I can feel the anticipation of the crowd growing, as they anxiously wait for The Sketch's arrival. I cling on to Noah so tightly I wonder if I'm going to cut off the circulation in his hand. He doesn't seem to mind, though. He takes me a few people deep into the crowd, and he was right: no one expects to see him, so no one takes any notice of us, except to gripe about us pushing through.

He comes to a stop in front of the stage, but several rows of people back. The way everyone around us is jostling our arms and stepping on our toes reminds me of the Brighton concert, but this time I have Noah's hands reassuringly on my shoulders.

Then the lights snap on, and The Sketch bound onto the stage. The screaming starts immediately and, caught up in the excitement of the crowd, I scream just as loudly. Even Noah lets out a loud whoop.

They play with frenetic energy, pounding through hit after hit. It's not just that their songs are catchy—and there's no doubt that they are—but they are also such great musicians, playing riffs on their guitars that you never hear on their radio tracks and hitting every note.

When Leah Brown appears, the screaming gets even louder—if that was possible. She enters in one of the most dramatic ways possible—from a harness suspended from the ceiling—and sings a feature chorus in one of The Sketch's most energetic songs. Her transformation from when I saw her earlier today is amazing: she's wearing a sparkling silver minidress, and her hair is blown out behind her like it travels with its own fan. On anyone else, her ensemble would look ridiculous, but on Leah it just *works*. As the song progresses, she's slowly lowered down onto the stage, and I even manage to snap pictures the whole time.

When she reaches the stage, the whole tempo of the performance changes. The bright lights go out completely, plunging us all into darkness. It feels like everyone in the arena is holding their breath. Slowly, tiny points of light appear in the ceiling, until it feels like we're standing beneath a canopy of stars. It's breathtakingly beautiful, and instinctively Noah draws me close, wrapping his arms round me. I lean into him.

Two beams of light appear on the stage, illuminating Leah and Hayden—the lead singer of The Sketch—who are now sitting on stools. Leah has changed into a black dress, sequinned to catch the light, and her hair lies flat, framing her face like a curtain.

"Hi, Berlin," says Hayden. "We have something a bit

different for you guys now. Something no one has heard before. We hope you like it."

He starts to sing a cappella, and without any backing music his voice is strong and clear. Leah picks up her lines, and together they sing a beautiful, haunting duet about lovers who are kept apart.

I feel tears prick my eyes and, even though no one here has heard this before, I know I'm not the only one. Emotion floods the crowd. It's like we're all connected through the music. This is a taste of the passion I know Noah feels when he writes his songs. This is what he wants to create: a chain of notes and words that can make a crowd of thousands move and feel as one.

"I love you, Penny," Noah whispers in my ear.

I squeeze his arms round me.

There's a roar from the audience when the song ends—it looks like Leah and The Sketch have another hit on their hands. The spell is broken—or, rather, the spell has been cast. The audience is completely with The Sketch now, and would clearly follow them to the ends of the earth. The lights come back on, bright and blazing in our eyes, and the beat picks up into a fast tempo.

Noah and I are no different from everyone else around us. We dance like wild people and sing at the tops of our voices, getting sweaty and silly and not caring for even a moment. By the time the band plays their final encore, I don't think I've ever been so happy.

Chapter Twenty

Still reeling from such an amazing night, Noah and I skip along the hotel corridor and back up to my room (I'm not even worrying if my deodorant has stood up to the task of all that dancing). We continue singing The Sketch's songs right up until we get to the door.

"I'll leave you here, Pen, as a proper gentleman would." Noah opens the door and gestures with his arm into the room like a bellboy, almost bowing as he does so. His hair is a lot messier and curlier than usual when he releases it from underneath the beanie, which he unceremoniously dumps on the floor. He looks at me with a twinkle in his eye and a cheeky smirk on his face, his dimples appearing as if by magic. I completely melt on the spot. I don't think I have ever been more in love with Noah Flynn than I am right now.

"Don't you have time to come in for a bit? Tonight was amazing, but we've not had much of a chance to chill out, just the two of us, yet." I try out what I hope is an endearing smile.

Noah chuckles. "Sorry, Autumn Girl—I've got to go back to the venue and make sure everything's set up for tomorrow. Dean loves a good debrief." I must not be doing a very good job of hiding the disappointment on my face, because he's right up close to me, his face soft with a smile. "We've got Magical Mystery Day tomorrow, Penny—a whole day, just you and me. I promise it will be amazing and completely cake-fuelled." He kisses me on the lips before I can reply.

"How could I forget?" I say, when I'm able to take a breath. How can any human being be *this* charming and desirable? It's going to end up killing me.

Then, against my wishes, my mouth opens into a yawn so big I could almost swallow Noah's head, messy hair and all. I'm embarrassed, but Noah just pulls me tight into his chest—which is shaking with laughter.

"You look as tired as I feel," he says. "You have no idea how much I want to just stay here with you, but you should get some rest . . . you're going to need it for tomorrow."

I feel my heart flutter at a million miles an hour as he turns to head back down the corridor.

"Goodnight, gorgeous!" he yells as he skips off and disappears round the corner.

I collapse in a giggly heap on my bed. The biggest smile creeps across my face and I feel myself almost well up with happiness. I let out a huge sigh and roll over onto my stomach and kick off my Converses. I grab my laptop from the bedside table and open up my emails. I start typing an email to Elliot.

From: Penny Porter
To: Elliot Wentworth
Subject: RE: Re: Re: Re: THE ELLIOT REPORT

Wiki, Wiki, Wa-Wa-West,

I think I'm on cloud nine and I can never imagine myself ever coming down. I've just had the best night with Noah. I watched him perform, he was amazing (as always), and then he dragged me out into the crowd to watch The Sketch perform with Leah Brown. She was actually pretty amazing. Noah and I danced and held hands and sang as loud as we could right up until the end, and I DID NOT PANIC! Amazing, right?

I've had one of those pinch-me moments about how perfect Noah is and how lucky I am to be here with him, supporting him and watching his success grow before my eyes, and that I'm the one he chooses to share this with. I can imagine you retching at the screen as you read this, but I really am SO happy right now. You'll also be pleased to know that I'm exploring Berlin tomorrow with Noah for MMD!

Will of course fill you in once I'm back.

Missing you a lot, but also having the best time!

Pen xxx

26 June

How to Survive Life on a Massive European Pop Tour

So, I know you're all dying to know the details, and guess what? I've survived my first day of life on tour! Not only that . . . I actually enjoyed it. After he'd finished his set, Brooklyn Boy took me out into the crowd to watch the headline act, and we danced all night until we were sweaty and gross. But it was wonderful.

I feel like I've learned so much already, even though I've only been on tour for a day! Here are my top tips so far.

1. Snacks are your best friend.

There's almost no time to have a proper meal when you're jetting from bus to hotel to venue and back again. I'm going to line my pockets with muesli bars in case I get peckish.

2. There are people EVERYWHERE backstage.

Who knew so many people were needed to run a tour? There's not just Brooklyn Boy's manager and band, but also his security guard, publicist, photographers, makeup artists, hair stylists, stage manager, his manager's assistant, his manager's assistant's assistant, and about a million roadies who all seem to know *exactly* what to do.

3. Sleep when and wherever you can.

Everyone seems to. Today I saw somebody fall asleep on top of a speaker that was blaring music from the stage! I feel like it's a warning of the lack of sleep that is to come . . .

4. Don't expect to fit in much sightseeing.

Even though tomorrow Brooklyn Boy and I are going to see as much as we can of Berlin, his schedule is so jam-packed that I can't even imagine how he's been able to carve out any time for me!

It's all so exciting and scary! But I'll try to remember to keep the blog up to date.

Girl Offline . . . never going online xxx

Chapter Twenty-One

The next morning my alarm goes off at 8 a.m. and I scramble around for an outfit that is comfortable yet cool and chic. I settle on a loose white T-shirt tucked into a pleated black skirt, and I make sure to wear my delicate gold-chain necklace with the words AUTUMN GIRL written in cursive on the pendant. It was my Valentine's Day present from Noah this year, and it's my favourite thing to wear. Noah texted me soon after he left last night and told me to meet him downstairs for breakfast at nine this morning to start Magical Mystery Day off properly.

I grab my camera and head down in the lift to reception. The lobby is what Elliot would describe as uber-modern—all glossy black countertops and white walls, with a bright, bold graffiti print hanging behind the reception desk. It's packed, and I walk past the long queue of people checking in, most of whom are trailing big suitcases. I start wondering what kind of adventures these people are on, or what adventures they've had. *Are they here alone? Have they been on a romantic European city break?*

I take a seat on a plush velvet sofa in the reception lobby and a beautiful spray of orchids catches my eye. I can't help myself—I lift my camera and start snapping away. Orchids are one of my favourite flowers, particularly white ones. Elliot once bought me an orchid for my birthday and it sat proudly on my dressing table, looking elegant and fresh. Unfortunately, its beauty was short-lived—I quickly realized how difficult it is to look after them, as I over-watered it and it died. The year after that he bought me a cute succulent in a miniature hanging pot and told me if I managed to kill that then I could never own another plant again! Thankfully, it's still hanging in the corner of my room, holding up despite the fact that I don't pay it any attention. That's about the level of care I can handle, and Elliot knows it.

I look down at my phone—it's 9:20 a.m. I look back up and scan the reception lobby for any sign of Noah. Nothing. Just the hustle and bustle of a busy Berlin hotel, but no sign of my boyfriend's trademark scuffed jeans and sparkling white smile. *He must still be getting ready*, I convince myself. *Or maybe he has something up his sleeve that involves a bit of planning?* I recline onto the sofa and wait a further ten minutes, watching people start their day.

"Oh, hey, Penny?"

The voice startles me out of my people-watching. I crane my head over the sofa and see a rather sorry-looking Dean, bloodshot eyes peering at me over the top of his gold-rimmed Ray-Bans. "Why are you hanging around in reception? Have you had breakfast yet? I think they stop serving at ten, so you should get in there quick if you want a croissant. They get snapped up pretty quick." His husky laugh turns into a cough. He really does look rough.

"No, I'm waiting for Noah. We're having breakfast together, then heading out to explore the city."

Dean cackles so loudly that it echoes throughout the lobby and a few people turn and stare at him with bemused looks on their faces. When he finally recovers, he says, "You won't be seeing him until at least midday. The boys were out until about four a.m. last night. It could've been later—I gave up at three thirty." He slumps down onto the sofa next to me. "It got really crazy, to be honest, hence the sunglasses. Man, I need a coffee. And I wouldn't say no to a bacon sandwich."

My heart sinks. I try to maintain a smiley demeanour while Dean is still beside me.

"Oh, of course. Silly me, I completely forgot. Noah did mention something about it changing to midday." I stumble on my words as I struggle to think of anything to say that will make me seem less of an idiot.

"Do you want to grab a bite with me instead? I mean, I'm nowhere near as good-looking, but I can play a few chords on the guitar." Dean stands up and tries to usher me over to the dining area but I shake my head.

"Actually I think I'm going to head back up to my room. I just realized I have to call my parents and let them know I'm still alive. You know what parents can be like . . . they forget you aren't ten anymore, and if they don't hear from me they might send the police, or the army . . . or at least my brother, Tom. But you enjoy your hangover cure. I'll see you later."

Before Dean can try to persuade me to grab some food with him, I jump up and head for the lift. Once inside it, I press my floor number and collapse against the wall, resting my forehead against the cool glass. I'm not sure what is more upsetting—the fact that Noah never told me he was going out, the fact that he didn't think to invite me, or the fact that he went out *and* still couldn't meet me for the one day we had together that he promised would be so special. I check my phone to see if he has tried to call or text me, but I already know there's nothing.

As I walk along the corridor from the lift, instead of taking a right along to my room, I turn left and head towards Noah's. I stand outside it and go to knock, but, as my hand is hovering inches from the door, I change my mind and walk back to my own room. Noah's never given me a single reason to worry before, and I don't want him to think I'm turning into one of those clingy girlfriends who needs to know my boyfriend's every move. What if he is still getting ready? What if he *does* have something else planned? He may not have invited me out last night, but I suspect it was all Blake's idea anyway and, knowing Blake, Noah wouldn't have had much choice in the matter.

When Noah's ready, he'll come and find me—nothing is going to ruin our Magical Mystery Day.

Chapter Twenty-Two

The clock ticks past midday and I accept that Noah probably isn't busy getting ready or planning something for the day. I've already painted my nails (fingers *and* toes) a summery coral pink that I'd been saving for the trip, checked Instagram and WhatsApp about a million times, updated my Snapchat story with clips and photos of the hotel room, and done everything I can to distract myself without leaving the room in case Noah turns up.

I text him again to ask where he is, but I get no reply. I call him too, but it's almost time for everyone to head back to the venue and do the soundcheck for tonight's show anyway, so the chances of Magical Mystery Day still happening are slim. It's not like Noah to be this rubbish with his phone, or be this rubbish in general.

I try not to think about it too much. Every time I think I'm calm, another question rises in my mind. *What if something happened to him? What if he's hurt? Or in trouble?* The questions threaten to grow bigger and bigger with every passing minute that I don't hear from him. I know they will drive me crazy if I stay in this room alone, with nothing to distract me. I can't even text Elliot—I've bothered him enough already, and he and Alex are having a date day. They don't need me dragging them down with my whingey texts. I need to perk myself up.

I think about trying Noah's room but then convince myself that he's just asleep and won't want to be woken up. That's not such a bad thing. This is his first tour after all; he's allowed to have fun. He probably forgot to set an alarm. That's OK.

I grit my teeth and push back any negative thoughts that try to take hold, bursting them like soap bubbles before they can land on my brain. I grab my bag, my camera, and my laptop, and make the decision to head to the venue on my own, instead of sulking around my hotel room. At least some of the crew will be there and I can take some shots for my project of everyone setting up before Noah arrives. I try his phone one more time before heading out, but it goes straight to answerphone.

When I arrive at the venue, Dean greets me with a huge hug. He looks more alive now—food and coffee must have revived him. "PENNY! What brings you here so early? Lover boy is still asleep, I take it?"

"Yeah, I just figured I'd leave him to sleep while I get a few shots here and then I might sit and edit some of them. I'm doing photography for my A levels next year and my teacher is not going to be happy if I come back with nothing to show for it."

"Hey, well, it's great you have a hobby. Remember, I'm here if you need anything. I think Larry should be bringing the boys over soon for a soundcheck."

I nod and make my way to the dressing room. I take the memory card out of my camera and transfer the images that I have so far onto my laptop. There are some goofy ones of Noah and me that I took at the airport, some of Noah in front of the tour bus, lots of backstage shots, and then ones that I took from the crowd last night. I've managed to catch one of Leah that makes it look as though she's floating above the stage. She looks amazing. I open the image in Photoshop and start playing around with the exposure and colour filters.

I've always loved taking photographs, right from the moment my parents gave me my first camera—a disposable one that I used in the playground. I liked trying to catch people unawares, winding the dial on the back of the camera to get the film ready for the next picture. Editing in Photoshop is something that I've only just started learning how to do in the past year, and it's addictive. Hours can pass as I sit on the computer, making the tiniest adjustments to my pictures. Most people think Photoshop is about turning spotty faces into flawless ones, but it's so much more than that: I can add filters, adjust the colour palette, fix poor exposures, and make the photos more vibrant. Miss Mills has taught me that less is more when it comes to editing my images, but I still love to play around.

"Wow, that's a killer shot!"

I spin round quickly to catch Leah peering over at my laptop screen from the doorway—I must have left the dressing-room door open when I came in. I instantly feel as though I need to slam my laptop shut.

"Oh, no, don't close it. Honestly, it's really cool. Can I

come in and take a closer look?" She doesn't wait for an answer, but strides in and sits down next to me. "You like photography, right?"

"Yes, er . . . I mean, yeah, I love it. I saw the show last night and it was truly amazing. You looked great—and you and Hayden sounded incredible singing that a cappella song." It feels weird to be giving Leah Brown a compliment. I'm not entirely sure she wants a compliment from me, but I also know that I am speaking the absolute truth. I feel a bit scared and more than a little intimidated by her, though. When she's on stage, she looks otherworldly—like a more perfect being from another planet, or a goddess blessed with unnatural beauty. She is still stunning in person, but with her sitting beside me I can hear her breathing and it reminds me that she's just like me. And I don't really know her at all.

"Oh, thanks, honey. That's nice of you. Hayden is a sweetheart. Have you met him?"

I shake my head.

"Well, The Sketch are kept on a pretty tight leash, you know? Their management are the absolute best in the business. You wouldn't catch them getting drunk on a work night." Leah winks at me, but my stomach flips when I think of Noah and Dean's late-night antics. Leah continues, oblivious to my discomfort. "You know, you really have a talent with those photos. I've worked with lots of photographers who don't get shots like these. May I?" she asks.

I nod and she scrolls through some of the other photos until she gets to the goofy ones with Noah. "You guys are cute. I'm glad it's all working out, Penny. I really do mean that." She places her hand on mine and I instantly feel warmth from her. Is the Leah Brown I thought I knew crumbling away right in front of my eyes?

"Thank you," I say. "I suppose we're quite cute! I still can't believe it's all worked out."

"I guess I'm jealous!" She smiles at me. Not a small, sarcastic smirk; a proper heartwarming smile. "It's so hard to meet decent people in this business. And, trust me, it was not fun for me either, having to pretend to be with a guy who didn't actually like me."

I suddenly realize how difficult it must have been for her, even though I've never thought of it that way. Noah retreated from the world, holing up with his grandmother in Brooklyn, completely abandoning Leah to handle all the speculation and gossip about their relationship on her own. She had to be professional, whereas Noah escaped by being the amateur who couldn't handle the pressure.

"I have no idea why you'd even need to pretend, though. Surely you have guys falling over themselves for you!"

She laughs. "It's not those types of guys who you want, to be honest! And I'll never pretend again. Did you know I dumped my manager after he made that arrangement? Being so fake just isn't worth it. I hope Noah knows how lucky he is. It's easy to get swept away in all the other stuff and forget what's real."

"I think I'm the lucky one that he even wanted me here at all. But we support each other, you know?" I look at her hopefully.

"Yeah, I know. You're so darn cute—it's hard to be mad at either of you. Oh, damn, I've chipped this nail." Leah jumps up from the sofa and calls out to her assistant. "CLAIRE,

I'VE CHIPPED A NAIL! CAN WE SEND THE TECHNICIAN OVER ASAP?" She turns back to me. "Penny, I've got to run. Let's catch up again before this tour is over, though. It's nice to have some female company. The male energy in this place is sometimes a little too much to cope with."

I can't help but smile, as I've had the exact same thought. Maybe having Leah around won't be so bad after all. "Yeah, it was nice to chat with you."

"No problem, doll." She blows me a kiss and walks out of the room. As I listen to the click of her heels, I hear another voice chatting back to her. I'd know that voice anywhere: it's Noah.

He emerges from the doorway, looking sheepish.

"Pen, I am *so* sorry." He sits down next to me and grabs my hand. "Blake practically forced me to go out to this bar he'd found and, before I knew it, it was four a.m. and we were walking back. Then I set an alarm for this morning and I must have turned it off in my sleep! I've ruined what should have been a perfect day out."

It's at this point that Blake strolls in, hood up, shades on, smelling like a rotten mix between a brewery and an ashtray. "Honestly, Penny, it was the *best* night. I hooked up with this German chick who I met after the gig last night, and we hung out with her and her friends. Dean was dancing on tables; Noah was *so* drunk. I've never seen him like that before—we had to carry him home!" He laughs hysterically.

Noah gives me a pleading look as Blake carries on chatting away about how crazy their night was. I can't tell if Noah wants the ground to open up and swallow him . . . or Blake.

Noah squeezes my hand. "We'll have an amazing day at the next city, I promise. All the cake and culture you could ever ask for." He's lowered his voice so that only I can hear, but he's out of luck—Blake has caught the last bit of the sentence.

"CAKE AND CULTURE? Are you joking, Noah? You're on tour, not a school field trip! How lame can you get?" Blake glares at Noah, then at me.

"Blake, please. Just be quiet for one minute." Noah looks exasperated.

"Why? Your head pounding?" Blake bursts into laughter again, but then mercifully leaves the room. Now it's just Noah and me.

Noah rolls his eyes and turns back to me. "Penny, please. Say something? I'm sorry, I really am. This won't happen again. I got carried away."

All I can think about while this is happening is what Leah said to me about how it's so easy to get swept up in everything. I can't stop him; I don't want to. I don't want to be that type of girlfriend. He's eighteen, he's living his dream and he's having fun. I have to be happy for him, or else I'll lose him forever.

"It's fine, don't be silly, Noah. I found lots to do and I had an awesome day regardless. I'm glad you had a fun night out." I smile, placing a kiss on his lips and ruffling his hair. Then I wrinkle my nose. "Not going to lie, though, you absolutely stink!"

Noah grimaces. "I didn't have time to shower. Larry woke me up and I came straight here." I throw him a towel. Noah grabs it and kisses me as he heads towards the shower, taking off his T-shirt. My eyes open wide and I can't help but gawp at his strong back muscles, honed by many hours jumping up and down onstage and working out at the gym.

He smirks and throws his smelly T-shirt at me, and I grimace as it lands square on my face, ruining the good view.

Chapter Twenty-Three

It's late by the time we get back to the hotel after the gig, but Noah is still buzzing with adrenaline. We order burgers from room service and we've barely sat down on my bed when there's a knock at the door.

"That was quick," I joke, as Noah opens the door to Dean.

"Hey, Noah. Hey, Penny—found you. I've got something for you. I think this is all of it," he says, and, with a grunt, he hauls a huge black bag into the room.

I turn to Noah and frown. I don't understand why Dean has brought Noah a bag full of rubbish.

"Oh, wow! Thanks, man!" Noah grabs it and opens the top of the bag. It's full to the brim with notes and gifts that Noah's received from his fans. "This is crazy! Is this all from tonight?"

Dean nods. "Yeah, they've been leaving stuff all day! Thought you might want to get a look at it now before there's even more. I know how you like to stay on top of this stuff. I think I even saw some envelopes with your name on it, Penny." Dean winks at me.

"For me? Really?" I stare at the black bag like it might be radioactive. Who on earth would write to me?

Noah lifts it and empties the contents out onto the bed. The notes and gifts cover almost the entire surface of the crisp white duvet. I pick out a piece of artwork that has caught my eye—it's a portrait of Noah, done in ballpoint pen. It's so incredibly detailed and lifelike, every feature, even down to the dimples in his cheeks, is perfectly rendered in dark blue ink.

"Wow, your fans are so talented!" I say, breathless—and a little overawed.

"Hey, look," Noah says. "There's one for you here."

He slides it across the duvet towards me. It's a pale yellow A4 envelope. I tentatively undo the sticky seal, and I'm filled for some reason with trepidation about what it might contain. Who would be sending *me* fan mail?

I tip the envelope upside down over the bed, and a few sheets of paper fall out. I open them up, and it's a printout of one of my blog posts from *Girl Online*. There's a hand-written note in the margins.

Dear Penny,
I just wanted to say what a huge inspiration you were to me when you were writing your blogs. I especially loved your blog about when you first started going out with Brooklyn Boy. It gave me hope that love could be real and maybe it will happen to me! I also thought you were so brave at the start of the year . . . but I am sad you had to close your blog.

I started writing my own blog, because of you.
It's nowhere near as good as GIRL ONLINE, but if
you want to check it out then I've left a link below.
Your friend,
Annabelle

I hug the letter to my chest. I can't believe someone has written to me! This fills me with a warm, fuzzy feeling, and I know I'm going to treasure this letter forever.

"All right, you crazy kids, I'm heading to bed," says Dean. "Remember, early start tomorrow—no one is missing that bus."

I didn't realize he was still standing inside the doorway.

"You got it, Dean-o," says Noah.

Dean grimaces at the nickname and waves as he shuts the door.

Noah is quiet, his brow furrowed in thought. I know he feels overwhelmed by all this attention—it's still not something that he's used to, even after all this time. I wonder if he will ever get used to it? In a way, I hope not. This could *never* be normal!

I look back down at the huge pile and I'm surprised to see another envelope with my name on it. This one feels slightly squishy, like it has bubble wrap on the inside. I tear into this one with more excitement.

But that excitement turns to fear when I read the note. I drop it like it's on fire, tossing it as far away from me as possible.

"What is it?" Noah looks up abruptly, his eyes wide with alarm.

I just shake my head and point to the letter.

He picks up the discarded note—it's a printout of some of our private text conversations. Some of the words have been circled, and when you read them together it says: *Go home, Penny, or else.*

At the bottom is the signature: *TheRealTruth*.

I feel shaken and confused—this is what I was afraid of. I thought the first message was just a one-off, but obviously not. Does that mean TheRealTruth is in Berlin?

To my surprise, Noah doesn't look angry or even vaguely annoyed. He looks relieved. He reaches over and grabs my hand, pulling me towards him.

I'm reluctant at first—why isn't he more bothered by this?—but then I know that nothing will make me feel better than a hug from Noah.

He kisses my forehead. "This has proved it to me—it's just a crazy person, nothing more. They can't hurt you, I promise. Now that we have this letter, we can give it to Larry and he can keep an eye out. This is kind of part of the deal."

I nod, and pull his arms tighter round me. This is real. We are real. That letter is just a sick fantasy. "You really think there's a fan out there who wants me gone?"

Noah gives me a funny look, and I realize how silly I sound. Of *course* there are some fans who would rather I wasn't on the scene. I've seen the adoration and the love for Noah in the crowd, which is bordering on the fanatical. How many of them picture themselves in my position?

"Please don't leave me tonight. I don't think I can sleep if I'm on my own." I know Noah is reluctant to break the rules my parents set, but I *also* know he's way too respectful of my feelings to try anything I'm not ready for. I trust him.

To my relief, Noah nods. "I'll clear all this up and then we can get some sleep. I can look at it on the bus tomorrow."

I head into the bathroom and wash my face. It feels good to scrub myself clean of the day—the reappearance of TheRealTruth makes me feel dirty, even if it is just some crazed fan, like Noah says. I brush my teeth and change into my cosiest pyjamas. I think of all the girls who would rather be here, and it makes me feel a little sad. Would they still want to if they knew how hard it is?

"Did you know you are the most beautiful girl I've ever seen?" Noah says, as I emerge from the bathroom in my pyjamas. "You keep me grounded through all of this." He gestures to the huge fan-mail bag, which he's tidied away into the corner of the room. I sit down on the bed next to him. "You don't deserve what's happening to you," he continues, "and I promise you that, when these crazy two weeks of tour are over, we can hang out, just the two of us. No more creepy letters and anonymous hotel rooms and non-stop travel. You can finally see New York in the summertime! It's just as magical as at Christmas—if not, dare I say it, even better."

"It sounds lovely," I say, drifting off to sleep as he strokes my hair.

"Just remember, Penny. It's you and me against the world."

★·★Chapter Twenty-Four★·★

When I wake up in the morning, it's still early. Our arms and legs are interlocked like we're a human jigsaw puzzle. I gently lift Noah's arm, which has fallen across my waist, and wriggle out from underneath it, sliding on the sheets until my toes find the carpeted floor.

I pick up my phone from its perch on the bedside table and quickly scroll through the updates from last night. On Instagram, there's a picture of Kira at Brighton beach, dipping her toes in the sea. I can almost feel the rush of the waves, the wind whipping through my hair, the screech of seagulls . . . I can't believe I miss that pebbly stretch of beach, but I do.

There are several WhatsApp conversations that I catch up on. Megan has been giving us a minute-by-minute account of her latest date with a former sixth-form boy called Andrew, who's taken her to the Sea Life Centre. There's a series of selfies of them together in front of colourful fish, their faces lit up by the eerie blue light. It's strange because I know that Megan would love to be where I am now—on tour with a rock star, living this crazy life—but sometimes I wish with all my heart that Noah and I could just have normal dates, like a normal couple.

A message flashes up on my phone.

> Are you up?

It's from Elliot. I type a reply quickly.

> Yeah! Literally just woken up. You're up early!

> Early start at the magazine. How are you this fine morning?

> Didn't really sleep very well. I got another message from TheRealTruth in Noah's fan mail. Noah's convinced now it's just some crazed fan, so hopefully it will go away

You're not famous until you have a stalker! Comes with the territory. Stay safe though. It's probably not a good idea for me to go through all the facts I know about other celebrity stalkers?

PLEASE DON'T!! I'm freaking out enough already! OK, I better go . . . Noah's just waking up

Wait?! He's there? Did you guys . . .

No!!!

Calm down—I'm only teasing! You guys are the cutest. Say hi to N for me

"Everything OK?" Noah leans forward and kisses my shoulder.

"Just Elliot being a nosy parker!" I say with a laugh. "And scaring me about stalkers . . ."

Noah shakes his head. "Don't let him—or, more importantly, that creep—freak you out. We'll get through this together. You and me against the world, remember?"

I smile. "I remember."

"Good. Now, we better get ready or else the tour bus is going to leave without us!"

On the journey from Berlin to Munich, we pass loads of amazing photo opportunities, but there's no time to stop. Instead, each sight just disappears in a blur through the thick pane of glass. The fields are filled with flowers, and each town we drive through is packed with lovely old buildings— even the little cafés on the roadside look picturesque.

The rest of the boys are sleeping in the beds at the back of the bus, but Noah and I take a seat on the sofa for a Disney-movie marathon to pass the time. Halfway through *Aladdin*, I realize the Disney marathon is a one-man race: Noah is out like a light, and he ends up sleeping most of the journey with his head rested on my shoulder. It is so nice just being with him, listening to his deep breaths as we trundle along through Germany. His hair smells clean and fresh, and every now and then I get a strong whiff of his aftershave. I take out my camera and get a few shots of the two of us.

"Penny?"

I look up as Dean says my name. He sits down in a chair next to me.

"Noah let me know about the letter in the fan-mail bag.

I'm so sorry—we try to screen as much of that stuff as possible, but it's not easy on tour. Is there anything I can do to put your mind at rest?"

I shake my head. "No, I guess I just need to learn how to deal with it."

"Well, remember I'm here to help you as well as Noah." He looks over at Noah, who is fast asleep, then he lowers his voice. "I can help arrange a trip home for you as well, if it's all getting a bit . . . much."

Instead of getting angry when I hear this, I simply feel relieved. I feel better knowing that there is an escape route if I need one—and hopefully I won't need it. "Thanks, Dean. That does make me feel better."

"You're welcome, Penny. I know this is all a lot to take in. I'm sure you don't want to be reminded of this, but you're still young. I spoke to your parents, remember—I feel a responsibility!"

I laugh. "How do you deal with all this? Don't you find it a bit crazy?"

Dean smiles. "Are you kidding? I live for this stuff! And Noah is my shining star. I knew it from the first time I saw him on YouTube. When was that? Almost two years ago now? I can even remember exactly what I was doing when I saw him playing for the first time. I was searching for this Fleetwood Mac song and Noah had done a cover—"

"Oh, of 'Landslide'? Noah's shown that to me."

Dean snaps his fingers. "Exactly! It wasn't what I was looking for, but it was magic. I couldn't stop watching, and I thought to myself, *This kid is something special.* Hey, a lot of managers and talent spotters get that feeling—but I'm lucky.

It just so happened for me that it was true. I went from managing a bunch of wedding singers to the big time."

"Noah's lucky to have you," I say.

He chuckles. "Hey, whatever I can do to make sure Noah's happy and singing, I'll do it. That boy means the world to me."

I nod. "I feel silly for worrying about a couple of little notes when it's Noah's career that's on the line. And it's not as if my relationship is the only one that has to face big struggles."

"What do you mean?"

"I mean real-world problems. Like, my best friend, Elliot, has this amazing boyfriend, except he's not out to all his friends and family yet. That feels like such a genuine issue, whereas my problems are superficial in comparison."

Dean shrugs. "They're both young. Some people are just more confident than others. I'm sure they'll work it out. Sounds as though you're a great support to Elliot too. You'd be surprised how rare loyalty is sometimes, Penny."

"I hope so. I just want Elliot to be happy. He's the most important person in my world—after Noah, of course."

Dean laughs. "Well, nudge your lazy boyfriend—we're almost here, and he's got work to do."

Chapter Twenty-Five

"I'm awake, I'm awake," says a sleepy Noah. "Whoa, Munich seems awesome."

I turn and follow Noah's gaze out of the window. The buildings are more picturesque here than the cooler, more modern vibe of Berlin. It's like a real-life version of the imitation German Christmas markets my parents drag Tom and me along to every year, in the centre of Brighton, where we drink glühwein (or hot chocolate, for me!), eat bratwurst smothered in hot mustard, and stick our hands in the mounds of fake snow. Looking down over a *real* German town, I realize this would be the perfect setting for a fairy tale, and I can't help wondering what it looks like in winter, covered in a layer of snow like frosting on a cake.

By the time we arrive at the venue, the roadies have already started setting up and getting everything ready for the show tonight. Noah holds my hand as we're shown through to the backstage area—and I really feel like I'm starting to get the hang of this whole tour thing.

Noah stops us outside the dressing room. "Hey, we're

about to have a big, boring meeting about some technical stuff that you won't want to listen to, but apparently some of The Sketch's friends and family are hanging around in one of the other rooms—do you want to check it out? I'll only be about an hour."

"No problem," I say, but I must look unsure because Larry comes over and throws a burly arm round my shoulders.

"Come on, Penny. I'll take you!"

"Thanks, Larry!" I say. Noah and I kiss goodbye, and I leave him to his meeting.

Larry leads me round a corner and out to a big, wide area just behind the stage. There are lots of people here, relaxing on multicoloured beanbags and drinking coffee out of paper cups. I spot a couple of members of The Sketch lounging around and it takes all my willpower not to whip out my phone and snap a picture of them for my friends back home. That wouldn't be very good backstage etiquette.

Larry nudges me towards a table that's laid out with drinks and snacks. "Go over and grab a bite to eat, then introduce yourself."

"Oh, I'm not good at that . . ."

"Sure you are. Just offer someone a cup of tea. They'll think your accent is so cute they'll be all over you." He gives me a gentle pat on the shoulder, then goes and plops himself down on one of the beanbags.

I giggle as he sinks deep into the bag—I'm not sure I've ever seen a security guard look so undignified, but somehow he pulls it off. It's even better when he slides a paperback out of his pocket, and it has a bright pink cover and a couple kissing on the front. Who knew Larry loves a good romance novel?

I take Larry's advice and walk over to the table. There really is a vast array of food and drink to choose from, including every type of tea under the sun, from normal English breakfast to camomile and peppermint. There are also huge vats of coffee, which I avoid—it just makes my anxiety spike. I'm tempted by some brightly decorated cupcakes and I wander down the table to take a closer look.

"Oh, those are *so* good," says a voice next to me. I look up and there's a beautiful girl with very long, very straight brown hair standing next to me. She holds out her hand. "Hi! I'm Kendra. I'm Hayden's girlfriend. You're Penny, right?"

I shake her hand and smile. "Yeah, hi! Wow, I didn't even know Hayden has a girlfriend." I suddenly realize what an awkward and uncool thing that is to say, and I clap both hands over my stupid mouth.

But luckily she throws her head back and laughs, her bright blue eyes sparkling. "Yeah, I know, right? I'm not like you—I'm a certified GUC."

"GUC?" I ask, confused.

"Girlfriend Under Cover," she says with a wink. "It's better for the boys' image if they're single, but, trust me, Hayden wouldn't last a day without me to keep him in line! I don't mind, though. I have a job on the tour team as a makeup artist, so it gives me a legitimate excuse to hang around. And to eat cupcakes, of course." She reaches out and grabs one. "You can come and sit with us, if you want?" She points at a table surrounded by a few other girls who all look pretty and glossy like Kendra.

"Oh, thanks." I follow her back to the table, cupcake in hand, but feel increasingly conscious of the fact that I'm wearing a pair of old jeans and a plain T-shirt while Kendra is cool and casual in a pair of chic black skinny jeans that are ripped at the knees and a floaty white top with cutouts in the neck. We arrived straight off the bus, so I haven't exactly given my outfit a second thought. "I love your top," I say to Kendra when we sit down.

"Thanks, it's Chanel," she says, with a smile. "Hayden's credit card goes a long way to making sure I always look my best!"

"Has Noah not kitted you out yet?" asks one of the other girls, who Kendra introduces quickly as Selene. She has gold eyeliner drawn in an elaborate cat-eye shape that pops against her dark skin.

"I, uh . . ." I'm about to say that I buy all my clothes from Brighton thrift stores, but suddenly that doesn't seem very cool.

"He's brought her on this tour; it's the least he could do to help her out a bit," Selene says, responding to Kendra's warning look. They continue to talk about me as if I'm not there. "I mean, she's not even a GUC—I know I wouldn't want *my* picture in magazines without some kind of preparation. But I guess we're the lucky ones." Selene and Kendra quickly look over at Pete—one of the other members of The Sketch.

"What do you mean?" I ask, following their line of sight.

"Pete's been with Anna for two years, but they hardly ever get to see each other. It's been three months now since he last saw her, and they've still got three months to go," says Selene.

Kendra sighs and stares at her nails. "Even more time on the road." They carry on chatting about what it will be like on the next part of the tour, which is going to even more far-flung places like Dubai, Singapore, and Australia. I can't help but think I'll be back home in Brighton by then, hanging out with my friends.

Kira has a giant scratch map of the world hanging on her wall, and every time she visits a country she scratches it off the map. She has a big dream to travel the world, and we used to talk about all our fantasy places to visit if we could. I used to worry about whether I would ever be able to travel with my anxiety, but it was still fun to dream about it together. I still can't believe that some of that dreaming is coming true for me, and in the most surreal way imaginable.

Selene's voice breaks me out of my daydream. "How are you enjoying life on tour, Penny?"

I cringe a little. "Oh, you know . . . it takes some getting used to!"

"Hey, we've been doing this for over a year now. You'll get into the rhythm eventually!" Kendra smiles at me, and I smile back gratefully at her attempt to make me feel better.

"You had that blog, didn't you?" asks Selene.

I nod. "I did, but I shut it down at the end of last year."

"That's good—you wouldn't be able to sit here and talk with us if you were just going to go and write about it all on your blog. The managers would probably have a fit!"

"No, I know—I'm not Girl Online anymore. I'm just plain old Penny." Suddenly I feel a warning prickle of anxiety heat on my neck and I realize I need to get out of there quickly or else things might go from bad to worse. I stand up from the table. "I'm just going to find the bathroom. It was nice meeting you guys."

"You too, Penny! Come hang out with us anytime. Then you can officially be a member of the tour WAGs!"

I nod and smile, then head off in the direction of the bathrooms. I push through the heavy door, locking it behind me. I lean up against the door for the moment. I know what was making me feel panicky: the more I hang out with other people who have done this for a long time, the more I worry that it's not going to be for me. I don't have any talents that would make me a useful member of Noah's entourage, and I don't like fashion or music enough to keep up with the other girls. I like my home, and my own bed, and having my family close by. But I like Noah too.

I glance at myself in the mirror. Just thinking about being with all those other girls leaves me feeling racked with inadequacy. My long red hair is curled loosely and looks a little messy. I pull a few strands away from my face and trace my freckles with my finger; they are a lot more prominent now that it's summer. My green eyes stare back at me and I squint in the mirror, making a funny face.

I wish I knew how to do more with my eye makeup, like Selene. My eyes are probably my favourite feature. They are the sort of green that you would probably only see on a vampire in a TV series, and they change colour in different lights. My dad calls them sea-glass eyes, after the smooth shards of glass that wash up on the shore at the beach. Mum and Dad gave me a bottle-green sea-glass necklace for my sixteenth birthday that perfectly matches my eye colour.

I think back to last night and how I'm completely relaxed wearing my comfy pyjamas with Noah. It doesn't matter what other people might think: Noah loves me the way I am, makeup or no. I look down at my watch and am surprised that it's almost been an hour already. I wonder if Noah's meeting is over yet.

I head back round the corner to the dressing room and knock tentatively on the door, which instead swings open at my touch.

I'm greeted by a completely unwelcome sight: Blake's bare bum.

Chapter Twenty-Six

Blake is completely naked, running around with Noah's guitar, and everyone is in fits of laughter. I have no idea where to look.

"Ahem ... HEY, GUYS!" I say, loudly enough so they know I've entered the room. It doesn't seem to make any difference. I spot Noah and quickly sandwich myself next him on the sofa, trying desperately to avert my gaze. He is practically doubled over with laughter.

"Oh, hey, P!" He pulls me in for a cuddle and kisses my nose.

"Spare us the PDA, Noah," Blake calls over.

"Spare me your naked body!" I yell back.

Noah bursts into laughter again and Blake just blinks back at me in absolute horror. I blush pink, but actually feel proud that I managed to respond to Blake's jibes.

When Noah finally regains his composure, he says, "Clear out, dudes. I want a bit of time with Penny before the show."

"Seriously, man? Can I not put on some boxers first?" Blake protests.

"Hey, you made this bed. Now you have to lie in it. But here—" Noah fishes out Blake's boxers with the end of a drumstick, wrinkling his nose, and whips them across the room. Blake snatches them out of the air and shuffles over to the door, just managing to cover himself with the rest of his clothes, which are rolled up in a ball.

"What was all that about?" I ask Noah, when everyone's finally gone.

"Oh, just typical Blake. He was threatening to play my guitar completely naked tonight." Noah laughs softly.

"Of course he was," I say, lifting an eyebrow.

"I'm so sorry, Penny." Noah lifts my chin with his fingers and gives me a small smile.

"What do you mean?"

"I thought we'd have so much more time to spend together. But the tour is a lot more full-on than I'd ever imagined." His hands drop from my chin and, instead, he runs them through his hair. "The press is becoming more and more interested in me—I have interviews flying in left and right, and I want this tour to be amazing for everyone, and for me. The reviews are all good, but I need them to stay that way. I want to practise twenty-four seven, and if I'm not practising or publicizing the tour I'm asleep. I feel exhausted already, and I'm only partway through."

"I know—" I try to reach out to him, to let him know that I understand how he feels, but it's like a dam has broken and the words keep rushing out of Noah.

"On top of that, I feel like this is such a weird time for me. I'm getting to do the one thing I've dreamt of since I was a kid, and I'm doing it with no family around me. I don't get

text updates from my mum and dad asking how the tour is going like the rest of the boys do. I don't have parents to Skype every day, who look out for me, like yours do. Sadie Lee's focus is on making sure that Bella is OK—I'm eighteen, I don't need her as much as Bella does. It's just me, on my own." He slumps down into the sofa and starts tracing the music-note tattoo on his wrist. "But tonight . . . tonight, I promise that we can go out for dinner after the show. I owe it to you. I know I do."

"You don't owe me anything, Noah. I love you! And you're not on your own—you have me. I can do whatever it is that you want me to do. I want to make this easier for you. I just want you to be happy."

"I am happy, Penny. I am the happiest I've been in a long time. It's just sad at the same time, you know?"

I put my arm round him and pull him into me for a hug. Why hadn't I seen that Noah wasn't OK? It's dawning on me just how much pressure Noah must be feeling right now.

"Let me help you. What can I do for you?" I jump up off the sofa and look around the room.

"Honestly, Penny. I don't need you to do anything. Just being here is enough."

"No, there must be something. At least let me do something to help? One little thing . . ." I turn to the mini fridge and grab a fresh-fruit smoothie. I run and grab a glass from the table, and pour the smoothie into it. Then I slice a strawberry and wedge it onto the rim of the glass—a little smoothie cocktail that looks like something you'd order in a fancy hotel, topped off with a pretty straw.

"Voilà!" I say, spinning round to reveal the smoothie to

Noah. It's as I'm taking a couple of steps towards him that I realize I don't have control of my footing. I look down in horror to see one of my feet is caught behind the leg of a coffee table, and suddenly the floor is getting closer to my face. As I hit the ground, the smoothie flies through the air towards Noah. I see his face frozen in horror as the pink pulp splatters over his entire outfit.

"NO! Oh no, Noah. I'M SO SORRY!" I leap up and start scraping the mess off his top with my hands.

Noah's expression is serious . . . until he bursts out into laughter. "That's it! You're getting a hug right now!" He opens his arms wide and takes a step forward towards me, his smoothie-covered chest looming.

I squeal and run away, and we end up in a game of chase around the dressing room. He catches up with me when I get caught between the sofa and a stack of empty guitar cases, and he squeezes me tight. I cringe as the smoothie dregs are squished between us.

He kisses the top of my head. "Hey, good thing all I own is black T-shirts, right? I'd better go change out of this."

He winks as he peels his T-shirt off, rooting through his bag for another. I can't believe I can be the silliest, clumsiest person in the world and Noah *still* loves me, no matter what.

In a fresh black top, Noah looks like the smoothie disaster never happened. He kisses me on the cheek and dashes out the door to get to the stage. A few moments later, I hear the crowd start to scream with delight.

He's in his element, and that's all that matters to me.

Chapter Twenty-Seven

When I've cleaned up, I watch the rest of Noah's set with Kendra and Selene from a little balcony in the wings of the stage—but I make sure to be back in the dressing room when Noah's finished. I'm hoping that we can head out straight-away to go to dinner.

My heart lifts as I see Noah walk in. His cheeks are red with exertion, but he has the biggest smile on his face. Dean follows not far behind, along with a man and woman I don't recognize. Neither of them is dressed for a rock concert—in their matching grey suits and stiff white shirts, they look prepared for the boardroom, not backstage.

"This is where I chill before and after the show." Noah gestures around the room, then plunges his hands deep into his jeans pockets. Weirdly, he looks nervous. Normally he rides high on confidence after a show, so I'm intrigued as to who these people are.

"Oh swell, that's just swell," the man chimes.

The woman tries to hide the fact she's wrinkling her nose

slightly. It makes me laugh—I'm used to the smell of stinky boy musicians now.

My giggle draws their attention. "Who is this?" the woman asks, looking at me. It's clear she thinks I don't belong. "Did you win a competition to be here, my dear?"

"Er, no, this is Penny. She's my—"

"She's a friend." Dean steps in, drawing the group together so they're standing in a circle, backs turned towards me. I can still see Noah's face, but he is studiously avoiding my gaze.

My stomach does a few flips. What's going on?

"So, Noah—Alicia and Patrick were wondering if they could take us out for dinner tonight, just to go through a few contract things with Sony, if that's OK?" Dean's voice is as smooth as silk.

Things are starting to make more sense now. These are bigwigs from the label.

Noah finally looks at me, his eyes filled with guilt, and then back at Dean, Alicia, and Patrick.

Please say no, please say no, I plead silently, even though I can already see it's a lost cause.

"Yeah, sure, that's fine!" Noah replies, and he even manages a smile. "I'm looking forward to it. It's honestly very nice of you both to fly here for the night to see me. I know you must be crazy busy."

My heart sinks. Now it's me who can't look at Noah, and I pick furiously at a loose thread on the cushion of the sofa. Why hasn't he introduced me as his girlfriend? I don't think I've ever felt more invisible and uncomfortable in my life. I don't look up even as they all leave the room together, not until I hear the click of the door closing.

I get goose bumps, even though it's warm inside the dressing room. Then I feel the sofa sag next to me—to my surprise, Noah's stayed behind.

He grabs my hand. "I'm sorry, Pen—"

I don't let him finish. "Honestly, it's OK. You do what you need to do. It's great that they came to see you." I smile, but I hope it doesn't look as forced as it feels.

His eyes dart around my face, looking for cracks in my facade, but I don't let my disappointment show. Not until he leaves again; then I feel the burn of tears pricking the corners of my eyes. I fight them back as I pack up my camera and laptop to head back to the hotel.

Chapter Twenty-Eight

There's only one person I need right now. Back in my hotel room, I immediately Skype Elliot. As soon as he answers the call, I feel a swell of relief.

"Penny, you're lucky. I was just about to begin my evening pamper routine, starting with sorting out these talons." A slightly pixelated Elliot appears, holding up his hands.

"Elliot, this is an emergency!"

"You went sightseeing finally?"

"No . . . but thanks for the reminder." I let out a huge sigh and put my head in my hands.

"Whoa, Lady P. What's up?"

I bite my lip. Where to start? "You know how I haven't had any time with Noah yet—how he's either asleep, performing, or hanging out with the band? Well, we were supposed to go out for dinner this evening, but two people from his record label flew in from LA so he's doing that instead."

"Well, that is a big deal . . ."

"It's not that. I'd understand if he needed to see his label. But . . . it was so weird. I was in the room with them, and he didn't even introduce me as his girlfriend. I guess I'm a certified GUC."

"GUC?" asks Elliot.

"Girlfriend Under Cover," I explain. "It was like he felt embarrassed or ashamed of me."

Elliot frowns. "That is so unlike Noah. That's not cool at all. I would have gone to dinner and pulled up a chair just to make a point."

I giggle despite myself. Elliot really would have done that. He has absolutely no shame.

But even laughing with Elliot makes me sad. It reminds me how far away he is, when all I want is for us to be back in Brighton, chatting away in my bedroom like normal. I pull my knees up under my chin and give myself a hug. "Maybe he's exhausted. Maybe he was in shock that they just turned up out of the blue like that? I mean, he can't say no to a dinner with them, can he? I need to stop reading so much into this."

I watch as Elliot lets out a long sigh.

"That's a lot of maybes, Penny. You have done nothing wrong here. He invited *you* along on tour, remember? He told you there would be Magical Mystery Days in every city. He told you it wouldn't be stressful, because it was his first tour, and that the team was great. He said he was so well rehearsed that he wouldn't need to practise too much between shows. He wanted you there—it wasn't the other way round. It's OK to feel disappointed."

"But he didn't realize how busy it would get with the press . . . and people just showing up for dinner isn't his fault. It must be hard for him doing this." Then I shake my head. "I just feel like I may as well not be here . . ."

"I'm not convinced, P. This seems a bit off, if you ask me. Just remember that no other man will ever love you as much as I do." He blows me a kiss and laughs.

"While I love you too, you know that's not exactly reassuring."

"Oh, shush. Just go ahead and do the things you wanted to do while you're there anyway. GO OUTSIDE, WOMAN. And take that camera of yours."

He's right. Noah is busy—there is nothing I can do about that—but, instead of feeling sorry for myself on Skype, I should be outside doing things and exploring this beautiful city. "I *will* have Magical Mystery Day," I say, "even if that means doing it by myself."

"That's the spirit!" says Elliot, but for some reason he doesn't look very spirited. I face-palm so hard I'm worried I'm going to have a red mark on my forehead. I've been so self-absorbed—*again*—that I haven't even asked Elliot how *he* is doing.

After I apologize profusely and redeem myself, Elliot beams. "Things are great. The internship is *amazing* even if I do have to commute to London every weekday! I can't wait to live there. I'm a bright-lights, big-city guy, that's for sure!"

He's so happy he's almost bouncing up and down in his seat—but the thought of him leaving Brighton twists my gut. It's another reminder that things are going to change soon, no matter how hard I wish they could stay the same forever.

"That's great, Wiki!" I manage to disguise my moment of sadness, and I smile back at him.

"And things with Alex are amazing. I went out to that rugby game with him . . . and I enjoyed it!"

"No way! I'm so happy for you. You'll turn into a right sports lover yet."

Elliot grimaces. "I don't think so. But we watched Noah's Berlin show on YouTube. It was so sweet when he gave you a shout-out before 'Autumn Girl'! I wish I could make big, romantic, public displays of affection with my boyfriend."

"Elliot . . ."

"I know, I know. I'm not complaining! I want him to come out to everyone when he feels confident. I just wish I gave him that confidence. It's silly, I know." I want to give Elliot a big hug and tell him not to worry about Alex—that it will work out in the end. They are made for each other; they are so perfect together. "So, where are you off to next, you globe-trotter? It's not more long hours on the bus-from-hell, is it?"

"Rome! And, no—we're flying."

"You lucky *signorina*." There's a pause as Elliot and I just stare at each other through the screen. His green eyes are enhanced by the purple rim of his glasses, and they start misting with tears. "I miss you," he says.

I can't help it; my eyes fill with tears right alongside him. "I miss you too."

We both hug the screen until, on a count of three, we hang up together.

Chapter Twenty-Nine

The late-afternoon flight from Munich to Rome is surprisingly pleasant. Blake and the rest of the boys are seated farther back, so Noah and I have a little bit of time together. Wrapped up in Mum's cardigan and snuggling next to Noah, I manage to keep my anxiety at bay, even though I grip Noah's hand throughout the take-off. During the flight we discuss the music industry and debate who we believe is the greatest rock band of all time. I don't think that Noah really understands my choice of Journey but I just can't help it: I love "Don't Stop Believin'"! He loves Pink Floyd and is shocked when I say I haven't heard of them. He plays "Wish You Were Here" on his iPod and makes me listen through his headphones. I agree on the need to expand my musical knowledge.

Stepping out of the airport, I feel a lovely warm breeze on my face. So many people have told me how beautiful Rome is and I am very excited to finally be on Italian soil. There is no show tonight and a whole day tomorrow to explore the city with Noah. The excitement bubbles up inside me as we are driven to our hotel. Rome really does look spectacular, even from a blacked-out tour bus.

When we finally reach the hotel, Noah flops down on my bed. "I've enjoyed today, you know, just us getting to talk about everything and nothing."

"I know what you mean. It's like New York all over again, before anyone knew about Noah and Penny."

He takes my face into his hands and kisses me as we lie next to each other. It's the sort of kiss that leaves me in knots and I feel like I may have to be scraped up off the floor as I've turned to jelly. Noah is a great kisser. Not that I've had many kisses to compare with his, but Noah feels older and a lot more mature and it's so different. It's not awkward or uncomfortable—it's just perfect.

Noah is exhausted so we order in room service and stick on a film to relax. It's not long before Noah falls asleep, his head resting in my lap.

When the film ends, I'm tempted to just let him sleep, but pins and needles are tingling up and down my trapped arm. As I shift to release the pressure, he stirs.

"Oh, what time is it?" he says, his voice groggy. "Is the movie over?" He sits up in bed, his hair flattened against the side of his face. I can't help but giggle.

He throws a pillow at me, then stretches and yawns. "I'll see you in the morning, Princess Penny."

He jumps up off the bed and makes his way to the door. All these rooms are beginning to look very similar and the novelty of staying in a hotel is definitely starting to wear off.

"Won't you stay with me? Please, like in Berlin?" I smile sweetly at him.

"You know the rules, Penny. That night was a one-off. Your parents wouldn't be happy if I did that—and Dean would kill me. Separate bedrooms was one of the terms of you coming along."

"My parents are so annoying and old-fashioned," I huff.

"They're just looking out for their little girl."

"LITTLE? I'm sixteen now! I'm venturing off into other countries without them—"

"You'll always be their little girl, Penny. You know that. Meet you downstairs tomorrow morning at nine. Love you." He blows me a kiss and disappears off to his room.

I distract myself for the rest of the evening by having a deep bath and checking some of my favourite photographers on Instagram, as well as the hashtags for Rome, with their sightseeing recommendations. I contemplate whether I should open an Instagram account for Girl Online—maybe it would be safer without words?—but then the warning bells start ringing.

Never going online, Penny . . .

Instead, I turn out the light and settle down under the covers, my mind filled with filters, photos, and all the treats that Rome has in store, and fall fast asleep.

The next morning I gather together my camera and bag, and head downstairs to the reception lobby. Noah isn't there. A worrying niggle gnaws at my stomach, and I pray that this isn't a repeat scenario of Berlin.

"Penny." Noah appears next to me with a somewhat less excited expression than the one I am wearing. He frowns. "I can't do today after all. Dean wants me to do a press junket and this is the only time I can do it."

I try to remain calm, but I can feel the anger rising and my face burns with heat. "OK," I manage through pursed lips.

"I'm sorry. Are you annoyed?" He tries to hold my hand but I snatch it away.

"No, really, I'm fine," I say. I play with the strap on my bag, trying desperately to think of a way to leave this situation before my emotions explode in a bubble of hot lava.

"Oh, all right then. I'm glad you're cool," he says, smiling down at me.

But, like a burst pipe, I can't contain myself. "NO, NOAH. I'M NOT FINE. CLEARLY I'M NOT FINE."

"You just said you—"

"GIRLS ALWAYS SAY THEY'RE FINE, BUT YOU SHOULD BE ABLE TO TELL I'M NOT FINE. THAT'S WHAT BOYFRIENDS DO! And do you know what else they do? They don't let their girlfriends down every chance they have." My voice is shrill and squeaky but I can't stop now. "Yes, this is big and scary for you, but this is big and scary for me too. I gave up a huge chunk of my summer holiday to be here with you, because you told me we would have the time to do these things, Noah. You promised me. I am jumping through hoops for you here and it's exhausting. I feel like a piece of your kit that's being carried from one venue to another."

By this point, Noah's mouth has dropped open and everyone in the lobby has turned to look at us.

I try to lower my voice, but the anger still comes through just as loud. "I'm *not* a piece of kit, Noah. I'm here and I want to experience this with you and I want to have at least *one* day with you where we can do the *one* thing you told me we would be doing." I stand there, breathless, waiting for a response from Noah, but instead he turns and walks out of the hotel's front door.

My feet are glued to the spot and I feel a heavy tear roll down my cheek as I watch him jump in a waiting taxi and drive off. Curious eyes burn into me from every corner of the lobby and, without making contact with any of them, I hold my head up high and strut to the lift. I walk in confidently when the doors swoosh open, then I stand back and watch the doors close, maintaining my poise . . . and then I burst into uncontrollable tears: snot, red face, heaving chest, and all.

The Inevitable: Our First Proper Argument

I hate arguing.

(No, I don't.)

Yes—I really, really do!

I go out of my way to avoid confrontation. Milkshakegate was the first time I've stood up for myself in years. And, even though it felt so good at the time, it hasn't made confrontation any more my friend.

When I get angry, I crumble. I cry.

And arguing with Brooklyn Boy?

That's practically unthinkable!

How can I argue with someone I love so much? We've been nothing but happy and carefree ever since we met.

I guess that means it was inevitable that one day our smooth sailing would hit a rocky patch.

Today just happened to be that day.

Imagine a luxurious and very grand hotel reception lobby in Rome: tall marble pillars and a domed ceiling painted with a beautiful fresco. Imagine the echo that would create. Now throw in an angry five-foot-five, auburn-haired sixteen-year-old and her cool, laid-back rock-god boyfriend looking charming and dressed down as always.

Now imagine my raised voice bouncing off the walls for the entire reception to hear. I don't have to imagine it—*I'm remembering it*. At the time, I didn't care about the commotion I was causing, but it has just dawned on me that I will need to go down through the reception lobby again to leave the hotel at some point. Mega cringe.

My parents hardly ever argue. I occasionally hear my brother fight with his girlfriend, but it's only ever over really stupid things like, "No, I told you I would call you back AFTER the football game." I feel like those things are little disagreements, while what's just happened between Brooklyn Boy and me was a rather large step up from that.

In fact, can you really call it an argument if there is only one of you doing the shouting? I think BB's sole contribution was a lot of blinking back at me. Was I being ridiculous?

All I know is that arguments sometimes need to happen in order for things to be OK again, and, like the mature, responsible grown-up I am, I am going to make sure things are OK. Find me a couple who haven't been through a simple argument. Actually don't. (Wiki, I'm looking at you.)

So, just for future reference, I'm going to make a list of things I've learned NOT to do in an argument:

1. Don't argue in the reception of a hotel—pick your moments and your location. Not everyone needs to know the ins and outs of why you're mad.

2. Understand that your voice is probably a little louder than it sounds in your own head.

3. Don't downplay how annoyed you are or say that you're fine. Not everyone is a mind reader.

4. Try to be cool, calm, and collected. Emphasis on the word *try* because by this point you may be about to explode.

5. When your boyfriend leaves without saying a word after your outburst, don't stand there cemented to the spot for too long. You will feel and look like an idiot.

6. When you have a big, snotty cry in the lift afterwards, expect that someone else might join you from another floor on your way up. That's what lifts are for.

7. Saying you have severe hay fever makes you look like a fool. It's pretty clear you are crying, so you may as well embrace it and accept the tissue from the middle-aged Italian man.

8. When making a grand exit, make sure you have your room key. After all, you will look ridiculous if you have to go back down to the reception to get another one issued.

9. Don't overthink the situation once you're sitting alone in your hotel room.

10. Don't eat ice cream in a hot, steamy bath—it's not that easy, especially when it's melting at lightning speed. I find pretzels to be a great alternative.

I'll leave it there for now. It's too cringey for me to want to write about it any more, and now that I'm seeing it all laid out in black and white I know I need to apologize for my way-too-public outburst.

Because, with any relationship, there will always be challenges that you might have to face together. It's just about being strong enough to know that an argument (even a mega-big one) doesn't have to mean the end.

Girl Offline . . . never going online xxx

★·★Chapter Thirty★·★

After publishing my blog post, I close my laptop and feel as though a huge weight has been lifted off my shoulders. There is a reason I love writing and filling my little (private) corner of the Internet with life musings and advice: it's so therapeutic. When I next see Noah, I'm going to apologize for how I acted in the hotel lobby, and I'm confident he's going to apologize to me too. We're going to get through this.

I look out of the small window next to my bed and notice all the people below wandering the streets in the blazing sun.

I'm in Rome.

Rome.

A city I've only ever dreamt of visiting. This is the home of Michelangelo and Raphael and Sophia Loren! I can sit here and go over our argument for the rest of the day, or I can make the most of Rome and clear my head—even if it means going it alone. I can hear Elliot's voice in the back of my mind, yelling at me to go out and explore the city. This time, I'm going to listen.

I roll off the bed and drag myself to the mirror. I look a

sorry state. I wipe a tissue underneath my bleary eyes, then have a confident Ocean Strong moment surge through me. *It's nothing a pair of oversized sunglasses can't hide*, I tell myself. I scrape my hair back into a messy bun, grab my bag (making sure to take my room key this time), and rush out of the door before I can convince myself otherwise. I pass Larry on my way out.

"Penny? Where are you going?" He frowns, concerned.

"Out, Larry. I'm going out. If I have to sit and look at the walls of my hotel room any longer I'll go insane."

"Let me come with you. What if you get lost? Do you have a map?"

A map? I hadn't even thought about it. My inner Ocean Strong wavers, but I tell her to pull herself together. I shake my head. "Honestly, I'll be fine. I think I just need a bit of time on my own to clear my head. If I get lost, I'll be sure to call you or grab a taxi and come straight back. I'm a big girl, Larry." I smile at him and move to continue down the hallway.

"At least take this." Larry digs a battered guidebook for Rome out of his jacket pocket. When I raise my eyebrow at him, he shrugs and says gruffly, "I just like to do my research. Have fun, won't you? My suggestion is to eat all the pizza and gelato you can. There's no problem that carbs and sugar can't solve."

Standing under the enormous dome of the Pantheon, I send a whisper of thanks to Larry for his guidebook—without it, I would have never found any of the sights. Rome is breathtakingly beautiful. It seems like there's something magical round every corner. When I first left the hotel, my camera might as well have been glued to my face. I kept wandering along the cobbled streets, thinking I was heading in the right direction, but when I ended up at the same fountain for the third time I decided to relinquish my pride and consult Larry's guidebook. I finally managed to make my way to the Pantheon. It's full of tourists, but the same feeling of sacred wonder descends on all of us as we enter the huge building, which is an oasis of quiet from the hustle and bustle of the streets outside.

From the Pantheon, I wander along the tourist trail down to the Colosseum and sit on a bench in the park outside to eat a huge slice of takeaway pizza. It's so surreal: I feel like I'm trapped in the pages of a history book, or maybe a TV show. I try to imagine what it would have been like to enter the Colosseum as a spectator, watching the gladiators enter the arena or maybe a dramatic reenactment of a sea battle. It would have been a bit different from the concerts I've been going to—but, then again, some of the fans at Noah's gigs are so rabid they might actually be out for his blood at times.

The illusion is suddenly broken when I am surrounded by a gaggle of Italian women dressed in their Sunday best. As they chatter away in feverish Italian, gesticulating wildly, I try to spot the object of their attention. Then I see her: a beautiful bride having her photograph taken with the Colosseum as a backdrop. Now *that's* an epic wedding photo.

The groom steps back into the frame, and the couple look so happy together, clutching each other's arms as they pose for their photographer. I snap a cheeky picture of my own, if only to show Mum. Weddings always make me think of her, and she would love to see these two in such a grand and dramatic setting. Next up, a line of bridesmaids sweeps across the grass, all in long pink satin dresses. They're much more flamboyant than the more traditional bridesmaids' dresses I'm used to seeing in England. Once again, I know it's something Mum would love.

I feel a smile spread across my face as I remember Mum and Dad's wedding album. Mum had just given up her acting career for wedding planning—so, of course, they had the most extravagant wedding ever! They opted for a Royal Wedding theme, which in the late eighties meant over-the-top-Princess-Diana style—not chic and understated Kate Middleton. There's no way Princess Diana would have been upstaged by her sister's bum! Whenever I see pictures of Mum's dress, I can't help but giggle. It was essentially reams and reams of cream satin, inlaid with clusters of tiny seed pearls, and had the biggest shoulder puffs I have ever seen, each one close to the size of her head. Apparently she bounced down the aisle looking like a giant marshmallow.

Mum always tells me that the guests were dressed just as extravagantly. All the women wore shoulder-padded dress suits with matching hats, and all ten (yes, ten!) of her bridesmaids wore puffy sleeves and white gloves and had their perms freshly styled. I am actually pretty gutted to have missed out on their wedding, despite the fact I wasn't even a twinkle in Mum's eye then.

Good job I have all three of their vow renewals safely nestled in my memory, and their thirtieth wedding anniversary coming up. Any excuse for a giant celebration in the Porter household.

Once the Roman wedding party moves on, there's another one ready to take their place. This is like a wedding-photo conveyor belt! As I watch each couple take their position in front of the Colosseum, I can't help but imagine what my own wedding day might be like. Mum will go to town and make it the most amazing wedding she's ever done, I know that much.

My favourite flowers, orchids, would be everywhere.

Elliot would be my man of honour.

Mum and Dad would give me away together, one on either side.

But would it be Noah waiting for me at the end of the aisle?

A week ago I would have said yes, but now I'm not so sure.

A wave of sadness washes over me as I go back through our argument in my mind. I feel all mixed up between guilt and anger, and I don't know what to think. Tears threaten my eyes, and my cheeks flush. I'm so confused.

This is exactly what I came outside to avoid. I stand up with purpose, frightening a flock of pigeons that had settled near my feet. One of the birds flies perilously close to one of the brides and launches a great stream of poop in the direction of her brilliant white dress.

"Watch out!" I yell, not sure if I'll be understood by the Italian bride. Her groom understands, and gallantly throws himself in the path of the pigeon poo. I scurry away as fast as I can.

The queue to get into the Colosseum stretches round the block, so I decide to forgo getting a close-up of the gladiator arena. I do feel some sympathy for the poor gladiators, though. Last year, I felt like I'd been thrown into the modern version of the Colosseum, with everyone on the Internet able to give me the thumbs-up or -down to decide my fate. Was I good enough for Noah?

Currently, I'd get a thumbs-down. I'd be fed to the lions, for sure.

The thought makes me shiver. I decide to head to another famous Roman landmark before I have to go back to the hotel: the Trevi Fountain. I somehow missed it on my meandering path to the Pantheon. I look up directions in the guidebook, and take a quick selfie in front of the Colosseum to send to Elliot, just to prove I am actually sightseeing.

When I finally arrive at the fountain, my jaw drops. Not because of how breathtakingly beautiful it is, but because of how busy it is. People are pressed round it like sardines in a large semicircle, all trying to get the perfect photo. I decide the best thing to do is to hang back a bit, but I also want to get a photo and leave. I manage to slip in a little closer to the front of the fountain and get my camera out to take a photo. All of a sudden the fact that the sun is blaring down on me and there are people everywhere becomes all too real, and I start sweating. I try to shake it off and slowly move away from the fountain, but I can't. I feel trapped against the pale stone of the fountain wall and all I can see when I turn round are the faces of other people.

My heart beats so hard inside my chest I feel like someone will be able to see it. My throat starts to close up and I can't breathe properly. I put my head down and run from the fountain, pushing everyone out of the way with my camera, accidentally snapping pictures as I go. Miraculously I find a nearby bench with nobody on it and lie down, looking up at the sky. There is barely a cloud to be seen, but I concentrate on counting even the faintest wisp of a cloud. I focus on my breathing and take a deep breath in and let a prolonged breath out. I don't even care at this stage if anyone can see me; I just need to calm down.

When my breathing returns to normal, I look through the photos I took while running through the crowd, deleting them to free up my memory card, but then a face catches my eye: a girl wearing a bright red scarf. Her dark hair is styled into a neat, chin-length bob, but there's something really familiar about her expression. I zoom in closer, but the tiny screen on my camera doesn't give me a good enough view.

I look up, scanning the crowd for the girl, and spot her striding purposefully away from the fountain, her scarf fluttering in the breeze like a flag. *It can't be . . . can it?*

I jump up from the bench and race to catch up with her. As I draw close, I reach out and touch her arm.

"Leah?" I say. "Is that you?"

★ *Chapter Thirty-One* ★

There's a moment of panic on Leah's face as she spins round, and a man behind me yells, "Hey! Stop right there!"

But the panic disappears as soon as she recognizes me, and is replaced by a warm smile. "Penny! Thank goodness it's you." She looks over my shoulder at the man behind me. "It's OK, Callum, stand down—it's only Penny Porter, Noah Flynn's girlfriend."

She pulls me over to a nearby bench and we sit down. Her security guard stands a short distance away. Leah looks up at him. "It's fine, Callum. You can go grab a drink or something. I'll be OK with Penny."

He hesitates for a moment, looking from me to Leah and then back again, then he nods.

"I almost didn't recognize you," I say, when he's gone.

"Well, that *is* kind of the point of wearing a disguise, silly. You must have a good eye!" She leans back against the bench so her face catches the full blast of the sun. The wig she has on changes her look from long blonde Hollywood hair to a short brunette bob, cropped at her chin. She's wearing bright pink lipstick that exaggerates the shape of her lips, changing her natural pout. Accessorized with a pair of cheap sunglasses like the kind you can buy at a pound store, she is almost completely unrecognizable as the pop star that I know. Almost, but not quite.

"Isn't Rome amazing?" she gushes. "Have you had any gelato yet? It's honestly unlike anything on earth. Pinkberry in LA just doesn't compare. I don't often indulge in sweet treats, but gelato is my complete weakness."

I shake my head. "Not yet. I don't really know where I'm going, to be honest. I'm mostly following the other tourists or trying, and failing, to follow the map in this beat-up guidebook." We both laugh, and it feels strangely natural and quite nice.

"OK, well, follow me," says Leah. "I know the absolute *best* place and you won't find it in any of those books."

I can only imagine Tom's face when I tell him I was rescued by Leah Brown in Rome and she took me for gelato. He might be into dubstep and electronic dance music, but I've caught him mooning over pictures of Leah Brown on more than one occasion. "Plus, if we move fast enough, I can ditch Callum." She winks at me, then grabs my hand and leads me through the narrow Roman streets.

It's so strange to be walking with Leah; of course she looks nothing like Leah, although there's still something in the way that she carries herself with confidence and poise that speaks the language of Leah Brown. That's not a look she can shake so easily.

We finally emerge into a large square, and I squeal with delight. There are artists and easels everywhere, painters selling their wares and drawing portraits of the passersby. There are fountains at either end of the square, and huge columns that stretch up into the sky. It's classic Rome.

"This is Piazza Navona," Leah says, giggling at my amazed expression. "Come on, the gelato place is just here." She pulls me inside a small shop that looks different from any other gelateria I've ever seen. Rather than large, fluffy mounds of ice cream, this gelato is in round metal bins and scraped down almost to the bottom—a sure sign of its popularity.

"This one is to die for. It's pistachio," Leah says, pointing to one of the round bins. "Definitely a firm favourite of mine." She orders a scoop in a cup. When the gruff server hands her the order, she takes a huge scoop with her little plastic spoon and puts it in her mouth, making a satisfied noise as she does. "Mmmmmm. The trick is to look for a pistachio gelato that's not overly green. It means it's made from fresh ingredients— no chemicals. What are you going for?"

"Uh, *gelato alla fragola*," I say, in a bad attempt at Italian, half to Leah and half to the man behind the counter. With my cup of strawberry gelato in hand, I follow Leah back into the square and we perch on the edge of one of the fountains, watching the people go by and the artists at work. It's amazing that no one recognizes Leah. But then I notice something *is* different about her: she's so relaxed.

"Can I take a picture of you?" I say, a bit out of the blue.

Leah looks up at me, her eyebrows raised in surprise.

"I won't share them with anyone," I say hurriedly. "It's just that you look so pretty and relaxed, and the sun is coming down against these old buildings—the light is just perfect."

To my relief, she smiles. "Sure."

I put my gelato down—moving it far enough away so that it's out of my shot—and then take a few steps back so I can snap a picture of Leah. There are people on either side of her, moving about their day, but the light is hitting her so perfectly it looks like she's surrounded by a warm, golden glow. Like it's her aura.

I can see why my brother and so many others have a thing for her; she really is very beautiful. Behind her is an elaborate statue, right in the centre of the fountain, with figures bursting out of the water. *Talk about an alternative perspective*, I think, remembering my A-level assignment. Here is Leah, who would normally have more in common with the statue—something ornate, isolated, something to be looked at and adored but not part of real life—sitting amid everything, like a normal person.

I look down at the photograph, pleased with the effect. I take a few more, and Leah's natural sparkle and innate posing ability come out in full force. I show her a few of the thumbnails on the screen of my camera, but I can already tell they're going to look way better blown up. Leah, for her part, makes appreciative noises.

"Would you ever sell any of your prints to the public?" Leah nods towards the many art stalls as I put my camera away.

"Oh, I don't know. I'm not sure they're good enough."

"Don't be ridiculous—you have serious talent. Is that what you want to be when you leave school? A photographer?"

I shrug. "I don't really know right now. I guess it depends on my GCSE grades and how well I do at college. I'm just not sure it's a career. I always thought by now I'd know what I wanted to do."

"What on earth is a GCSE?" she says. "Is that like an exam or something for you Brits?"

"Yeah . . . they're kind of important."

"Well, an exam is an exam, but your talent is forever! Of course photography is a career. Surely there are famous photographers you admire? Anything is possible if you really believe in yourself, as corny as that sounds. It could very well be a lyric of mine, but there's a reason why I sing it." She laughs at herself. "You need to aim higher than you think you're capable of."

She goes back to her gelato and we're both quiet as I reflect on what she's just said. She's right: I'll never get there if I don't at least try. And I'm going to need to really apply myself if I want to succeed at something.

"Leah? Quick question." I finish my gelato and wipe my hands with the napkin. "How do you cope with being so incredibly famous?" I let out a little laugh, trying to dissipate my nerves at asking such a direct question.

She laughs along with me, but I can sense a deeper emotion beneath it. "It's certainly something that takes a bit of getting used to. Which is why—Look, I hope you don't take this the wrong way, but I do worry about you and Noah. The music industry will chew you up and spit you out if you're not ready for it, especially if you're on the sidelines." She looks at me with a deep frown on her face, and a hint of sadness follows it. "I'm guessing that's why you're out here on your own?"

I nod. "We had this big fight—"

"In the lobby? Yeah, I heard."

"You did?" I want the fountain to swallow me up whole.

"Well, I didn't hear the fight but I heard *about* it. Word travels, I guess. I don't want to make you feel uncomfortable, Penny. I just genuinely don't want this crazy whirlwind to suck you up. You are a really great girl, with such pure, individual talent, and it's so easy to get lost in all this. Before you know it, you're just following someone else's dream and not your own."

I think about the tour so far, and how after each city I have felt less and less inspired, less *me* and more a piece of the furniture. How I have been content to be labelled "Noah's girlfriend." Now I'm not sure if that will be enough. What label *do* I want though?

"I know what you mean," I say, trying to inject as much confidence into my voice as possible. "But I do think Noah is different. Or, rather, that he will be different. It's new and exciting for him now, but I truly believe he's still the same guy I met at Christmas."

"You're right. Noah is great, Penny. Honestly, I mean that one hundred per cent. But no guy is worth changing your life for. An ex-boyfriend told me that singing was never going to happen for me, and I believed him. He worked in Manhattan as a very successful stockbroker, and I lived with him and made sure he had a meal to come home to every evening. One day I realized I was living his dream and not mine. I was unhappy—not in my relationship necessarily, but with the path I was going down. I decided to move back to LA and work hard on my music. My boyfriend left me, and I became a successful pop artist with two platinum albums. Sometimes you have to look out for *you*. It will really pay off if you want it badly enough."

I'm in awe of the woman sitting opposite me. I had no idea that Leah could have had any hardships in her life, or hurdles to struggle over. I guess you only see the glossy side of fame, but everyone has their demons.

The sun goes down as we stroll back to the hotel and chat about how Leah became famous.

Callum catches us up, looking red-faced as if he's been running. He glowers at Leah, but he can't be angry for long as she jokes, "You can always find me, honey. Just follow the gelato!"

Once I get back to my hotel room, I decide to type a blog post about how I'm feeling about the Noah situation and my conversation with Leah. This is something I need opinions on. My fingers hover over my keyboard as I try to convey all the thoughts that are whirring around in my mind.

30 June

Life . . . and Other Big, Important Things

OK, guys, after that post this morning, I've just had the most amazing day in Rome—but I don't want to talk about that right now.

Right now, it's time for the big question.

The one I'm almost certain every girl my age asks themselves on a regular basis, and one I've found myself asking more and more.

Do I need to know *now* what I want to be when I leave school?

I'm turning seventeen next year and starting my A levels in a few weeks . . . and I feel lost.

When I was a little girl, I wanted to drive an ice-cream van, because I knew how much joy it brought to others. Now that I'm older, I feel like I still want to spread that joy, just not in the form of ice cream (let's face it, ice cream brings joy to people regardless, especially Italian gelato . . . but more on that later).

Someone once told me that if you love the job you do, you will never work a day in your life. It might take you a while to find that job, but ultimately you have to love what you're doing.

I think this is why I'm finding it all so overwhelming.

I know what I love—my camera—and it seems as though my photographs bring people a lot of joy. But how do I turn that into something real?

Right now, it's like I'm caught in a rip current. My friends are all doing something to further *their* passions, and even though I'm right where I wanted to be—next to Brooklyn Boy—I can't help but feel like I'm being swept away from my passions and my identity. After speaking with someone very influential this afternoon, my eyes are well and truly opened about the importance of following your own path in life. Yes, people may join you on the path, but you have to remember that it's yours and it can go in any direction you choose.

Girl Offline . . . never going online xxx

Chapter Thirty-Two

After typing up my post, I lie back down on my bed. I still haven't heard from Noah since our argument, so I haven't had a chance to apologize, and I feel like if I check my phone any more than I already have been I'll start getting blisters. Just as I'm imagining what Elliot would be up to right now back at home, my phone buzzes next to my head. I jump up and grab it like it's Willy Wonka's Golden Ticket—a ticket that will entitle me to Noah's complete forgiveness for my embarrassing outburst, so we can go back to being disgustingly in love.

However, it's not Noah. It's a text from Leah.

> Hey, Penny. I want to say thanks for this afternoon. It was great to have some downtime, and it was fun getting to hang with you. Please don't mention the disguise to anyone for now. It's just not something I want too many people finding out about. I'll reveal all when I'm ready. Again, I don't want you to feel uncomfortable with anything we talked about. One sister looking out for another. KISSES, L

I smile down at my phone and feel somewhat comforted by Leah's text, and less alone in this crazy whirlwind. It's nice to know that I can trust her.

I've downloaded the pictures I took onto my computer, and there's one of Leah that is magical. She looks almost like a Roman sculpture herself; she is that perfect. Even the disguise can't hide how magnetic and beautiful she looks. I send my favourite to her with a message.

Thank you for today x

Then there's a knock at my hotel-room door. Throwing my phone down on my bed, I call out, "I haven't ordered any room service this evening! Wrong room."

"I haven't got any food, sorry." It's a voice I know all too well. That husky American drawl with a hint of charm can only belong to one person.

"Noah?" I open the door in surprise and see him standing there, one arm leaning on the door frame. His face is sullen and sad, and he looks more tired than I've ever seen him. But when he sees me it raises a small smile on his face, and his eyes light up. He's wearing a pair of shorts with a long, baggy crochet jumper and his old, beat-up Converse. A beanie pulls his hair back off his face and he has a necklace on that almost reaches his stomach. He looks breathtakingly gorgeous, in his own infuriatingly effortless way.

"Can I come in?" he asks, as he tucks a stray piece of hair into his beanie.

I shrug, and open the door a bit wider. "Yeah, sure."

He walks into the room and plops himself down on the bed, not caring about putting his dirty Converses on my duvet as he crosses his legs. He begins to speak. "Penny, I—"

"Noah, please. Let me say something first. I'm really sorry. I mean that. I shouldn't have said the things I said. I was being immature and I know you have bigger fish to fry than to entertain me like I'm your kid sister. I just felt a bit let down, and I know there are better ways to communicate that to you, but it all boiled up and I exploded, and I'm sorry that it was so public, and I'm sorry that it was so awkward, and I'm sorry that—"

"Stop." Noah places his finger over my lips. "You're word-vomiting all over the place." He smiles. "Penny"—now he is holding my hands, and he looks up at me from the bed as I stand in front of him—"I love you. I love you when you're happy; I love you when you spill smoothie all over me; I love you when you are sad; I love you when you slurp milk-shakes; I love you when you eat more pizza than I could ever imagine a human eating; I love you when you fall asleep at eight o'clock; I love you when you're anxious; I love you when you get so excited about things like you're a big kid; and I love you when you're mad."

I feel a small tear forming in the corner of my right eye, and I try with all my might to hold it in. I'm almost sure it's twitching at this point.

"I don't want to argue with you. I want us to be good, you know?"

"Me too. I'm sorry about everything. I—"

"Stop saying sorry! We're fine," he interrupts me. "Now,

let's put all this behind us and move forward. I wish I could stay in and watch a movie with you tonight or go out together, but Dean and I have another meal at a restaurant with a really huge newspaper. I just wanted to drop by before I left to make sure we were OK."

I nod, and let him pull me into a hug. It's too short—milliseconds short. Before I know it, he's pulled away from me. "I also brought this." He steps back out into the hallway and picks up a large wicker basket. "I know it's not the same as having me here, but I hope it makes this a tiny bit easier for you—and I know that none of this has been easy."

I take the basket from him, and set it down on the bed.

"Think of it as a substitute-Noah present," he says, with a wistful smile. "I better head off and at least try to make myself look presentable for this dinner tonight." He leans in and kisses me lightly on the lips, then heads out the door.

This is not a view of him I like: his back, as he walks away from me.

I turn to the wicker basket, which is covered with something I recognize: Noah's favourite hoodie. I immediately slip it on over my T-shirt, lifting the edge of the collar to breathe in the scent of his aftershave.

I roll up the sleeves, which are way too long, and peer into the basket. There's a DVD in the bottom with the words WATCH ME written on it, and an array of delicious-looking pastries filled with fluffy white cream.

I put the DVD straight into the player on the TV in my room, then sit back on the bed.

Immediately an image of Noah pops up on the screen.

He's wearing the same clothes I saw him in just now, so he must have filmed it today.

"Dear Penny," on-screen Noah says. "I know I've made you angry. I know I've made you sad. Those are two emotions I never want you to associate with me. I'm running out of ways to say sorry, but I hope you know how much I mean it.

"Hopefully you are now sitting there wrapped up in my hoodie and about to eat one of those pastries in the box. I asked at reception, and apparently those are called *maritozzi* and they're the most romantic pastry in Italy.

"Now, I know you're thinking that this video is *still* no substitute for the real me. And you're right: it's not. I wish that I wasn't talking into a camera right now. I wish I was there with you, taking you on a romantic stroll around Rome . . . but I'm quickly realizing how little I know about life on tour. How little I know about this career I've somehow fallen into. I'm basically just a big, ignorant doofus at the moment, and I keep making promises I can't keep.

"Penny, there are some things I do know. I know that I love making music, and I know that I love you. Those two things have got to be enough to get me through anything.

"And so, just in case you were starting to doubt point number two, I've put together this little montage just for you. You're my Inciting Incident, Penny. But I want you as the leading lady in every scene of my life. I hope this shows you that."

What follows next brings proper tears to my eyes. It's a movie montage of some of my favourite moments of our time together: the big orange moon Noah showed me in New York; Christmas morning opening presents on Sadie

Lee's living-room floor with Bella; my sixteenth birthday at Easter when Noah came with my family to Cornwall; snippets of our Skype conversations that he's recorded; and footage that I didn't even realize was being filmed, like me watching Noah onstage for the first time.

The montage is set at first to "Autumn Girl," but then it morphs into a new version of the song that I've never heard before. It's haunting and beautiful—just Noah's voice and a guitar, the way I like to hear his voice best. The words plant seeds in my heart that I know will continue to grow as long as my heart is still beating.

> *Forever girl*
> *You changed my world*
> *You are the one*
> *I know for sure*
> *That we will be together*
> *Forever, girl*

Chapter Thirty-Three

A flashing light catches my eye, and I realize it's my phone, abandoned on silent mode on my bedside table. I stretch across the covers and grab it, still running over the conversation I just had with Noah in my mind. I turn on the phone and the screen shows that I have eleven messages waiting from Elliot. My stomach drops. Elliot never sends this many texts. Something must be seriously wrong. I open them up as fast as I can.

PENNY

PENNY, PLEASE CALL ME

WHERE ARE YOU?

I NEED YOU

> PENNY, PLEASE CALL ME!

> PENNY, ON A SCALE OF ONE TO URGENT
> WE'RE AT ABOUT 100

> I'M ON SKYPE

> I'M WAITING

> Please, Penny, I hope you're there soon . . .

I text him back straightaway.

> I'M HERE! I'm so sorry. Are you still on Skype?

I don't wait for him to answer, but flip open my laptop and
Skype him. It dials for what seems like an age and my anticipation spirals. I feel a sense of panic, which is replaced with
relief as I see Elliot's face finally appear on the screen.

"Penny, FINALLY!" I can't quite work out Elliot's
expression as he glares at me from above the green rim of
his square glasses. It's an expression that I don't often see
from Elliot.

"Elliot, if you've panicked me with nine desperate texts in

order to tell me off for the small amount of sightseeing on this tour then that isn't funny. You got me worried." I start searching Elliot's face for any small signs of humour, and wait for him to ease up and laugh, but he doesn't.

"Penny, what was the name of that stalker person you were worried about?"

My heart feels like it stops beating within my chest.

"You mean TheRealTruth?" I ask, willing it not to be true.

Elliot's face falls.

"What? Why are you asking?"

"I don't think they're a fan," says Elliot, looking miserable. "Not unless they're *very* committed."

I clutch at my temples, fearing the worst. "What's happened?"

Elliot sighs. "On the train back from the magazine shoot, I got this weird email from an unknown address. I've forwarded it on to you." He places his hands on his head and sinks into them.

I quickly open a browser window for my email and I can see that Elliot's forwarded me a message from TheRealTruth. I don't even want to open it, but I have to see what's scaring Elliot so badly.

From: TheRealTruth
To: Elliot Wentworth
Subject: READ ME

Penny breaks up with Noah, or this goes viral.

ATTACHMENT: image1052.jpg

I click on the attached image, and my heart sinks even further. It's the photo of Alex and Elliot kissing on the balcony at Noah's concert. It's a really lovely photo and I almost want to smile a little bit at how cute they are. They are so clearly in love, lit up by the stage lights and surrounded by other people who are all watching Noah in awe. Almost like, in that very moment, it was only the two of them in their own world.

But since Alex isn't out to his friends or family yet, a picture like this . . . it could shake up his entire world.

"You took this photo, didn't you? At the Brighton gig?" He crosses his hands and rests them on his knees.

"I did, but—"

"But you didn't think to tell me about the fact that this was on your phone too when it was stolen, and now someone is threatening to make it public! Alex is going to be furious that we could be blackmailed this way. And of course you didn't think there was anything incriminating on your phone because you didn't think about me and my relationship at all."

I've never seen Elliot like this before. He's angry and sad and frustrated all at once.

But I'm angry too. "OK, I'm sorry. I wasn't thinking straight when it happened. Elliot, I feel awful that you're being dragged into this. I didn't know exactly what this person's intentions were then, but now I guess it's pretty clear. *Penny breaks up with Noah*. Someone wants us apart, no matter what."

"Penny, I don't know what to do! I have to tell Alex. If this gets out . . ." Elliot lets out a huge sigh. He sounds defeated, like this has sucked all the energy out of him. "You know how he is about us, Penny. He isn't confident about coming out to his friends and family. Even when we're away from Brighton, when there's no one we know around, it's rare that he holds my hand. That concert was one of the best moments in our whole relationship. And your house is our safe place. If he thinks we're not even safe around you . . . he's going to be so upset."

Visions fill my mind of Alex's absolute horror at knowing the photo exists full stop, let alone in the wrong hands. Although this sort of picture would be no big deal to lots of people, to Alex it will be a very huge step—one he certainly isn't ready to take.

Yet I know too that Elliot secretly wishes he could have the photo as his profile pic. This is the happiest I've ever seen him in a relationship. The only thing that makes Elliot sad is being unable to express his feelings in the way he'd like. He'd love to be able to hold hands and cuddle up on a picnic blanket in the park in the summer, but Alex just isn't in that place yet.

"I don't know what to say, Elliot. I'm so sorry that I took the photo, and that they stole it from my phone. They must have had enough time to download the last lot of photos I had taken before I changed my passwords and everything. How do they even know that Alex is this private?"

It's quickly occurring to me that TheRealTruth isn't some obsessed fan. But what are the chances of my phone falling into the hands of someone who knows me, and has an agenda like this? It was an accident.

I start racking my brain for any evidence of who this could be? Maybe it was Megan? Was it too convenient that she found me in the crowd, just after my phone went missing? She would have been surprised at seeing the picture of Alex and Elliot on my phone, since no one knew they were together. Could she still be annoyed about our confrontation and jealous of my relationship with Noah? Surely not, especially considering the conversation we had after the concert. It all seems too weird.

"I thought you understood, Penny. Taking a photo like that in the first place would have always unnerved Alex." Elliot looks awkward.

"I know. I'm sorry, E. You know what I'm like—I take photos of everything. I didn't think anyone would see it. And I would *never* have posted it anywhere without asking you first." I continue to try to put Elliot's mind at ease, but he remains downhearted and distant. "I can come home if you want? Try to make it right?"

"No, no, it's OK, Pen. I'll deal with this. And, whatever you do, don't let it come between you and Noah—it's just some stupid bully. I better go call Alex and let him know . . ." He ends the conversation, waving sadly at the camera.

For a few moments I stare at the blank screen, paralysed with indecision. But Elliot's right: this is just a bully, and they can't break us. I also decide that I can't deal with this on my own now.

I pull up my email again and send a note to all my closest friends and family, warning them about the bully and potential stalker, and let them know that I am gathering all the evidence to go to the police. That way, if it really *is* Megan or someone else who knows me, they will also know that I mean business.

I am Ocean Strong, and no bully is going to threaten my friends or stop me from living my dream.

Chapter Thirty-Four

I'm just about packed and ready to leave Rome when a wave of sadness passes over me. Even though I got to do a little bit of exploring yesterday, I feel like I've hardly scraped the surface of this amazing city. I stare out of the window and make a vow to come back.

There's a frantic knocking at my door, and for a moment I think I must be late—but there's still lots of time left.

"Penny? Are you in there?"

"Coming!" I open the door for Noah. He's got his backpack slung over his shoulder, and I can see a little tag with Dean's details scrawled on the side. He's so used to being ferried from one place to another that he doesn't know where he's staying in each destination or what time his planes are. Dean keeps track of all that life admin for him.

"I saw your email this morning—did that creep really strike again?"

I nod. "This time with Elliot."

"I can't believe that! Good idea to keep a note of all the

incidents—we can give it all to Dean and he can handle it with the police."

"That sounds great," I say, relieved that I can share the burden.

"Now, *ma chérie*, are you ready to go?"

"To Paris?" I pull a face, attempting to look sophisticated and Parisian. "*Mais oui!* I've never been more ready."

Landing in Paris, I feel so excited I want to run about like a child at Disney World. As we drive from the airport to our hotel, I gawp like a fish in a tank at the sights we're passing.

My mum has always loved Paris—especially as she thinks she is living in the film *Amélie* when she's there. It's her favourite place in the world to be, and when she was eighteen and a young, aspiring actress she ran away to live the bohemian life in the Latin Quarter for a few months. Now she and Dad make a special point of coming here for little breaks away, and now finally I'm able to see why they love it so much.

I'm in the city of love, with the guy I love. Could it get any more perfect?

"Paris is going to be the best, Penny. Tonight at the gig, all the top music journalists are going to be there, reviewing the show. We're going to have to be better and play harder than ever," Noah says, as we exit the car in front of the hotel. It's the grandest hotel we've been to yet, with porters collecting our luggage and hauling it up a wide staircase. It's exactly how I imagined our Paris hotel to be, and I know it's going to be so romantic. I turn and look at Noah, his face eager with excitement, and I smile a big, toothy smile—the kind you only do when your grandparents ask you to pose for a photo with your siblings. I'm not sure if it's an attractive smile, but at this point I don't care.

"And, after that, AFTER-PARTAYYYYY!" yells Blake from behind us, completely incongruous in the otherwise grand and peaceful scene.

Noah turns round and high-fives Blake. It's the night that everyone has been super excited for: the night of the biggest after-party of the tour. It's taking place at a hot Paris nightclub—one I normally would never be allowed in (not least because I'm underage) but, since it's a private party, it's OK. I've never been to an after-party before—not unless meeting up with your best friend after the complete disaster of the Year-Eleven ball and then gorging on a month's worth of pizza can count as one . . .

Noah drops me at my hotel room, then dashes off to the venue—they have only hours before their set begins. I take a deep breath—the hotel room is stunning, with a wide bed that has a burnished-gold headboard and crimson velvet covers. Tall windows open out onto a little balcony, from which I can *just about* see the tip of the Eiffel Tower. It's perfect.

I've got a few hours before I need to leave for the concert, so I take the opportunity to dump the entire contents of my suitcase onto the bed. Tonight is different from any other night, because tonight I'm going to be seen at Noah's side by a lot of people.

The problem is, I have no idea what to wear to an after-party. And this is not just any old after-party, but the sort of after-party where everyone cool will be: all the guys from The Sketch, their girlfriends (undercover or not) and their management, Leah Brown and her entourage, Noah and the rest of the guys from his band, and every single crew member who is on the tour. There will probably be paparazzi and media lining the streets—not to mention all the fans.

I stare at myself in the full-length mirror, its ornate gilded frame perfectly matching the gold headboard of the bed. It's the type of mirror I could imagine Marie Antoinette staring into—but, unlike her, I hope this isn't the night before *my* execution. In my mum's big cardie and leggings, I feel anything but Parisian chic. To be honest, none of my clothes feel right. This is not the time to be wearing a tea dress. Everything I own feels very young and very uncool.

I know that Noah loves me no matter what, but tonight I don't want to feel like the sixteen-year-old girl who probably shouldn't be in cool bars with her famous boyfriend. I want to feel sexy and chic. Maybe makeup can solve all, but I've never exactly been a whiz with it like Megan and some of my friends are.

I grab my makeup bag out of the suitcase and sit down cross-legged in front of the big mirror. I take out my black eyeliner and smudge a little more round my eyes and attempt to add some false lashes. After wrangling with both sets of eyelashes for a good twenty minutes, I finally give up and try to apply more eyeliner to even everything out. I'm not sure that it works.

Next, I know I have to tackle my pale complexion. I'm starting to think I look slightly more gothic than I was hoping for. What would a makeup artist like Kendra say? Would she tell me to add a bit of bronzer? Would she recommend a red lipstick? Or avoid red lipstick with lots of eyeliner? It's times like these I could actually do with having Megan here, and I *never* thought that wish would *ever* cross my mind. Then someone else pops into my head.

"Hi, Leah. It's Penny . . . Um, I'm just doing my makeup, and I wondered . . . do I go with an orangey-red lipstick with a smoky eye, or more of a pink red—"

I don't get any further before Leah interrupts.

"PUT DOWN THE LIPSTICK, HON. What room are you in? I'm on my way."

Chapter Thirty-Five

Rushing around Paris with Leah Brown in a chauffeur-driven car is up there with my highlights from this tour so far. After ripping my poor attempt at false lashes off my eyes and removing my thick layer of black eyeliner, Leah insists on taking me out to help me get ready. Our first stop is makeup superstore Sephora, where she hands me product after product that I then stack neatly in my basket.

"Leah, I don't know what to do with half this stuff. I mean, I think I can guess . . ." I turn over a pack of copper transfer tattoos and it suddenly dawns on me that I really have no clue at all. "When did transfer tattoos come back into fashion, and where do they go?"

Leah snatches the pack off me and places it back in the basket. "Penny, you aren't going to be putting this on by yourself. I'm going to get my makeup artists and hair stylist to come and help you. And these tattoos have been the in thing for a while now, Pen. Don't you read *Glamour*?" As we walk around the store, I try to avoid noticing that everyone else is noticing *us*—or, rather, noticing Leah. I think there's a crowd gathering outside the windows, and I notice that the shop assistants have moved to the entrance to stop anyone else from coming in.

"Well, obviously, I love *Glamour*. It's my favourite." I smile weakly and pray she can't sense my lies through my wonky voice.

"Oh, thank goodness, you almost had me fooled there." She laughs and gives me a friendly nudge, while adding something called "bronzing dry oil" to the basket.

Once the basket is almost overflowing with beauty products I didn't even know existed, Leah takes it to the checkout, where the girl behind the counter starts beeping it all through. It comes to well over a thousand euros and my chin almost hits the floor.

"Leah, thank you so much for helping me, but I can't afford all this . . ." I go to take the products and put them back on the shelves, but Leah grabs my arm.

"You British are always so polite. It's cute." She hands over a black credit card and the sales assistant swipes it through her machine.

"Thanks so much," Leah says, grabbing everything, which is now packed in two huge paper bags tied up with black-and-white string.

"*Bonne journée*. I love your music, by the way," the girl says in an amazing French accent.

I definitely wish I sounded that sexy. Maybe I should work on my accent and bowl Noah over? I attempt an *Au revoir*, but the shop assistant gives me a strange look that I think means I should never attempt to speak French again.

We hop back into the car and Leah instructs the driver

where to go next. He turns onto a wide boulevard lined with shops bearing designer names I've only ever seen in Mum's fashion magazines. Each store seems to be attempting to outdo the one next to it with fancy window displays, mannequins contorted at different angles, and explosions of brightly coloured flowers everywhere. I swear I see a dress made entirely out of baked goods. Judging by the women I see walking in and out of the shops, though, that is probably the closest they come to a cupcake.

As we slow to a stop outside one of the fancy stores, I realize Leah's about to spend a whole lot more money on me and I can't help but feel awkward. "Leah, this is too nice of you. I wish there was a way I could pay you back."

She puts her hand on mine. "Penny, please just let me do this. I like being able to do it—I don't get a lot of time to go out shopping with my friends, and I needed a spree anyway. What better way than to do it with you, for you? I have everything I need and more, so shut up and enjoy this." She opens the car door, grabs my hand, and pulls me out onto the pavement.

We run into the nearest shop, and I glance down the street to see a crowd of paparazzi storming our way. Once we're inside the safety of the store, the bright flashes of camera bulbs illuminate the front window.

"Wow, Leah, no wonder you sometimes go around in disguise!" I say.

"Tell me about it," she says, rolling her eyes. She walks straight over to the racks and starts pulling out dresses for me, bundling them into my arms. I end up trying on dresses that are more expensive than some of the entire wedding budgets Mum has had to work with. I hobble out of the fitting room in a hot-pink cocktail dress and snakeskin stilettos that are way too high—I feel like a strong wind would knock me over.

"I'm not sure. I feel silly." I look down at my hips and skinny ankles and grimace.

"Penny, you have a body to die for," says Leah. "You have curves in all the right places. EMBRACE THEM."

"It's not my body I'm worried about. In these heels, I'm a liability to everyone else!"

"*Mademoiselle?* Perhaps you wish to try on something *un peu plus élégant?*" The small Parisian man who runs the store is dressed head to toe like he is about to meet the Queen. "Something more . . . sophisticated?" He hands me a little black satin sleeveless dress that has a big satin bow at the waist and a lace insert across the entire back and along the bottom.

I feel as though this man is handing me a newborn baby. I don't know how to hold the dress, how to feel about it, how it will look, but I take it into the fitting room with me. After struggling for a while with the whole stick-on-bra malarkey, I finally walk out of the fitting room. I'm met with stunned silence and then a flurry of applause. Even Callum, Leah's bodyguard, is clapping wildly.

"Oh, Penny, you look absolutely beautiful! You really can never go wrong with an LBD."

I put on a pair of slightly lower black stilettos (four inches high as opposed to six), then stare at myself in the mirror—and not in complete horror, for a change. I've never been glamorous in my life. Even when I've dressed up for weddings or end-of-year balls, I normally go for vintage-quirky over sophisticated and cool. But standing here in this shop, look-ing at myself in this outfit, I feel like a grown-up for the first time. In this dress, I look like I belong on Noah's arm.

"*Mon Dieu!*" exclaims Leah in unsurprisingly perfect French. She's staring down at her watch in horror. "Look at the time! I have to be back at the venue or my manager will have my head. Jacques, will you have the dress steamed and sent to the hotel ready for this evening? Penny, how many times have you seen the concert?"

"Oh, like four times now, I guess."

"Well, if you can stand to miss one night, do it. Let my makeup and hair people work their magic on you, then put on this dress, and I'll come and get you after the show so we can go to the after-party together. You'll knock 'em dead."

I can't help myself: I launch a full-blown hug at Leah, throwing my arms round her neck. "Thank you so, so much!"

"Aw, honey, you are so welcome! Now, watch the dress. I don't want *anything* to happen to it, or you, before tonight. And that's not a request—it's an order!"

★ ·*Chapter Thirty-Six*· ★

I have strict instructions from Leah for once I'm back at the hotel: take a bath, scrub myself clean, shave my legs, and await the arrival of her glam squad. Not having to worry about being backstage feels like a weight has been lifted from me, and it's a genuine pleasure to be able to use the impressive claw-foot bathtub in my beautiful bathroom. I turn the golden taps and hot water streams out. I drop in a fizzing bath bomb I discovered in the haul from Sephora and watch as rose oil tints the water a soft shade of pink.

While the bath is filling up with hot, steamy water, I text Noah.

> Hey, nothing to worry about but I feel the need to chill out tonight, so I think I'm going to stay at the hotel before the party instead of coming to watch you. Is that OK? xx

Almost immediately I get a concerned text back.

Are you sure? Is everything OK? Do you want me to send Larry to pick up some chicken soup for you or something? You know I would much rather be with you right now!

I know. And I'm fine, honestly. Not sick, just relaxing. I'll see you later xx

You'd better—I'm not going to the after-party alone

Love you xx

Love you too

A bath is exactly what I need to clear my head. I lie back and let the bubbles pop against my skin, sifting them through my soapy fingers. As much as this is enjoyable, I ache for home. I couldn't survive this life permanently—zipping from place to place, barely stopping to smell the roses or, in my case, see the sights and taste the food. I know I could just say the word and Noah would take me away with him forever. I could be by his side, living this life of luxury. The shopping spree I just had with Leah, that could be the norm, not a once-in-a-lifetime event. That could be *my* jet-black credit card. I could hang out with Kendra and Selene, and focus on looking glamorous all the time.

Megan would do anything to be in my position. Heck, so would Elliot, if it meant having all the clothes and hats he was able to buy. But would *I* be me right now?

I sit in the bath until my fingertips begin to look like prunes. Somehow, I don't think Leah would approve. I wrap myself up in the snuggliest, fluffiest white dressing gown in existence, then fold my hair into a bath towel to dry. When I open the door back into the main room, I gasp. There's a beautiful bouquet of roses sitting on the table. One of the hotel staff must have come in while I was having a bath.

I read the little card that is sitting beside them: YOU ARE ALWAYS IN MY HEART, MY FOREVER GIRL. N.

I grin from ear to ear at Noah's note. I can't believe I doubted whether we were right together for an instant. Of course we are. Whatever obstacles there may be in the future, Noah and I can overcome them.

I know we can.

There's another knock on the door, and I wonder if Noah

has more surprises for me. Instead, I open the door and find myself face-to-face with five fierce-looking women who have identical slicked-back ponytails and are armed with black cases of varying sizes. One of them has a hair dryer tucked under her arm. It's Leah's glam squad.

They sit me down and start trawling through the Sephora bags, ripping the freshly bought products from their cardboard packaging and applying them to my face. I learn more than I ever thought I would about whether primer comes before moisturizer (it doesn't; it goes after) and whether to put concealer on before foundation (you can do either, but the lady doing my makeup prefers foundation first). I try to keep at least one eye open at all times, making sure to take mental notes of what they are doing so I can at least have a hope of re-creating the look on my own.

At one point, I have a girl curling my hair with a hot iron, another one brushing purple eyeshadow onto my eyelids, and someone else applying a transfer tattoo to my wrist. I feel like a canvas rather than a human being. These are artists at work.

When they're finished, one of the girls asks me unceremoniously to drop my dressing gown. I want to cling to it with my life, but when she holds up the dress and I remember how beautiful it looked when I tried it on in the store I relent. These girls have probably seen a lot more women in their underwear than just me!

It turns out this particular girl is also an amazing seamstress. I thought the dress fitted perfectly in the store, but she pins it and sews it until it fits like a glove. I hold on to her shoulder as I slip my feet into the stilettos. Then she spins me round and walks me towards the full-length mirror. I almost do a double take at the girl staring back at me. Her expression may be blank—or, I should say, stunned—but the rest of her is . . . well, magnificent.

The stylists behind me high-five and hug each other. I turn round and hug the girl who helped me with my dress.

I don't have any words; the only ones I can grasp are a jumbled mess inside my head. The feeling I had in the shop when I first tried on this outfit was nothing compared to this. I have dry bronzing oil on my legs, which makes them glisten in the light. My hair is full of volume and curled beautifully—there is none of that cotton-wool frizz I'd usually have at my roots. My eyeshadow is a smoky purple to complement the colour of my eyes, and the new, perfectly applied fake lashes are so curly and pretty I can barely stop blinking. My lips have a beautiful pink shade to them and I have an amazing, intricate rose-gold feather transfer tattoo on my wrist.

One stylist whips out a little black bowler hat and pops it gently on my hair, and the outfit suddenly feels complete. I don't think I've ever felt so cool in all my life, not even when Elliot styled me, and he *knows* his fashion. I get one last spritz of Chanel perfume and the women surrounding me all grin.

Finally I find my words. "Thank you, thank you, thank you!" I say.

There's another knock at the door, and Leah walks into the room. She looks slightly dishevelled—but still stunning. I guess I would probably look a bit out of sorts too, having just come offstage. Catching sight of me, she gasps audibly. "Oh. My. God. Didn't I tell you these girls were the best in the business? Penny Porter, you look absolutely beautiful.

Noah is the luckiest guy I've ever known. You are going to knock him *dead*."

"I feel a million dollars. Thank you, Leah." I give her a huge hug, probably squeezing her a little too hard, but I don't care.

"You are so welcome. Now, ladies, I need you to fix me up too! I am a disaster and I need to look unbelievable for this after-party!"

Amid the huge array of feelings I have at that moment, one of the main questions that buzzes around my head is how I can find my own glam squad to do this for me every morning. But I decide that even if this Penny Porter is for one night only, she intends to have the time of her life.

Chapter Thirty-Seven

I wobble nervously towards the door of the nightclub where the after-party is being held, holding on to Leah for dear life. She probably thinks I'm getting a little *too* appreciative and wants me to stop being so clingy, but I know that if I let go, or loosen my grip even slightly, I'll probably fall over. The cobbled streets of Paris are very beautiful, but *wow* are they hard to walk on in four-inch stilettos! I'm determined not to start this evening off by falling flat on my face.

I'm the epitome of sophistication right now. Clumsy Penny has retired to the hotel room and is staying tucked up in bed this evening. Instead, Parisian-chic Penny is out on the town and, although she probably won't be the coolest girl at the after-party (Leah still holds that title), she at least stands a good chance of feeling like she belongs—and her boyfriend might think so too.

We are ushered straight past the bouncers at the entrance to the club, with Callum holding up his jacket to shield Leah from the flashing cameras of dodgy paparazzi. For once I've left my camera at home. In fact, I don't even have a clutch bag with me—my hotel-room key is tucked into a tiny pocket inside my dress.

I'm actually somewhat disappointed once we pass through the darkened doorway and into the club. I start to think all this hard work might not have been worth it since it's so dark and dingy.

Leah spots Noah first, over in a VIP booth. Luckily, the lighting is slightly brighter over there—all the better to show off who is in the club, I'm assuming. She nudges me towards him. "Go on, this is your big moment. I have to go find my manager."

I give her hand one last squeeze. "Thank you so much for everything today, Leah."

"Honestly, don't mention it. Now, go show him what he's been missing." She winks, and I take a deep breath.

Noah is sitting in the centre of the booth, with his band mates and friends in a semicircle round him. I force myself to unclench my fists and walk nervously towards him. I jerk to a stop as a waiter carrying a trayload of champagne flutes filled to the brim with bright, effervescent liquid swerves in front of me. It's a breathless moment, but nothing spills.

Yet my gasp must have been loud enough for attention to be swayed in my direction. Then, the moment I've been waiting for is unfolding. It's exactly like something from a movie, a scene where everything is happening in slow motion. Noah looks up from his drink and locks eyes with me. I watch as his mouth falls open, then the mouths of his band mates following suit. They look like a shoal of fish all sitting there together, faces agog, not saying anything and just staring in disbelief.

"Penny . . . HOLY COW. I—how—you look—" Noah jumps up from the booth to greet me. He clings on to my elbows and looks me up and down. "You look absolutely breathtaking," he says, finally finishing his sentence.

He kisses me so passionately it's like we haven't seen each other in months. It feels absolutely electric; the hairs on my body stand on end and my goose bumps are so intense it feels like the air around us has dropped a few degrees.

"I missed you," he says. "You had me worried when you said you weren't coming to the concert."

"I might have . . . bent the truth a bit. I felt fine, if only a little scared of Leah's glam squad!"

"Leah did all this for you? Tell her I say thanks!" He wraps an arm around me and we walk over to the booth. I sit down next to him and he introduces me to everyone as "my girl-friend, Penny." He even introduces me as his girlfriend to the Sony execs who we had a run-in with last time.

I do my very best, most polite handshaking and greeting, but I can't seem to wipe the giant grin from my face. I have a feeling that this is going to be the best night ever.

"Well, Penny, let me just tell you—we are very impressed with your boyfriend here," one of the Sony execs says with a smile. There's something about the way she says *boyfriend* that jars—like she's talking to a child. I grit my teeth and smile back. The way Noah is clinging on to my waist, like he's ter-rified to let me go, is definitely *not* childlike.

"I think he's all right too," I reply, not sure what to say.

"You should tell Penny the good news," the exec contin-ues, looking at Noah intently.

Noah shifts in his seat, then with his free hand laces my

fingers in his. "Oh, yeah, right." He looks me straight in the eye. "The Sketch and everyone are really pleased with how things are going on the tour . . . with the dynamic, you know? It's just working for all of us. So they want me to continue with them—like, beyond Europe—on their world tour. Dubai, Japan, Australia . . . for the next three months."

I can see behind his sparkling eyes how excited he is, and I throw my arms round him. "Noah, that's great!" I'm genuinely excited for him. This is his dream come true all over again.

"That's not all, though," he says, looking hopeful. "I want you to come with me."

Chapter Thirty-Eight

He wants me to come with him? Immediately all sorts of questions pop up in my mind, like moles in the whack-a-mole game on the pier. *What about my A levels? My parents? My life?* I bat them all away. This is Noah's big moment.

Luckily, I'm spared from having to reply when a jumping song comes on and as everyone leaps to their feet to dance, Noah and I are pulled along with them. Judging by the way he's leaping around to the music, Noah doesn't seem to be worried about not getting an immediate response from me, so I decide to embrace my makeover and enjoy myself too.

As the night draws to a close, I'm starting to think my feet have swollen to the size of an elephant's—the stiletto heels have been the biggest style challenge of the evening. Thankfully, it's not long before we all head back to the hotel together. Noah even gives me a piggyback for the small walk from the taxi to the hotel lobby.

As I'm on his back, I look up and catch sight of the tip of the Eiffel Tower. It is covered in sparkling, dancing lights, and reminds me of a grand version of the fairy lights Noah set up for me in Sadie Lee's basement in New York.

"Look at that," I whisper in his ear.

Noah tilts his head back and immediately lowers me to the ground when he spots it.

"My feet! My *aching* feet!" I protest.

"It's not that," he says, grabbing my hand. "I have an idea. We haven't had a Magical Mystery Day yet. Why not a Magical Mystery Night? Let's go see the Eiffel Tower right now. Then we can go to this twenty-four-hour restaurant that Larry told me about and watch the sun rise over the Louvre . . ."

Only moments before, I felt so tired I could have slept for a thousand nights, but now I am wide awake. Excitement spreads from the top of my head right down to the tips of my toes. "It sounds perfect," I say.

"Come on, let's go before anyone notices," he says.

"Um . . ." I look down at my feet. "I don't think I can walk anywhere in these shoes."

Noah laughs. "OK, just a minute—give me your room key and wait here."

"Can you grab my bag too? It's got my camera in it."

"Anything for you."

Everyone else is already dispersing into the hotel bar and the elevators. Noah directs me over to one of the seats in the lobby. I hand over my room key and my stilettos, and Noah races off. "Back soon!"

It feels like just a couple of minutes before he's back, with my beloved Converse in his hands. I slip them onto my feet with a mixture of relief and amusement.

"Penny Porter, you look even cuter," Noah declares, admiring my new styling and pulling me from the seat. He passes me my bag and I slip the strap over my shoulder, putting my room key back in the pocket of my dress.

The pain in my feet disappears as we jog hand in hand across the street, the Eiffel Tower pulling us closer like a magnet.

"Noah? Hey, Noah, wait up!" The moment shatters as Dean shouts from the hotel entrance.

I don't want us to stop. I want to keep running down the street, and I can feel the hesitation in Noah's hand. But he slows to a stop and turns back.

"Yeah?" he says, the word laced with reluctance.

Dean hurries towards us. "I told you, I need your approval on some photographs and design elements for the World Tour. It needs to be done tonight or else it won't go to press."

"Seriously? Can't it wait until morning?"

Dean just stares at him, and Noah hangs his head.

I pull back on his hand. "Wait, can't you just approve them, Dean? Surely Noah doesn't need to look at everything?"

Dean grunts. "Noah approves everything that his fans will see. Right, Noah?"

"Dean's right," Noah says, sounding dejected. "I'd better go back and check on the photos. These ones are going to be everywhere—the whole design and look needs to be right. I don't want to let anyone down."

I almost laugh out loud.

"I mean . . . I know I'm letting you down, Penny. But—"

"I understand," I say, stopping him. At the same time, though, I think: *I'm trying really hard to understand, Noah. Really hard*. Then I'm almost laughing again at the thought that, even in the middle of the night, we can't find time to hang out together. Is this really what I signed up for?

We walk back towards the hotel, at a much slower pace than before. After the huge adrenaline rush, I feel the tiredness hit me again like a freight train.

"Let's talk over here," says Dean, striding across the lobby to the hotel bar.

"I think I'm just going to go up to my room," I say.

"Should we try again tomorrow?" Noah asks, his voice soft. I just nod.

Then his hand slips from mine, and I'm left alone, standing by the lift and watching Noah walk away.

Chapter Thirty-Nine

I lean up against the slice of wall between the two elevators and try to diffuse my disappointment so I don't lie awake all night, going over and over what just happened. I'm not even going to email Elliot about it; I'll pretend the night ended when we came back to the hotel the first time. Until then it was perfect.

"Why the long face?"

Blake's voice in my ear makes me jump. He's drunk and sways slightly as he tries to focus on me.

"Oh, you know . . . these lifts take ages." I take a step back. "Did you have fun at the party?" I ask tentatively.

"That party rocked!" He stumbles as he mimes playing the drums in the air in front of us, smashing an imaginary cymbal. "*Ba-doom tish!*" he shouts.

The lift doors open and he straightens up and links arms with me. "C'mon, pretty Penny, let's go!"

I walk with him in slight disbelief that he is being so friendly. The lift is funky and modern, designed to emulate the night sky. There are glowing planets on the walls and stars on the ceiling, and there's calming music playing.

"You look *so* amazing tonight, by the way." He starts trying to hold my hand and I realize very quickly that this isn't a comfortable scenario. I try to pull my hand away, but he reaches for it again.

"Blake, you're very drunk. Let's get you back to your room, shall we?" My head is spinning in panic, and I'm not sure where *his* head is at right now. "What floor are you on?"

"Eighth," he says, still slurring. If Noah knew that Blake tried to hold my hand he would be furious. Blake is his oldest friend; I might not get on with him, but I respect that he's like a brother to Noah, and I know immediately that this is not something I'm going to mention to Noah. Blake is drunk and stupid, but it's not worth ruining a friendship over.

The lift seems to move agonizingly slowly, but eventually we reach the eighth floor. Blake points towards his room at the end of the corridor and I follow him at a safe distance, just to make sure he actually gets into his room. As we approach it, he turns to me and smiles sweetly. "Thanks, Penny. I'm sorry I can be such a douche. I like you really. You're great." The silence feels awkwardly long as he just stares at me.

"Thanks, Blake, it means a lot—"

As I'm finishing my sentence, he pulls me near him and, before I know it, his face is looming towards mine. I whip my head to the side as he pushes his lips against me—missing my mouth but still catching my cheek. My bag slips off my shoulder as I throw my arms against him. "BLAKE! Get off! What are you doing?"

He tries again. I drop to the ground as he leans in for another kiss, and he ends up banging his head against the door. I take advantage of the moment of confusion and back away from him. In a split second, my entire night has flipped upside down. Trying to hold my hand was one thing—I was prepared to let that slide—but this is unforgivable. How dare he do this to me . . . or to Noah?

He rubs his head. "C'mon . . . I know you're into me." He puts his hand out, trying to entice me to come back towards the door.

I don't want to move, but he is standing between me and my only exit route: the lift.

"No. No, I'm *really* not into you. That isn't a thing."

"Well, Noah doesn't have time for you, so you might as well be with someone who does."

Something inside me musters the strength I need to push past him and run down the hallway, toward the lift. I hear Blake shout behind me: "Penny, wait! I'm sorry!" But I don't take the time to stop and listen to him. Instead, I don't even bother with the lift and I launch myself into the stairwell. I don't have my camera anymore—my bag is lying back in the corridor, but I don't care.

I run until I reach my room, thankful that I kept my room key with me, rather than putting it in my bag. I slam the door and lock it with the chain in place, my heart pounding in my chest. I lean against the wall and tears stream down my face.

My perfect night is officially ruined.

Chapter Forty

I'm not going to let Blake get away with this. I stand up, wipe the makeup from under my eyes, and try to put on my fiercest Ocean Strong face. I head straight down to the hotel bar to find Noah and tell him exactly what has happened, but the server lets me know that he and Dean have gone back upstairs.

I choose to take the stairs over the lift, not wanting to be trapped in any enclosed spaces if I can help it. As I approach Noah's room, I can see that the door is ajar. I can just about see the back of Noah's head, and even the sight of his messy dark hair makes me feel better. I'm about to barge in when I hear Dean's voice and it stops me in my tracks.

"You see, Noah? You really should have consulted me first. It's not the image we want to portray for you. And now this . . . she's just so young."

He's talking about me. I know he is. I wait for Noah to leap to my defence, but he doesn't. There's a deafening silence instead. My blood runs cold inside my veins, turning my fingers to ice. It's like all my worst fears are coming true.

Noah Flynn would be better off without me.

That exact thought has crossed my mind many times, but hearing the sentiment said out loud is truly horrible. Tears start rolling down my cheeks again, but then I hear another voice in the room that turns my blood from ice-cold to fire-hot. It's Blake.

"Sorry, man. I didn't know what to do. She just showed up at my door."

I let out a loud gasp, and Noah's head spins round. But I can't do this now. My Ocean Strong courage has evaporated. I turn and start to walk down the hallway.

"PENNY! How long have you been there?" Noah runs after me.

"Long enough to hear what you're talking about!" I try to wipe away a few tears before he can see them, but it's too late. My whole face feels as though it's on fire and my tear ducts are doing their best to try to put it out.

"Penny, please, can we talk? Just stop for one moment." Noah tries to grab my arm but I carry on charging down the corridor, back to the stairwell. I will not have another confrontation for everyone else to hear. I race up the stairs to my room, with Noah following me. When I'm finally inside, I try desperately to clear the anger that is clouding my ability to think or speak straight.

Noah stands in front of me.

"Penny, Dean is just being a manager. You know how these things are in the music industry. They're all crazy lunatics who think they know what's best . . ." He runs his hands through his hair, and starts pacing the room. He's nervous, but for once I can't be the one to calm him down—because *I* am the one who needs comforting right now.

"You think it's Dean that I'm mad about?" I say. I catch sight of my furious face in the mirror, and suddenly my glamorous get-up feels like a sham. I've been crying so much my false eyelashes have loosened on my lids, so I rip them off and throw them in the bin. I miss, of course. They cling to the carpet like squashed spiders. I throw on my Rolling Stones hoodie and scoop my hair up into a massive bun that Elliot and I like to call "The Pineapple."

"I promise he didn't mean anything by it." Noah looks at me pleadingly.

For the first time in a very long time, I'm looking at him and I don't want to jump on him and kiss him to death.

"Noah, I get it. It's not cool to have a girlfriend in this industry, especially when you're starting out and you're the screensaver on most girls' laptops and the wallpaper on most girls' phones, but do you not get how this is hard for me too? Do you not think I've noticed how frosty the Sony execs acted around me? And you didn't even defend me to Dean. I'm an embarrassment to you." At this point, I feel myself start to tremble. My hands are shaking. I think this is the most real conversation Noah and I have ever had. He stares back at me blankly, just like when I shouted at him in the hotel lobby in Rome, but I'm not shouting this time.

My mind rages that I've allowed Noah to derail me from the real source of my anger: Blake. I shudder even more. What story was he telling Noah and Dean?

"Penny, you're shaking! Are you having a panic attack?"

Noah's words bring home what is happening to me. I *am* having a panic attack.

My breathing is speeding up, like I can't seem to get enough air in my lungs. My heart feels like it is beating visibly through my chest, and I feel hot—so hot it's suffocating. My palms are slick with sweat and my feet burn with pins and needles.

Noah tries to speak to me—I can see his mouth moving—but I can't focus on him at all. Instead, all I can think about is breathing in cold, fresh air. I dart up from the bed and run to the window. It's old and the handles are refusing to budge, even though I feel like I'm pushing with all my might.

I give it one last heave with my shoulder, when all of a sudden I realize I'm going to throw up. I turn to run to the bathroom, but it's very clear I'm not going to make it. The bin next to the wardrobe is the next best thing.

I don't really feel or register anything until Noah wraps his arms round my shoulders and brings me back onto the bed. There's now a fresh breeze swirling into the room and I feel myself begin to relax. Noah must have opened the window while I was facedown in the bin. Usually I'd be mortified, but right now I don't care.

Noah brings me a damp facecloth, which he pats around my forehead and the back of my neck. My body is still shaking, and my insides feel jumbled from all the throwing up, but my pulse finally slows, along with my breathing. Noah sits with me, just holding me until I feel stronger again.

"Do you need anything?" he asks, his voice soft.

"Maybe just some water?"

He nods and fills up a small tumbler with water from the bathroom tap. I take a few sips and try to regain my composure, but I know the panicked feeling isn't truly going to go away until I tell Noah everything.

"Noah, it *wasn't* just about Dean . . ." I say, continuing to sip the water as Noah sits next to me, rubbing my back. I take a deep breath. "Blake tried to kiss me. He was really drunk and I was making sure he could get to his room but then he leaned in for a kiss. I managed to run away, but it was horrible, Noah." I look at him for any sign of shock or anger, but there is nothing.

Instead, Noah pulls away from me a bit, taking his hands off my back and putting them both in his lap.

"Blake said you might say that."

I almost choke on my next breath. "What?" I barely manage to say.

"He told me what happened. That you showed up at his door saying I didn't want you anymore and then tried to kiss him. He said he wanted to let you down gently but you ran away."

"No . . . what? That's completely wrong!"

"Jesus, Penny—I know things have been tough, but Blake's my friend. You didn't think he would come to me straight-away? Is this some kind of plea for help? Dean said something like this might happen . . . but I always defended you to him. I said you would never do something like this. I guess I was wrong."

I'm astonished. I'm too stunned for words. The boldness of Blake's lie has hit me like a runaway train and I don't know how to convince Noah how wrong he is. "Noah, are you being serious? I would never do that. It was Blake—he was the one who came on to me."

Noah then does something he's never done before: he shouts at me. "Penny, give it up! Blake's told me what happened, and he has my back no matter what. Why can't you just be honest and say you did it to get my attention? I know I haven't been there for you, but I expect us to at least be able to be honest with each other. I could forgive you if you said this was a mistake but I will never be able to forgive you if you keep making up lies, especially about my best friend. How old are you?"

I stare back at him in disgust and anguish. Right now I don't feel like I'm looking at Noah, the amazingly talented musician with the most gorgeous smile, the most romantic gestures, and the most beautiful mind. I feel like I'm looking at a normal, arrogant, eighteen-year-old boy.

It leaves me speechless. Why am I wasting my breath on this? I know what happened, but my boyfriend—the one person who is supposed to look out for me and trust me—refuses to believe me.

"Just get out, Noah. If you think that little of me, I really can't be bothered with this. It's a waste of time. I told you what happened. If you don't believe me . . . I don't know what to do."

Noah stands up abruptly. "Dean warned me that being on the road changes people. I just didn't realize he meant you." He glares at me, his mouth twitching in anger.

I almost want to laugh out loud at how ridiculous this all sounds coming from him.

"No, Noah, that's nowhere near right. In fact, it's very, very wrong." I take a deep breath. "I can't do this anymore. I can't be with someone who thinks these things of me, who's constantly juggling me in their life, and who won't believe me about something as serious as this. I thought I knew you, but obviously that's not the case. I just don't know how this can ever work."

I can't quite believe those words have just left my mouth. I'm not sure Noah can either. He turns and walks out of my hotel room, slamming the door as he leaves.

.

Chapter Forty-One

Immediately after Noah leaves, I pick up my phone and call Elliot. I don't even care about the European phone charges. After a few rings, he answers.

"Hello?" Instantly I can tell that something is wrong. He sounds quiet and far away—but then I realize it's almost 2 a.m. and I've probably woken him up.

"I'm sorry to call so late," I say. I try to make my voice sound as normal as possible, even though I feel like all I've done for the past hour is cry and argue.

"It's fine," he says. "I was awake." He still sounds cold and distant.

"You were?"

"What's up?"

"The sky?" I say, making a meagre attempt at a joke. It's the sort of thing Elliot would usually at least chuckle at, but he doesn't make a sound. I guess neither of us is in the mood for joking around.

"Elliot, I think that Noah and I may have just broken up." I sit and twiddle with my hair as I'm met with an eerie silence.

The only thing letting me know the call is still connected is the fact that I can hear Elliot's nineties power ballad playlist on in the background. It's currently Bon Jovi's "Always," which makes me feel rubbish. I can't keep the tears silent now, and I start sobbing down the phone.

Elliot takes a deep breath down the line. "No way."

I make a small sound of affirmation and then the ball seems to drop with him. "But . . . but why? What on earth happened? What did he do now?" Elliot immediately falls into defensive best-friend mode. Now *this* is the Elliot I need.

"His sleazeball of a best friend tried to kiss me, and when I went to tell Noah, I overheard a conversation that he and Dean were having about how Noah shouldn't have a girl-friend. Blake then lied and said *I'd* made the move on *him*. But guess who Noah believed! He said I'd made it up for attention, and that Blake would never do that. I'm in shock. I feel so alone."

I catch sight of myself in the mirror opposite me, the very mirror in which, earlier on in the evening, I had looked at myself and thought, *Wow, Penny, you are hot stuff*. Now, all I can think is, *Wow, Penny, what a hot mess you are*. There's black mascara and eyeliner running down my cheeks, my beautiful black lace-and-satin dress is hanging out from underneath my ragged old hoodie and my Pineapple is no longer looking very fresh.

"I can't believe that Noah didn't believe you . . . Are you OK? Do you need me to send someone to beat that Blake guy up?"

I giggle through my sniffles. "Maybe you and Alex together could take him?"

"Well, this is weird timing," Elliot says. There's a long pause on the phone. "I was going to wait till you got home to tell you, but . . . Alex and I have broken up too."

Now I understand why he is listening to that playlist. "Oh no, Elliot . . . what happened? I'm so sorry." I am genuinely in shock. I honestly didn't think I'd hear those words come from Elliot's mouth. The distance between us seems so wide in this moment. I want to reach through the phone and give him a hug that will last forever. Then it clicks. "Oh my god, was it because of the photo?"

"That set the wheels in motion, but there's more to it than that. I need to tell you in person. It's too much for over the phone. I wish we were together right now." Elliot sighs, as Whitney Houston belts out from his laptop in the background.

"Me too. I don't think I've ever wanted you on the other side of the wall so badly. I could just knock and you'd come straight over."

We continue to tell one another how much we miss each other and play out the things we'd be doing if we were together right now. Elliot even says he'd go as far as bringing me a box of twenty chicken nuggets from McDonald's, and I know he understands how serious this is. He hates McDonald's—except in dire emergencies.

I sigh as I stare out of the window. The Eiffel Tower, which only hours ago seemed so romantic and beautiful, is now just a stark reminder of how far away I am. I want to be at home right now, listening to Tom's dubstep music pounding through the floor, Mum singing all the wrong words to pop songs on the radio, and Dad telling bad jokes about everything.

"Oh, Elliot, what am I going to do?" I say, feeling completely lost.

But, to my surprise, Elliot gasps in excitement and I'm almost sure I hear him clap his hands together. I can hear him typing away furiously on a keyboard. "Penny, I have an idea. It's a bit crazy, but you have to trust me. Be at the Gare du Nord station tomorrow morning at nine thirty with all your stuff. I'm going to get you home."

My heart catches in my throat. "Wiki, I've been let down a lot recently. Please don't say that if you don't mean it."

"Lady Penelope, when have I *ever* let you down? You can trust me."

And, of course, Elliot is right: he's never let me down. I feel so relieved at the thought of going home that I don't even care if it means having to get the train on my own. Tomorrow, I can be asleep in my own bed.

"I love you, Elliot."

"I love you too, Penny. Remember: nine thirty tomorrow morning, Gare du Nord. Write it down. There are eight major train stations in Paris, and I don't want you going to the wrong one!"

"I've got it, Wiki," I say, trying to sound more confident than I feel. But Elliot has succeeded where I thought no one could: my spirits have lifted just a tiny bit. At least now I have a plan: I'm going home.

★ ·Chapter Forty-Two ·★

By the time I manage to crawl into bed, it's gone 4 a.m. The four hours of fitful sleep I have are barely enough to reduce the bags under my eyes, which are the size of small balloons.

Even though I'm excited about going home, I can't help but keep checking my phone, desperately wishing for a text from Noah to pop up, telling me he was wrong to assume I was lying and that he doesn't want us to split up. But there's nothing.

I rush around my room, quickly tossing all my belongings into my suitcase. My stomach clenches when I remember I left my bag with my camera in it somewhere outside Blake's room—but I can't worry about that now. I'll ask down at reception if anyone has handed it in. According to my phone, it will only take ten minutes to get to Gare du Nord in a taxi, so I have a little bit of time.

I sit back down on the bed and tear a piece of paper from a notepad. I've never written a goodbye letter before, and I never expected I would have to write one to Noah. I don't quite know where or how to start. I scribble down my thoughts numerous times, but everything I write sounds wrong. I scrunch up the rejected letters and toss them towards the bin (which I had cleaned out to avoid the room smelling bad all evening).

Finally, I feel happy with what I've written.

Noah,

I don't really know where to begin. There are a lot of things I want to say, but all I need to say is that I've gone home.

I'm sorry that all this happened, but I feel like I'm in your way here. Hopefully now you can experience everything that fame has to offer, and you won't have me dragging you down.

I can't hide that I'm hurt and upset. I put everything I had into this relationship, and you threw it all back in my face. I'm hoping one day you'll realize I never lied to you and that all I wanted was to make you happy.

You'll always be my Inciting Incident, but maybe Inciting Incidents always lead to The End?

Penny x

PS Please don't contact me. I need some time to clear my head.

I place the letter next to my phone, which I check one more time. There's still nothing from Noah. I probably don't need to tell him not to contact me; he most likely doesn't intend to anyway.

I do one last check of the hotel room, then drag my suitcase out into the hallway. It's more than a little bit of a struggle—this is the first time I've had to move my suitcase myself, without anyone to help me, and I've collected a lot of souvenirs to take home, including at least twenty miniature bottles of shampoo and body lotion from all the hotels.

When I get down to the lobby, I hear my name. "Penny?"

In that split second my heart leaps, thinking that it might be Noah. Maybe he's going to apologize? I turn and see a shiny, bald head and a cheery smile.

"Larry!" I smile at him and hope that my sunglasses are doing a good job of hiding my puffy eyes.

"I've been looking for you everywhere. I thought you might want this back." He hands me my bag, with my camera still inside. I can't help it: I throw my arms round his waist. Larry seems to be the only person on this tour who has always looked out for me. My head barely reaches his chin, and he chuckles.

"Thanks, Larry," I say, sniffling, and eventually I let him go.

"Glad I caught you! But where are you off to, miss? Would you like a hand with that?" He takes the suitcase off me and carries it out to the front of the hotel.

"Actually . . . I'm going home." I look down the road, searching for anything that remotely resembles a taxi I can flag down to take me to the station.

He frowns. "But—"

"Please don't ask, Larry." I can feel my bottom lip starting to tremble, but I refuse to cry; I've done enough of that. I pray for a taxi to come. One seems to be free, but it whips past me and stops at the feet of an effortlessly glamorous woman carrying a poodle. Looking down at my button-up shirt and black leggings, I'm frustrated. I didn't realize you had to look chic in Paris just for the taxis to stop for you.

"Does Noah know?" Larry asks gently.

"Of course he does," I say. It's not a complete lie—he'll know as soon as he sees the letter.

"Well, then he wouldn't want you to go to the station on your own. At least let me drive you."

He might not care what happens to me, I think, but I know I'm being petty. And a ride wouldn't hurt. Larry gestures towards the blacked-out Mercedes sitting just along from us and I look back at the traffic on the road.

"OK. Thanks, Larry." It's enough that I've just broken up with my boyfriend; the last thing I need is to get lost in Paris with a heavy suitcase in tow. "I appreciate it."

Larry is kind enough to just make small talk in the car, telling me all about the trip he took to Notre Dame yesterday. Once we arrive at the station, Larry helps me with my suitcase and wishes me luck, and I thank him for everything he has done for me on the tour.

"You're welcome, Penny. And don't worry—Noah will come back to his senses," he says with a friendly wink.

I smile weakly and nod. Then I spin round and face the imposing entrance to the station. I take a deep breath and walk in as confidently as I can.

Once I'm inside, I let the facade drop. I also realize that I'm not entirely sure what I have to do. In hindsight, I should have asked Elliot for a little more detail, but at 4 a.m., after one of the worst nights of my life, I wasn't exactly asking the right questions. All Elliot said was that I had to be here for 9:30 a.m. I look up at the departures board and see there isn't a train leaving for London until 11:30 a.m. Maybe Elliot wanted to give me plenty of time? I start looking around for any signs that may have my name on them, with no luck.

Breathe, Penny, I tell myself. *What would Wiki do?* I try to put on my most sensible, logical head—which is difficult, because that part of my brain seems to be lurking underneath a cloud of emotional fog.

"*Excusez-moi?*" I stare at the small woman in the glass-fronted ticket booth and she smiles at me politely. She has a petite face and her eyes are framed with round glasses. She has overdrawn her red lipstick. "*Parlez-vous anglais?*" I ask, hoping I'm not mangling my French too much. When she nods at me, I smile with relief. "I need to get to England. My name is Penny Porter. I don't suppose you have a ticket for me?"

The lady looks at me with slight confusion on her face. "*Pardon?* My English is not very good. You have a reservation?"

"Yes! Maybe?" I hand over my passport. She smiles as she turns to her computer and starts tapping away.

She frowns. "I do not see anything here for you."

"No, sorry. I think my friend may have booked me a ticket. Elliot Wentworth?" I realize how dramatically I'm using my hands to express myself and I turn tomato red. Clearly this lady will not understand who Elliot is based on hand gestures.

"*Mademoiselle?* You need a new ticket?" She points at her computer and then to a train, smiling like she's just won the lottery.

I smile back at her just as sweetly and shake my head. "Never mind. It's OK. Thank you. *Merci.*"

I lug my bright pink suitcase back over to the departure boards. What on earth am I thinking, trying to make my own way home? It doesn't matter that Elliot has somehow arranged plans for me; I am clearly an absolute liability, an accident waiting to happen. I sit down on my suitcase and call Elliot to ask what exactly I'm supposed to be doing, but his phone goes through to voicemail. I mutter at the screen. "Not now, Elliot, you complete and utter—"

"Pen-face! You're here!"

I spin round and see Elliot standing there in his checked trousers and red loafers. His brown hair is styled to perfection and his crisp white shirt and black bow tie look perfect with his tortoise shell-rimmed glasses. I run at him and jump up, wrapping my legs round his waist in an elaborate movie-style hug.

"OK, calm down! This isn't *Dirty Dancing*! I'm not built for this type of affection," Elliot says.

He drops me and I just about land on my feet.

"Sorry, but I'm so excited to see you! Are you really here? Was this your plan all along?"

"Yes. I considered bringing you home for about a millisecond, then I thought, *We're going to be heartbroken, sad losers. Do I want to be a sad loser in my bedroom in Brighton? Or a sad loser in Paris?* New York pulled you out of a slump, so I thought maybe Paris could do the same for me. It felt like fate: I had days off from *CHIC*; I used the credit card that Dad gave me for emergencies to buy the tickets; and I had just enough time to head to London to get the Eurostar this morning. I've had NO sleep. I need a shower though, because I feel so gross."

"Elliot, you're the best. What's the plan?"

"I have a hotel booked in the fifteenth arrondissement."

I love Elliot so much! "What's that?" I ask.

"It's an area of Paris—did you know there are twenty

arrondissements in Paris in total?" Elliot takes my arm and we walk out to find a taxi.

Even though sadness hovers over me like a rain cloud, it's as though a few of the grey clouds have parted slightly and this big beautiful rainbow has appeared to take away some of the gloom. I feel so different now I have Elliot with me.

"I did not know that! Elliot, you look amazing considering you've had no sleep. You should see my eyes under these sunglasses."

He pulls up my glasses and peers at me with a look of concern on his face. "What designer are they?" he asks, still looking.

"The sunglasses? Oh, they're not designer. I bought them at Topshop two years ago."

He laughs as he puts the sunglasses back over my eyes. "No, the bags, *daaaahling.*" Elliot bursts into a cackle of laughter and drags me over to a taxi. I muster up a little giggle as I jump into the car next to him.

The taxi begins to pull away from the station when I spot a head of messy brown hair and a familiar silhouette. I can't work out if it's shock or undeniable delight that pulses through my body. Noah's come for me.

"Stop the taxi!" I shout.

Chapter Forty-Three

Except it's not Noah. When the guy turns round, he doesn't look anything like Noah. It's just my desperate imagination playing tricks on me.

The taxi driver harrumphs as I slump down into my seat, and Elliot pats my hand gently.

Thankfully, the ride isn't too long, but when we pull up outside the hotel that Elliot's booked I can't help but be dubious. It's a far cry from the hotels I've been staying in on tour—the exterior is shabby and the walls are covered in graffiti.

Elliot shrugs. "It's all I could find at the last minute. It has a good rating on TripAdvisor though!"

I squeeze Elliot's hand and we walk into the hotel. Just the fact that he's here is something no amount of money could ever buy, and I'd be happy to stay in a cardboard box as long as we are together.

Even though it's early, the receptionist hands us the room key, and we lug my suitcase up three flights of stairs to our room. We are in fits of laughter trying to drag the heavy suitcase up each step and I can barely breathe. The combination of being unfit (I definitely shouldn't have skipped as many PE lessons as I have) and our giggling is making this task a lot more difficult.

The exterior isn't the only thing that's different about this hotel: it is also a lot more cramped. The two single beds in our room are pushed up against one another and the ends of the beds pretty much touch the wall. There is a tiny window, but no hope of a view of the Eiffel Tower—instead, I'm greeted with the sight of a brick wall and a fire escape. There's graffiti on the outside wall that reads: L'AMOUR EST MORT. Elliot translates it: "Love is dead." I know how that person feels. In the bathroom, the showerhead hovers over the toilet, and I have to hunch my shoulders to fit in.

"Well, that kills two birds with one stone." Elliot laughs as he pokes his head round the bathroom door.

We both fall back onto the beds in an exhausted heap. Although I have been absorbed in my own misery about Noah and I breaking up, I've not really taken into consideration how Elliot must be feeling right now. Alexiot is no more, and a part of my heart breaks for him as I lie there thinking about it.

I reach out and grab his hand. "Wiki? Did you see this coming with Alex? Have you guys been arguing a lot?" I roll over onto my stomach and prop my head up with my hands.

Elliot lets out an exaggerated sigh and interlaces his fingers over his stomach.

"You know that Alex isn't out yet, and of course I didn't mind in the beginning. I would never pressure him into coming out—he needs to go at his own pace. But, as stupid as it sounds, I thought by now we would have jumped that hurdle together. That maybe I would have been the one to change him and give him the confidence . . . I sound like a bad movie. I know I can never change anyone but, Penny, I'm tired of playing second fiddle. The photo of us kissing just magnified everything. He completely freaked out and demanded to know how on earth I ever let this happen. He said,"—Elliot's voice sounds so small, my heart squeezes inside my chest— "he said he wished he had never kissed me at all. I felt so embarrassed."

I look over at Elliot and he's squeezing his eyes really tightly shut. Then he opens them again, blinks, and for the first time his voice sounds harder. He sounds more like his father, which is weird because he never sounds like his dad. "It's just sad to invest so much in someone and not feel like that investment has had a good return. So it had to end."

Elliot rolls over and, despite his words, I don't think I've ever seen him so upset about anything. I know that if he's dealing with something sad he'd rather turn off the emotion tap completely than let the world know how badly he is hurting.

"Oh, Wiki, that's horrible. But you have to know it's not to do with you. This is something Alex needs to work out within himself, and that's really awful for you because all you can do is sit and wait at the sidelines. But you haven't done anything wrong by wanting your relationship and your feelings to be respected. He can't hide you away forever." I look at Elliot and smile a little, just to see if I can inject a bit of positivity.

To my relief, he smiles back at me. "I know, Penny. It's just . . . I really like him. Like, *really* like." He raises his eyebrows at me.

"Like, really *like* like?" I wiggle my eyebrows back at him and we find ourselves giggling a little bit. Then he jumps off the bed.

"Like *really* like *like* like. Look at us, Penny. We're acting as though the world has stopped turning. We're stewing in our own sadness and it's very unattractive. We're in Paris, for goodness' sake—we need to forget about guys and go out and have fun. You might not have had any Magical Mystery Days with Noah, but you are sure as heck having one with me."

"Ooh, I know this great fashion street you will *love*," I say, thinking back to my day out with Leah. Was that only yesterday? It feels like a million years. "It has all these fancy boutiques on it—"

Elliot frowns. "Wait, how do you know about a great fashion street?"

I blush. "Leah took me. She dressed me up for the after-party last night." I take out my phone, even though it pains me to scroll past pictures of Noah and me together, looking so happy. I find one Leah took just after we left the hotel, when my hair, makeup, and outfit were all perfect. I show it to Elliot, whose jaw drops to the floor.

"Oh, Penny, you're telling me Noah gave you up after *this*? Honey, he's a fool."

I take back my phone and put it in my pocket, tears threatening to fill my eyes again. "I guess if I knew how to look like that all the time maybe I would be enough for him."

"Oh, no," says Elliot. "That is *not* the Penny I know. If he can't love you like this"—he gestures at my schlubby leggings, shirt, and messed-up hair—"then he does not deserve to have you. Penny, you're not a princess; you're a queen. And queens deserve hot chocolate and croissants for breakfast, so let's go."

Chapter Forty-Four

Flaky, fluffy, melt-in-your-mouth croissants dipped in velvety smooth hot chocolate should be requisite morning-after-a-breakup food for everyone. I'm pretty sure the waitress gives us a disapproving look as we order their last six *pains au chocolat*, but we don't care.

Elliot soon wins her over with his French chat, and before long they are exchanging tips on where to find the best macarons in Paris. Elliot sounds so cool; I swoon every time he speaks, which he starts to find really annoying after a while.

After breakfast, we walk the strip of very expensive shops that Leah took me to, and I feel a wave of sadness creep over me as I remember how much effort I went to for Noah last night only for it to all go so horribly wrong. Every time I start to look sad, Elliot pulls out the bag of leftover *pains au chocolat* and makes me take a bite while he does the same.

It works—until we run out of *pains au chocolat*. That's when we sit down for lunch and I have the world's cheesiest *croque-monsieur*—and, of course, a massive slice of apple tart.

Who says that food can't solve every problem? Food and best friends are officially the ideal combination.

After lunch we head to the Pont des Arts on the Seine River, otherwise known as the love-lock bridge. Elliot is determined to get a padlock, write both our names on it, and attach it to the bridge forever as a little homage to our friendship, but when we get there we see that all the padlocks have been taken away. In their place, there's a big sign asking people not to keep putting locks on because the weight of them is damaging the bridge.

Although Elliot is disappointed, I'm not. I don't think I like to imagine my love as a lock. Instead, I prefer to think of it as being like the bridge we're standing on—something that connects two hearts together that otherwise would never meet. The love locks are a bit like all the problems Noah and I had: each one was small, but together they were enough to make us buckle, and eventually break.

Despite the fact that the love locks are now banned, we are still surrounded by happy couples taking photos on this bridge which for so long has stood as a symbol of unending love. I wish Elliot hadn't brought me here. The last thing I want to see are couples making kissy faces at their phone screens.

"OK, so no lock, but how about a romantic stroll along the Seine?" Elliot brings me back into the moment as he scurries along the bridge, dragging me by the arm.

"Did you know there are over thirty bridges that cross the Seine in Paris?" Elliot says, linking his arm with mine.

"I can believe it," I say. It seems like we've passed half a dozen in our short walk. I lean my head against Elliot's shoulder and we follow the path alongside the river, watching as long boats packed with tourists glide serenely by.

"Look! Look!" Elliot points up at the Eiffel Tower, which is now looming in front of us.

Even though it instantly makes me think of Noah, and how close we got to having a Magical Mystery Night, I can't help but be awed by how majestic it is up close, with its iron body stretching into the clear blue sky. It's so iconic that my heart catches in my mouth as I look up at it. Elliot grabs my hand and we pick up into a run, desperate to get closer.

There are hundreds of tourists milling around us and we're forced to slow down to a halt. Elliot lets out a low whistle, clearly impressed. Now my heart has stopped for a different reason: a group of Japanese tourists has just moved away, revealing a line of posters taped to a temporary wall, and on them is Noah's face. They're the first posters for the tour I've seen: he is holding his guitar and smiling at the camera, his picture just below a big photo of The Sketch. Although the headline band takes up a larger portion of the poster, it's Noah's face that stands out to me like a sore thumb.

He looks so rock-god-tastic—except he's not my rock god anymore. Just as I feel like I'm about to have a breakdown, I hear "I Will Survive" booming from some speakers nearby. I turn to see a middle-aged guy singing and dancing in the street next to a boom box. There is a part of me that wants to cringe—I mean, how many people do you know who would rock out to a seventies disco anthem in the middle of Paris? The absurdity of it makes me want to cry and laugh at the same time.

There are so many different emotions running through my body and I can't work out which one to convey, so I turn to Elliot for a bit of guidance. His face makes it a little easier for me, as he smiles so big I can almost see his fillings. He reaches out and lifts me into a dance. I follow his lead and, before we know it, we're dancing around like absolute idiots under the Eiffel Tower along with the Frenchman, and we're belting out the words to "I Will Survive" just as loudly as he is. Soon everyone around us is also joining in. It's like we've created one giant Parisian breakup flash mob.

I feel like a lunatic, I feel crazy, but I feel free. And it's the first time in a very long time that I feel like me again.

3 July

Songs to Cure Your Heartbreak

You know that day I thought would never come?

The one I could never picture in a million years?

It's happened.

Brooklyn Boy and I are no more.

I can't write more than that at the moment. I will say this, though: heartbreak is never easy, but they do say that music cures the soul. Along with Wiki, I've been compiling a list of the best songs to get through the emotional roller coaster that is a breakup.

1. "Someone Like You" — Adele

2. "Irreplaceable" — Beyoncé

3. "We Are Never Ever Getting Back Together" — Taylor Swift

4. "End of the Road"—Boyz II Men

5. "I Will Survive"—Gloria Gaynor (courtesy of a French busker we danced with under the Eiffel Tower yesterday)

6. "Since U Been Gone"—Kelly Clarkson

7. "Forget You"—CeeLo Green

8. "Without You"—Harry Nilsson cover

9. "I Will Always Love You"—Whitney Houston

10. "You Could Be Happy"—Snow Patrol

11. "The Scientist"—Coldplay

12. "With or Without You"—U2

13. "Survivor"—Destiny's Child

14. "Single Ladies (Put a Ring on It)"—Beyoncé

15. "Losing Grip"—Avril Lavigne

Listening to the following playlist could make you feel better, or it could make you cry, or it could make you feel all of the above—in which case, you and your best friend can finish with a dance-off to "Single Ladies" by Beyoncé, jumping between two single beds in the smallest hotel room in Paris.

Girl Offline . . . never going online xxx

Chapter Forty-Five

As the Eurostar train pulls out of Gare du Nord to make its way back to England, I rest my head on Elliot's shoulder and watch Paris disappear through the window. It feels weird to be leaving Noah here, on a journey that started out with us together and is now ending with us . . . broken. I guess TheRealTruth got their way after all: Noah and Penny are no more.

So much promise and anticipation seems to have spiralled into all of this. It's a runaway train I can't control.

Now that I really am on my way home, I can't help but feel a pang of sorrow at the fact that we never had a final hug, one last conversation, or a kiss goodbye. It's almost as if Noah woke up one morning not remembering who I am or that I ever existed.

"What are you thinking about?" Elliot asks. When I don't reply, he takes a guess—and, of course, he knows exactly what the answer is. "Hey, don't worry about it too much. You asked Noah not to contact you. At least he's respecting that."

I make a non-committal grunt, and wrap my mum's

cardigan tighter round myself. I can't wait to replace this cardigan with a real-life hug from her. I really need it now—and I definitely need to not think about the fact that this train travels through a tunnel beneath a great big channel of water.

The point isn't that I asked Noah not to contact me; the point is that I could be anywhere, with anyone, and he doesn't appear to care. For all he knows, I could be lying in a ditch on the side of a Parisian road. I'm sure Larry told Noah that he dropped me at the station, but Noah could have at least challenged the fact I was leaving or that this was over—anything but this great big nothing.

I keep replaying a moment we shared up at the top of the Waldorf Astoria in New York at Christmas. It was when Noah kissed me for the first time, and I remember thinking that nothing and no one could ever be more perfect. Another memory pops into my head: the first day we spent together, when he completely embraced the spirit of Magical Mystery Day and took me to a secret Italian restaurant where we slurped up spaghetti and laughed about the same things. People say that it's impossible for two people to fall in love so quickly, but the chemistry between us was impossible to ignore. We . . . clicked.

It was never just a casual thing. Of course, I tried my best to *act* casual, but my heart beat at a million miles an hour whenever he walked into the room. I was his Inciting Incident—it was our movie, and we changed our lives forever.

I rewind even further, to when I first saw him in the spotlight onstage, pretending to be a wedding singer. He'd seemed so vulnerable and mysterious. I didn't realize then that he would be this amazing, goofy, romantic, perfect guy. *No*, I tell myself. *Not perfect. Not perfect at all.* Where did it all go so wrong? How did we let it get to this point? Where did that Noah I first met go? It feels as though on each leg of this tour he has shed something that I loved about him, until all that was left was someone I don't know.

As the train hurtles along and Elliot drops off to sleep, I also think about how this is all my fault. I should have known this would happen. I dived headfirst into this entire thing, thinking it would be like it is in the movies. The rock star gets famous, falls in love with a girl, and they live happily ever after. But this isn't a Hollywood script. This is real life, and *newsflash*: sometimes real life sucks.

My phone buzzes, snapping me out of my thoughts. It's a text from my mum.

> Penny darling, Dad and I will be waiting for you at St. Pancras station. We're so excited to see you. We've got Dad's cottage pie for dinner tonight—your favourite. We'll also sit down and watch Elf, even though it's July. Can even go as far as wearing our Christmas jumpers if you want? ☺ xxx

The text makes me smile. My parents don't know all the details yet—but they know me well enough to guess. Initially I tried to get away with simply telling them that the tour wasn't quite what I imagined, but they grilled me like a suspect over Skype.

I got about as far as telling them that things with Noah weren't the best before my bottom lip started to shake. They could see that I wasn't quite up for an in-depth question-and-answer session yet, and any further questioning would have to wait until I was safely back at home.

I love my parents—they're so caring, if maybe sometimes *too* caring. I know what they'll be like: they'll be baking me cookies every morning, noon, and night, taking me out to all my favourite shops, and trying too hard to make me happy. I'm so grateful to Elliot for taking the sting out of that first night by coming to visit me in Paris. I think if I had gone home straightaway I would have been crushed under the weight of my parents' sympathy. There's nothing bad about being loved—my parents just want me to be happy—but sometimes it can be smothering.

At this point, the only smothering I want is from my own duvet. I want to wrap myself in it (even though in the heat of summer my attic room is like a sauna) and bury myself away from the world. To just wallow in the deep pool of my own self-pity. To eat my body weight in ice cream (to counteract the sweltering bedroom, of course) and disappear from real life.

I sigh and tap out a quick reply before we head into the tunnel (which I am NOT thinking about) and I lose signal for a while.

> Thanks, Mum. Excited to see you both too. No Christmassy stuff, please, but cottage pie does sound good xxx

I don't want to taint my favourite season with sadness. They know how much I love Christmas, but right now all I can think of is spending Christmas at Noah's and helping him to decorate the tree with Bella. I flick through my texts and my finger hovers over the conversations with Noah. There is a part of me that really wants to go through them all and relive them. The *I love you*s and the *forever*s and the *Inciting Incident*s, but I don't. Stepping off this train needs to feel like the beginning of something else, not the end.

Noah will be getting ready to pack up and head to Norway right about now, and then he'll be heading off for the World Tour. Our lives feel so different already. Noah has everything in place, but a nagging question still haunts me.

What am I going to do now?

Chapter Forty-Six

News travels fast when it comes to Noah Flynn. As soon as we pull into the station and I *finally* get data on my phone again, I'm bombarded with messages and alerts.

"Wow, Penny, have you seen this?" Elliot holds up his phone, where a popular online magazine is shouting the headline: NOAH FLYNN IS SINGLE. QUEUE UP, LADIES, YOUR FAVOURITE BROOKLYN BOY IS FINALLY UP FOR GRABS.

I guess the PR machine doesn't waste any time. But *up for grabs*? Really? Like he's some prize at a local fete? I thought I was starting to get the hang of the media, learning the hard way that they are always trying to grab attention with their completely twisted, magnified, and sometimes blatantly untrue headlines. This time, though, they're right on the money. I guess Noah Flynn *is* single. I just didn't think he'd want to make that so clear, so quickly.

It feels like every person on my contacts list is messaging me with condolences. It's way more than when I got dragged through the mud last time. I guess getting dumped is easier to empathize with. I scroll through the messages and most of them make me alternate between smiling and cringing.

Kira:
OMG! Penny, I just heard the news. That SUCKS. Let me know when you want to see people and I'll bring over sweet treats and my fave horror movies! Nothing like an Insidious + Paranormal Activity movie marathon to get over heartbreak . . . xx

Amara:
BOO! I thought you guys would be forever. Kira said she'll bring the horror flicks . . . I'll bring the popcorn! xo

Megan:
TELL ME IT'S NOT TRUE!! xx

There's even a message from Pegasus Girl.

To: Girl Online
From: Pegasus Girl
Subject: Noah Stuff

Hey, Penny,

I wanted to email you to say that I'm thinking of you. I'm sorry to hear about you and Noah. I want you to know I'm always here if you ever want a chat. I know it must feel like the whole world is against you at times, but I wanted to reassure you that I absolutely love what you do, and think you're very talented and extremely brave. I would never have been able to jet off on tour, and I bet you never thought you'd be able to either. Anyway, I'm sure he will come to his senses and whisk you off your feet. Don't most guys do that in the end?

PG xx

I smile at her message, but only manage a small one. I don't think Noah is going to come and whisk me off my feet any time soon. More importantly, I don't think I want him to.

I'm still staring at my phone when Elliot plucks it out of my hands. "Pennylicious, your expression has changed so many times while looking at your phone it CANNOT be good for you."

"You're right," I say, trying to put on a good face to see my family. "I'm not going to let this get me down."

As soon as we get through the Eurostar gates at St. Pancras station, I fall into my mum's arms and all my good intentions slip away. I can't help it; the tears stream down my face. Now that I'm officially back on British soil, I have to acknowledge that it's over.

Really and truly over.

Chapter Forty-Seven

Things go from bad to worse in the week that follows. I spend way too much time sitting on my window seat, head pressed against the glass, wrapped up in my duvet. If someone took a photograph of me during this week, they'd have to call it *Portrait of an Impossibly Sad Girl*.

As promised, the twins come over for a horror-movie marathon, but I'm so spaced out that I don't even jump during *Paranormal Activity*. That is *not* normal activity for me—I'm usually the one clutching the arm of the sofa until my knuckles go white, and screaming down the house at every appearance of a ghost. Even the wind rattling at the window freaks me out.

I don't hear from Noah either. Despite telling myself I don't want to, I keep looking online to check he isn't signed in on Skype. I follow his tweets, Instagram, and other social-media posts like one of his obsessive fans. Elliot comes over after he's finished at *CHIC* every day. My Internet stalking has become so bad that he makes me log how many hours I spend each day checking up on Noah online.

The day I log almost ten hours is a bad day.

I find myself wanting to see Noah go into meltdown mode, for him to write something moody on Twitter, to see that he's struggling to cope without me. In reality, though, I know he is incredibly private about that kind of stuff, so there aren't any personal updates anywhere. Instead, there are endless posts about his tour dates, and the occasional thank-you to his fans for continuing to support him as he embarks on the World Tour.

Sometimes I wish I could be more like Elliot. His way of making himself feel better about breaking up with Alex is just to blank him out completely—delete his number, block him on social media, avoid the vintage store—then carry on as normal. But it's almost impossible for me to do that. Whenever I leave my room, I seem to hear "Autumn Girl" on the radio in the car or in the supermarket. It's as if now that I'm not with Noah I'm surrounded by him more than ever.

That's why, even though it's now been over a week since we got back from Paris, I've retreated to my little window seat. I know I'm wasting the last few weeks of summer freedom by being a walking zombie. I know I can't turn off every radio on the planet while I try to get over Noah. I know I shouldn't be refreshing his Twitter feed every thirty seconds. But, without Elliot to distract me during the day, there is nothing except the occasional squawk of seagulls or Dad shouting at the football to pull me out of this mind-numbed state.

Whose fault is that, Penny? You were the one who decided to trail around after your boyfriend instead of pursuing your own passions.

I hate my inner voice sometimes.

12 July

How to Stop Obsessing Over Someone

When going through the highs and lows of a breakup, it's all too easy to become modern-day Sherlock Holmes. Instagram, Twitter, Snapchat—it's so easy these days to see what people are up to, and I'm not sure how I feel about that. There are impulsive moments when you want to sit and read through everything until you find some incriminating evidence to suggest your ex has moved on and doesn't care about you anymore. But, in reality, can we really judge these things by a 140-character sentence?

I have to admit, it's hard. You want to know, but you also don't. It could crush you into a million tiny pieces. Obsessing over someone is unhealthy, we all know this. Obsessing over someone who is an up-and-coming international rock god is an emotional roller coaster, because I'm not Brooklyn Boy's only stalker: there are hundreds of Tumblrs and fan sites doing that for me. I could know his every move if I wanted to . . .

There have been some dark days when I've lost myself down the rabbit hole. I even started following Brooklyn Boy's friend's Twitter feed, which is just a steady stream of prank videos and the occasional pseudo-motivational tweet, like *LIVE HARD, DIE YOUNG*, almost always in shouty capital letters. That was a new low for me.

I've found that the best way to stop obsessing is to turn off every radio in sight, refuse to enter a car unless whoever's driving puts on a cheery CD, and avoid the Internet as much as possible.

In reality, I can't tell you how to stop obsessing over someone, because it's one of those things that only *you* can do, and only when the moment is right. All I can say is be strong and fight the twitching urges to refresh everything all day, every day.

Girl Offline . . . never going online xxx

Chapter Forty-Eight

I banish my laptop to the bottom of my laundry basket to stop myself from looking at it, and decide to distract myself by finally unpacking. My suitcase has been sitting unopened in the corner of my room. I'm too afraid of the memories I might have tucked in the case alongside my socks and underwear. With a deep breath, I unzip the case and open it up—but then I get a blast of unmistakable aftershave: Noah's. I push the case away from me like it's on fire. Absolutely everything reminds me of him. Perhaps a brain transplant at this point would help?

I sigh and look out of the window. At least I have a great view from my window seat over the other pastel-coloured terraced houses; in the distance, I can just about see the whitecaps of the waves. Ordinarily, I might have picked up my camera to take a shot, but not today.

"All right, Pen?" Tom appears in my bedroom doorway, making me jump. I was so engrossed in my own pity party that I didn't even hear the creak of the third-from-top stair that normally alerts me to anyone coming up to my room.

Tom comes in, wading through the dirty laundry sprawled all over the floor, and perches on the end of my bed.

"Hey. What's up?" I slide off the window seat and sit down next to him.

"Your floordrobe is looking a little unorganized . . ." He kicks up a pair of crumpled jeans.

"Yeah, I know, it's a bit of a mess. I just . . . *urgh*. I don't feel motivated to do anything. Today is the first day I've brushed my hair this week. I don't even remember when I last washed it."

Tom grimaces slightly as I attempt to run my fingers through my knotty hair.

"Penny, you might not want to hear this, but you need to: you have to snap out of this funk you're in. No one is worth this, and I hate seeing you this way."

I look at Tom, almost expecting him to laugh or say he's joking or do something that's not so serious, but he doesn't. "It's like you've come back from this tour a different person. You need to find *you* again. I mean, do you even know where your camera is?"

"Of course I do!" I protest. "It's . . ." But then I look around my room, and I can't see my camera.

"Of course you don't, because I stole it to see if you'd notice. You didn't." He takes it from behind his back, putting it in the space between us. It sits there, taunting me.

Remember when you used to like to use me? it says. *Remember how many pictures of Noah you took with me?* I almost want to throw up. I push the camera lens away.

"Keep it. I don't want it."

"What? Why? Is it because of Noah?"

I roll my eyes at him. "You're a mind reader."

He picks up the camera and places it firmly on my lap, wrapping my fingers round it. "You're a Porter, and Porters don't give up on their passions. They keep going until they succeed. Apart from the time Dad tried to learn to dive— that didn't actually go down so well . . ." He lets out a little laugh. "If you're going to waste away the rest of the summer, at least do it while doing something you love."

I feel my whole body seize up. Tom's words chip away at the wall I was happily building in my head to help myself get over Noah; the wall that I am now realizing I began building on the very first day of the tour, when everything started going wrong.

I don't like crying in front of Tom. He's strong and caring, but very practical, and deep down I wish I could be more like him. He sees the world very differently to me, and it's so refreshing to hear him say these things.

"So? What do you think?"

I put the camera back down on the bed, prompting Tom to sigh. Then I look around my room and spot the magazine clipping I taped up on my wall—the one that labels me "girl-friend of Noah Flynn." Once upon a time, that clipping made me proud. Now it makes me feel a little angry.

Tom's right: I'm losing myself in all this. I am allowing myself to feel completely inferior but, actually, I also have things I'm good at. I take down the clipping and stare at it for few moments before scrunching it up in my hand and drop-ping it in my bin. I sit back down on the bed in silence.

Tom leans over and wraps his arm round me, giving me a squeeze. "Welcome back, Penny. The world is waiting for you."

"Thanks, Tom. You're the best."

As Tom leaves I hear my phone go off on my bedside table. I'm hoping it's Elliot on the train from London with a humorous rundown of his day.

> Penny, I heard what happened. I'm SO sorry. I really hope you're OK. Listen, this might cheer you up: I've got an offer you may want to accept. Take a look at your email. Leah xx

I put down the phone and rush over to my laptop, digging it out of my laundry basket. I pull up my email and, sure enough, there's a message from Leah.

As I'm reading it, my mouth steadily drops open.

From: Leah Brown
To: Penny Porter
Subject: HUGE NEWS

Dear Penny,

I was really hoping that I'd get to ask you this in person, but, since that's not possible anymore, email will have to do! This is all TOTALLY confidential, obviously, so please don't let anyone know except your immediate family.

I didn't get to tell you about my new album, but I've decided to call it *Life in Disguise*. I've been writing a lot of songs about how, in order to deal with fame, I've had to disguise so many things— my love life, my friends, and sometimes even my identity.

We shot the album cover with François-Pierre Nouveau, but I wasn't happy with any of the pictures he took. They just all looked too staged. I want this to be natural. Light. Real.

So I had my design team mock up a cover using your photograph—the one you took of me in Rome, while I was in disguise. Do you remember? I absolutely love the picture; it is so perfect.

And it's even more perfect on the front of my album cover.

Why not take a look for yourself?

Do you think I could use it? I've attached a contract—it contains details of the fee and royalties and other things. I can put you in touch with a lawyer if you want to get someone to look it over. Then, if you're happy with everything, you can send me the high-res image and this can happen!

I really hope you agree that it looks perfect. You're an amazing photographer, Penny!

I miss seeing your face on tour already. You can bet that as soon as I'm back in the UK I'll be down in Brighton to visit you—and I won't accept no for an answer!

Your friend,

Leah xx

My hand is shaking as I click on the attachment and open it.

There it is. My photograph of Leah, on her album cover. ON HER ALBUM COVER. They've cropped the top corner so you can't tell that it was taken in Rome—and, even though she looks so different with her cropped bob and bright lipstick, there's an aura round her that is distinctly *Leah*. Down at the bottom of the cover are the words LIFE IN DISGUISE in neat type, and Leah's distinctive signature, with a heart on top of the *a*.

This is real.

Tom's words echo in my brain: *Do something you love.* Photography is my passion. I can follow this dream.

I grab my phone and reply to Leah with a big string of emoticons that are barely able to describe the combination of excitement, honour, and amazement I feel.

I hit send, and my phone buzzes immediately.

But it's not Leah or Elliot.

It's Alex.

Penny, can we meet up?

Chapter Forty-Nine

I agree to meet Alex the next morning at the Flour Pot Bakery in the Brighton Lanes. I can see why he chose it: it's the perfect place to have a quiet, private conversation. My fingers are tingling with anticipation. I'm not sure why Alex wants to speak to me. I swallow down the other feelings—the ones that are screaming *BETRAYAL* for meeting Alex behind Elliot's back. But Alex had one *other* request for me, and that was to keep our meeting a secret until I've heard what he has to say.

A large part of me wants to tell Alex where to shove his meeting request, having seen how badly he hurt Elliot, but I'm also intrigued. Alex has become a friend to me over the past year—a good friend—and he deserves to at least be heard. I don't have to like what he says, but I owe him enough to listen.

I walk into the bakery and lock eyes with Alex. He is sitting towards the back at a small table with a cappuccino.

It takes all the self-control I have to contain the look of surprise that threatens to spring to my face. Alex is the type of guy who usually makes a lot of effort on the appearance front. Elliot used to call him *preppy-chic*, even though it didn't seem to fit with Alex's day job at the vintage store. Today, though, it's like I'm meeting a stranger. He looks forlorn, and his eyes are so empty and sad. He's wearing a hoodie and I swear the cuffs have holes in them. His hair clearly hasn't seen a shower—let alone any product—in days, and his cheeks are sunken. I immediately feel my heart swell for him. I haven't looked much better myself over the past week and, as much as I love Elliot to pieces and he's my number one, I can see Alex is taking this hard too.

"Thanks for meeting me, Penny," he says, moving his rucksack to one side so I can sit down.

"Of course." I drop down into the chair, and there's a moment of awkward silence. "How are you doing? It's all been a bit . . . difficult, hasn't it?"

"Difficult is probably an understatement." He lets out an exasperated sigh and takes a sip of his cappuccino.

I decide to get straight to the point—I know that Alex wants to speak about something, and I don't want to dart around the issue. "So, what was it that you wanted to talk to me about?" I look at him and muster a smile, hoping he feels able to talk openly with me.

"I've screwed up, Penny. We both know that. Elliot is everything to me, and I threw it all away because I was too afraid to deal with my emotions and I cared too much about what everyone else would think. This relationship hasn't been easy for me—Elliot is the only guy I've ever been with." I watch him as he swirls the cappuccino froth with his spoon. "After everything ended with us, I finally told my close friends and family that I'm gay."

My breath catches in my throat. "Really? I know what a big step that is for you. How did it go?"

A smile tugs at the corner of his mouth and he shrugs. "Honestly, I don't know what I was so scared of. They've all been so supportive and are happy for me. It turns out that the only person I was ever hiding from was myself."

"Wow, Alex. I'm really proud of you. That's amazing," I say, and I mean every word. I can't believe how far he's come.

"Yeah, but now the one person I want to tell won't listen. I've been trying to contact Elliot and he won't respond to any of my calls, texts, or emails . . ." He rests his chin in the palm of his hand and gazes at me, his face full of both hope and despair.

My heart goes out to him. Elliot is an all-or-nothing kind of guy. He will be dive-in-at-the-deep-end-with-both-feet in love, but he can also be ruthless in shutting people out. He just builds a fortress round his feelings that's more impenetrable than Gibraltar.

"Elliot takes a bit of time to warm up . . . he's like Elsa from *Frozen*." I smile, but Alex doesn't smile back. Clearly now is not a good time for *Frozen* references. "I just mean it takes a lot to make him come round. He's really stubborn."

"You think I don't know that?"

"I know he really likes you, Alex. I've never seen him as happy as when he was with you, and I mean that."

Alex leans back in his chair. "What will it take for him to listen to me? If he won't answer my texts or calls, what else can I do? I don't want to just show up at his house, because he'll only shut the door in my face." Alex sighs dramatically—almost as dramatically as Elliot does. "I need to do something that will capture his attention."

"Something big. A grand gesture."

"Something *epic*." Alex reaches forward and grabs my hand. "That's why I asked you here today, Penny. Will you help me? I need you on board if I'm going to have a hope of pulling this off. You're his best friend, and you know him better than anyone."

It's clear that Alex is really regretting his actions, and I know Elliot isn't over this relationship either. I nod; I'll do it. "Maybe I can take him on a "decoy day," so he thinks he's doing something with me but actually you have a surprise planned for him?"

Alex sits bolt upright and his eyes are as big and bulging as a pug's. I can sense the optimism rising in him and, before I get swept away, I just have to say one more thing: "Whatever you end up doing, he needs to know you're serious about being in a real relationship, out in the open."

"Of course. I want to be with him. I want to show the world I'm in love with Elliot Wentworth!" He says it so loudly the other bakery customers turn and stare at us.

I laugh. "Save some of that for the surprise! This is so romantic. You need to get your thinking cap on."

"Well, I have a few ideas already . . ."

Alex and I sit for another half an hour, thinking about every aspect of Elliot's surprise. It brings me so much joy to see Alex motivated and passionate about winning Elliot back. By the end of it, we have a list of Elliot's absolute favourite things, including (but not limited to):

- sunsets
- the beach
- fashion
- general knowledge
- things with sparkles

"There's got to be some way to pull this all together," says Alex. "The sooner we can, the better, as I don't think I can wait much longer." He puts his hand on top of mine. "Even if . . . even if he doesn't take me back—which I would deserve, I know—I want him to know what he's done for me. How he's made me want to be true to myself."

This is what true love is: admitting that you've made a mistake, and going out of your way to make it right. Even if Elliot doesn't take Alex back, at least he's trying. If even half of what we have planned comes off, it's going to be like something from a movie.

I can't help but think of Noah.

Why doesn't *he* want to make it right?

Chapter Fifty

When I leave the bakery, I head straight for To Have and To Hold, Mum's wedding boutique in the Lanes. I need to ask for her advice on the Elliot surprise.

Mum is always the best person to go to at times like this. She is a true expert when it comes to big celebrations and planning (hence her successful wedding-planning business), but she's great at the small stuff too.

Mum and Dad are hopeless romantics with each other. Dad will often come home with a bunch of flowers, or a random card filled with love and admiration for Mum or, sometimes, an inside joke that neither Tom nor I understand. Mum will always make sure she gets Dad's favourite treats from the bakery for dessert, and runs him baths with scented bubbles, which he secretly loves.

Their over-the-top PDA used to make me cringe, but now it melts my heart. I hope that, whoever I end up with, we always take the time to be romantic with each other, just like my parents. They are my ultimate relationship goal.

I take a deep breath. I haven't been back to the shop since

before I left for Berlin, and my nerves are tingling. I take a moment to shake them off, then head into the shop.

Mum is finishing up a consultation with a bride. There are scraps of tulle and strands of pearls everywhere, and the bride is grinning from ear to ear. "I love all of these ideas, Dahlia—I can't believe it's only a few weeks away!"

"Time flies . . ." Mum catches sight of me in the doorway and her eyebrows rise in surprise. "Oh, Penny! You're here! Have you met Miss Young?"

I extend my hand. "Nice to meet you."

"It must be so nice to work surrounded by so many images of love and happiness all the time!" She disregards my hand and kisses me on both cheeks instead. I'm used to this from brides—they tend to be quite touchy-feely. Before I have time to say goodbye, she's out the door.

"Penny, it's so nice to see you here!" says Mum, squeezing me tightly into a hug.

I'll admit it: I've been avoiding the shop. There's probably no place anyone would want to go to less after a breakup than a wedding haven. All those symbols and images of love and happiness . . . Yeah, that's not exactly what I've needed.

But I'm surprised. I don't feel the urge to throw up while I'm in here. Maybe it's because I have a mission now. Mission: Get Alexiot Back Together.

"Darling, did you have a nice coffee with Alex? Is he OK? I can't imagine he's coping well. He walked past the shop earlier in the week and he looked terribly blue." Mum starts gathering up armfuls of tulle. "In emotion, I mean, not clothing." She winks at me. "Can you turn the sign on the door, sweetie? If another bride comes in here we won't have time for lunch! Now, I know it must be around here some-where . . ." She flings open one of the cupboards and starts rooting through it.

I flip the sign on the door to OUT TO LUNCH and sit down in one of the armchairs. "Alex is OK. Well . . . no, he's not OK. He's broken up about being broken up. But I'm proud of him—he told me he came out to his parents."

"Oh really, honey? That's wonderful news."

"It *is* wonderful. And he wants to share the moment with Elliot, but he's not taking Alex's calls. So Alex knows he's going to have to do something big—a *grand* gesture—if he wants to have a chance at winning Elliot back. So I thought I would come and ask you for help, since you are a woman of many ideas, most of which are usually grand—What are you doing?" I watch as Mum dives headfirst into a basket of shoes and handbags.

"I can't find my gold clutch bag at home so I thought maybe someone had brought it in. Do you remember? The one your brother got me for my forty-fifth birthday? I think I might have left a ten-pound note in it the last time I used it." Her legs are practically up in the air as she throws bags and shoes out of the basket and continues her frantic search.

"Of course . . ." I say, raising an eyebrow as I watch her from my seat by the window.

"Well, I *am* the queen of grand gestures, Penny, so you have come to the right place. What exactly is he thinking? AHA! HERE IT IS!" She stands up, her curly auburn hair all flipped over to one side of her head and her face a deep beetroot red. She puts the gold clutch bag down on the counter, then sits next to me.

"I'm not too sure. He wants it to be romantic. He's thinking of taking him to the pier or something, but Elliot isn't the biggest fan of the pier—too much bad fashion. I don't think he wants the soundtrack to their big moment to be the ringing of the 2p machines either. I just don't know where else there's such an amazing view of the sea at sunset. Alex doesn't exactly have a big budget . . ."

Mum claps her hands together and breathes in theatrically. "I know the *perfect* place! How about the bandstand? I've planned many wedding ceremonies and photo shoots there, so I've got a contact. I can sort that out for you. There's a sea view *and* privacy. Alex can have whatever soundtrack he wants! Elliot will love it."

This is the exact reason why my mum was the perfect person to ask. She knows anyone and everyone when it comes to planning parties.

"Sounds amazing! We can decorate it and make it look all Pinterest-perfect! That would be so great—thanks, Mum." I throw my arms round her and kiss her on the cheek. "Do you think we can make it happen for next Thursday?"

"That's soon . . . Let me see what I can do. But this is a *big* favour—maybe I can ask for something in return?"

"Of course! Anything!"

"Help me out here tomorrow? Jenny's still not feeling well and Saturdays are my busiest days . . ."

I hesitate, but only for a moment. I really am OK with being here in the shop. "Sure, Mum. That's fine."

She smiles at me. "It's so good to see you like this, Penny. You seem back to your normal self. Your dad and I have been so worried about you since . . . since you got back from

Paris. You know we both liked Noah very much, but also you do know you can talk to us any time, don't you?" She cups my face and kisses my nose.

"Yes, I know. I'm all right now. I wasn't before, but if it wasn't meant to be then I can't force it. It was so hard, and if it's *that hard*—"

"Then it's not right."

"Then it's not right. I think I just needed a bit of space in order to figure out what I really wanted, you know?" I rest my head on her shoulder and she brings me into a hug.

"You're a very strong young woman, P. You must get that from me . . ."

We both laugh, and I thank my lucky stars that I have such amazing and supportive parents who stand by me through everything.

I text Alex.

What about the bandstand?!?!

I love that idea!

Great! Next Thursday then?

The only piece of the puzzle left is the fact that I need to plan a distraction in order to have Elliot in the right place at the right time.

Alex has been brave.

Now it's my turn.

"Mum, can you grab our lunch while I send an email? It's an important one."

"Sure thing! I'll pop out to the deli and get us both some sandwiches. Sausage baguette with scrambled egg, like always?"

I nod, and start a new email on my phone.

From: Penny Porter
To: Miss Mills
Subject: Photography Showcase

Dear Miss Mills,

Thank you for your note about Noah. I'm sorry I didn't reply sooner—I've been living under a rock recently. I feel like I'm doing much better now, though. How are things going with the school showcase? Actually, I was wondering whether it was too late for me to join in? I'm trying to take steps to be brave, and I think this might be a good first step.

Yours,

Penny

Once I send off the email, I absentmindedly open my Twitter feed. I catch sight of a headline that's been retweeted by someone I follow—it's about Noah, but I'm pleased to notice that my heart doesn't twinge *quite* as much as it did even yesterday.

HAS NOAH FLYNN FOUND HIS SUMMER GIRL?

My heart might not twinge, but I still can't control my fingers. I click on the link, which leads to an article on a trashy gossip website called *Starry Eyes*. There's a dark, grainy picture of Noah and Blake walking out of a club somewhere in Europe. Blake is caught in the middle of his normal punching-the-air pose and Noah is just behind him. His face is half-hidden by shadow, but his mouth is downturned and he looks like he's frowning. There are two girls walking next to them, both with bright blonde hair. One looks like she is holding Noah's hand, but it might just be the angle of the photograph.

It is strange to see Noah not looking as fresh and happy as I thought he would. Seeing the girls doesn't make me angry, or even incredibly sad—I just feel empty.

The article continues.

> Will rising superstar Noah Flynn find another English rose when he's back on UK soil? Recently confirmed to be playing the PARK PARTY festival in London this weekend, Noah Flynn is set to rock the socks off the English capital. But will these lucky ladies spotted out with him and his band mates

in Stockholm be coming with him? Starry Eyes will have all
the gossip . . .

I decide to put myself out of my misery and quickly close
the browser window. Instead, I open Pinterest, and start
browsing ideas for decorating the bandstand. I scroll past
photographs of beautiful weddings and engagement photos
galore, but my heart isn't in it. Everything looks beautiful,
but also generic. If this is going to work for Elliot, it needs
to be personal.

My phone pings with an email. It's from Miss Mills.

From: Miss Mills
To: Penny Porter
Subject: RE: Photography showcase

I thought you'd never ask!

Of course you can still display your photographs in the showcase.
It would be an honour. Drop them off at the school when you can.

And I meant what I said, Penny: I'm proud of you.

Miss Mills

I can't believe I'm really doing it. I'm finally going to show
my photographs to the public.

★ ★ Chapter Fifty-One ★

I am knee-deep in leopard-print wallpaper.

It's my first day back in To Have and to Hold, fulfilling my promise to Mum, and I'm tackling my favourite task: the window display. There are two huge bay windows on either side of the door, and Mum always has a new theme to draw in customers.

Last week was an underwater theme with a mermaid-blue dress, lots of shells dangling from the ceiling, sand on the ground, and a tiara that was full of the most amazing blue and green gemstones.

This week, though, it's a safari theme: a completely new one for Mum! She definitely gets top marks for originality. The dress we are centring the theme on is lacy with a subtle zebra print on the underskirt. It's pretty, but not exactly my cup of tea.

I'm clearing out a giant seashell and replacing it with an oversized stuffed toy of a leopard (Mum found it at a car-boot sale and finally has a place to put it) when Alex walks in.

"Penny—What on earth is that?" Alex almost jumps out

of his skin as I spin round to greet him with the giant leopard under my arm.

"Don't ask. It's for our safari theme this week, and of course Mum has a life-sized stuffed leopard that would look perfect."

He laughs and grabs my hand, helping me out of the window. "I just dropped in to go through plans for Elliot's surprise. Everything OK?"

"All good! Mum confirmed this morning that the bandstand is free on Thursday night, so it's all systems go."

"He doesn't suspect anything, right? And you're OK to distract him for the evening? The sun doesn't set until later, so you'll need to make sure he doesn't go home early . . ."

"Stop worrying! He suspects nothing. He thinks he's going to the photography showcase to look after me, so he won't leave me. This will totally be the best surprise he could ever imagine. I can bring him to the bandstand at nine o'clock. I'm so excited. This could bring Alexiot back together and then the world will feel right again."

"I really hope so. But there is still a chance he could hate everything and never want to speak to me again."

I reach out and take Alex's hand. "We'll try to do everything possible to make sure that doesn't happen."

"Penny, that's just it—I think there's something missing. But it will involve asking you another huge favour, and I feel like I've asked too much of you already."

"No, please ask. This is the biggest thing in your life right now, and, if I can, I want to help you in whatever way possible. Unless you're asking me to rob a bank or something to pay for a giant diamond—"

"No, nothing quite like that!" He squirms awkwardly and beams at me, showing off all his teeth.

Now I'm starting to feel a bit nervous. What could Alex possibly want me to do that is making him go all awkward? I really hope he's not going to ask me to do a weird naked photo shoot of the two of them or something.

"You know how 'Elements' is my and Elliot's song? I just wanted to check that it would be OK for me to play it on some speakers at the bandstand? I know how you feel about Noah, and I know it could bring up a lot of pent-up emotions, so I just wanted to check . . ."

I feel a huge sense of relief that I'm not going to have to see Alex in his birthday suit. "Of course, that's fine." I smile, especially seeing my look of relief mirrored in Alex's face. It will mean a lot to Elliot, I know—it was the song that was playing when I took that photo of them.

"Elements" means so much to so many people. I've seen Noah play it so many times onstage and I've seen the effect that is has on the audience. It's the perfect song for anyone who is in love.

I let out a long sigh, and now it's Alex's turn to try to comfort me. "What about you, Penny? Is there no hope for you and Noah?"

I shrug. "I don't know. I really doubt it. We haven't spoken at all since we broke up."

"Well, you will never know if you don't *try* to speak to him. Even if things don't work out, you need closure."

He's right, of course. I have to speak to Noah at some point. I've tried to block out the reality for so long, but seeing Alex doing all this for Elliot is really pulling on my heartstrings. We may not be together, but maybe we could be friends?

But would he even want to talk to me now? He's doing a good job of respecting my last wish not to be contacted—too much of a good job. Maybe he's really angry at me for leaving. Does he still think I was making up the whole Blake thing? There are too many unanswered questions, and I'm not even sure I want to know the answers to them. But, if there was ever an occasion to be brave and bite the bullet by speaking to Noah, it is now, before he jets off on his World Tour and I lose the chance—maybe forever.

"I know. I found out recently he's going to be in London, so I can get in touch with him and maybe we can meet up and at least clear the air. It's not like we have to go from being in love to being in *hate*, is it?"

Alex leans over and kisses me on the cheek. "You can do this, Penny. I believe in you."

Back in my bedroom my fingers are hovering over the keypad on my phone, with an empty text-message screen. Why can't I find the words? *Oh, hey, Noah, remember me? That girl who left you in Paris during your tour. The one you wrote that song for . . .*

I bury my head in my pillow and let out a frustrated whine. *WHY IS THIS SO HARD?* I'm absolutely terrified that the wounds, which are just starting to heal since I left Paris, are all going to rip open again once I send this text. What if Noah responds like Elliot and doesn't reply? But I can't ignore this forever. If I don't try, then I'll never know. Noah was—*is*—so special to me, and we have to talk at some point. I can't keep putting it off.

> Noah, I know it's been a couple of weeks, and it's been hard not contacting you. I heard you were going to be in London, so I thought maybe we could talk? It might be too much to ask, but I have to try. Can we be friends? Penny x

I put my phone down on the bedside table, almost expecting there to be no reply, when it lights up instantly. It's from Noah.

> I want to talk to you too. Come and meet me at the festival tomorrow, if you can. I'll get you a ticket—and one for a friend so you don't have to come alone. I miss you. N

My heart skips a beat at the end of the text. *He misses me.* Has he really been waiting for me to contact him? My flood of feelings for Noah comes pouring back and I instantly feel my face flush.

I remember us dancing in the crowd like complete fools while The Sketch played; I'm remembering his little kisses on the end of my nose, the nights he would text me from his room to say he wished he was cuddling up with me instead, and the way he would dart me a glance in the wings as he sang "Autumn Girl" to a stadium of people. The wonderful memories I've been trying to lock away are quickly replacing the angry, frustrated ones that have been helping me through the last few weeks.

I try to push the happy memories away, because I know if I let those feelings in I'll fall completely head over heels back in love with him. What if he does just want to be friends? I'm totally doing an Elliot and wanting to close up and never talk about my emotions, but it's just making me more and more confused about what I actually want.

OK, I think I can do that. P x

I hit send. I've done a lot of nerve-racking and ridiculous things over the past year, but, for some reason, the thought of talking to Noah again fills me with the biggest nerves of all.

Chapter Fifty-Two

I'm up at the crack of dawn, and I can't believe I'm back to this—not being able to sleep, not letting my mind rest.

I've been a jittery, vibrating bundle of nerves all night. I can't wrap my head round the fact that I will be seeing Noah today. It may have only been a couple of weeks, but it feels like a lifetime. I've paced back and forth so many times that Dad has already popped his head in to check I'm not going crazy.

I've also chewed my fingernails down to the quick, but that's for a different reason. Noah was right when he said that I wouldn't—*couldn't*—go to the festival alone. My initial instinct of course was to take Elliot, but he's already agreed to go to Bath with his parents for a historical tour (an attempt by them to cheer him up). Besides, he would have asked way too many questions as to why I decided to go and talk to Noah *now*, and that would have brought up Alex and the surprise. So, in a way, it's better not to ask Elliot at all. I feel a little like I am cheating on him by being so sneaky behind his back, but I know it's all for a good cause.

Then I tried to invite Kira, but she is already going to the festival with Amara. They booked their tickets months ago because they are huge fans of The Halo Pixies, an a cappella girl band based in Sweden that is also playing.

I was comforted when I knew the twins would be going too, so I bit the bullet and invited Megan. Her messages to me since Noah and I broke up have been nothing but sweet, plus part of me wants to figure out the mystery behind TheRealTruth. There haven't been any more emails or letters since Noah and I split up so I chose not to go to the police in the end. Maybe if I spend a whole day with Megan, I'll be able to reassure myself that she wasn't behind all those nasty threats.

I really hope she wasn't—I'm just starting to feel as though the Megan I grew up with is making more and more of a reappearance. She's going to her drama school in September, and a part of me will even miss her. I won't miss her ending all my sentences or wanting to be the centre of attention at every given opportunity, but I will miss little things like her always being there to meet me after English so we can walk to lunch together and her sarcastic sense of humour.

So, now, she's here in my room, perched on my desk chair and looking at me with a slightly concerned expression.

"Penny, I know you said you're fine, but I'm starting to think you might be lying. I've been counting how many times you've paced back and forth and I'm up to fifty-six already. That's far too much exercise for one day, let alone when you're feeling stressed and anxious." She looks down at her nails and traces the little daisy transfer that she has on her thumb.

"Megan, are you sure I look OK? No, not *just* OK. Do I look *really* OK?" I scan myself in my full-length mirror and stand up on my tiptoes.

"As long as you stand like a normal person, you look great. I mean, it's not exactly what I would have chosen . . ."

I've gone for a black skater dress with a bright-red poppy print, paired with my little black ankle boots—because we are going to a festival after all! My hair is down and tousled and I have a pair of aviator sunglasses perched on my head.

"Where did you get all this makeup anyway? It's awesome!" Megan picks up my pot of NARS foundation and a gold bronzing palette.

It's all the stuff I got from Leah at Sephora. "Oh . . . a friend helped me pick them out. To be honest, I don't know what half of it does."

"Well, if you ever want to donate any of it to a worthy home—"

"I know where to find you." I finish her sentence.

When it's time to leave, we hop into a taxi that takes us straight to Brighton Station, where we meet up with Kira and Amara. We all buy smoothies from Marks & Spencer, then jump on the train to London. Surprisingly, we're able to get a table seat. It's really nice being with all three of them, like old times. It's refreshing to have friends I can just talk to about normal stuff—discussing boys from school, Year Eleven dramas, and what we are all going to do now we are venturing into kind of serious, grown-up territory.

"Do you think Blake will be there today?" Megan looks at me from across the table and does a strange winky face.

"Um . . . as in Noah's drummer?" Just hearing her say his name makes my skin crawl.

"Yeah, he's really hot. I might stand a little bit of a chance there, especially since you can introduce me again." She smiles and laughs.

"Yeah, of course I can, but . . . he's not good news, Meg. He's more of a bad boy."

"PENNY! I sometimes wonder if you know me at all!" She laughs again, but this time a lot more loudly. "You know I love a bad boy. They're always far more interesting. You will introduce me again, won't you?" Her tone changes slightly towards the end of her sentence and I feel the old Megan could be rising inside her like a demon.

"No, really, Megan. Blake came on to me when we were in Paris. He tried to kiss me but I managed to get away before it got too far."

I can see the confusion on Megan's face—and the insecure voice in my brain says it's because she also can't believe Blake would go for someone like me. But then Kira speaks up. "Seriously? That's awful, Penny!"

"Is that why you and Noah broke up?" Megan asks.

"Sort of . . ." I say.

"I can't believe he broke up with *you* and didn't dump that greasy hanger-on of a friend," says Megan. She's obviously decided to turn on Mega-Bitch mode towards Blake, and I couldn't be more grateful. "Noah better apologize today. You're way too good for him."

"That's so true," says Amara. "No guy is worth you if he won't stand up for you!"

I can't help the blush spreading across my cheeks. I've

never been more happy to have such great girlfriends by my side.

A voice comes over the train PA system, letting us know that we are minutes from London Victoria.

"I'm *so* excited to get there!" says Kira. "This festival is supposed to be awesome. What time are we heading back later?"

"I don't know," says Amara, "but The Halo Pixies aren't on until five."

"I probably won't stay for the whole day, guys. I'm just going to find Noah and then come back home," I say, watching the world speed by outside of the train window. I know that the conversation with Noah is going to be enough to send me into an exhaustion coma. "I don't think I can stand to be at the festival for very long. Crowds aren't really my thing, remember? Shall we meet to say goodbye at three, after I've spoken with Noah?" I look down at my phone. That definitely gives me enough time to get out of there before he takes to the stage.

"Sure thing!" Kira says, smiling widely. "Maybe we can go get waffles? I had the best food last time I was there."

"I heard they have a pop-up blow-dry bar!" says Megan. "Maybe we can get our hair done before we see the boys?"

I tug at my hair, which hasn't seen much styling since I left Paris. It certainly doesn't have the beautiful sheen that Leah Brown's stylists managed to get into it. But I'm not going to waste any time faffing around—I just want to see Noah, get out, and go.

My phone buzzes with a text.

The tickets are waiting for you at the east gate, under your name. See you soon—come to the VIP area to the left of the main stage and Larry will find you when you arrive. N

Suddenly the swarm of butterflies in my stomach that has been lying dormant the whole train journey wakes up in a complete frenzy. The train pulls into Victoria Station and I prepare to be face-to-face with Noah once again.

Chapter Fifty-Three

We stop just outside the east gate of Hyde Park, and wait in line to pick up my and Megan's tickets. Thankfully they are behind the desk, just as Noah said.

As we walk through the gates of the park, I'm amazed by how big—and busy—it is. I'm grateful that Kira and Amara squeeze me tightly between them, making a Penny sandwich and protecting me from the crowds.

I can hear the tinny blast of music rising from the stage, which is still quite far away from us. Food trucks and stalls selling band T-shirts and feather headbands line both sides of the path that leads through to the main stage. It's chaotic and frenzied and basically exactly the kind of atmosphere that I dislike. I wish Noah and I could have arranged to meet somewhere outside the festival. Why didn't I just meet him at his hotel? Or at the airport? Or anywhere other than here?

As we near the main stage, Kira and Amara head over to the blow-dry bar, but Megan sticks to my side like glue.

"Do you know where you need to go?" Megan looks over at me.

I pull out my phone. "Noah said that the VIP area is to the left of the stage, and that Larry should be there to meet us."

Megan is playing with her waterfall braid, trying to make sure that every strand is perfect. "Who's Larry? Is he another band member?" She pulls out a tube of pink lip gloss and reapplies it for the millionth time.

I laugh. "No. *That's* Larry." I point as Larry's lumbering, imposing form strides across the park to meet us. He parts crowds of people as if his bald head is the sparking prow of a ship cutting through the waves. He spots me and a grin breaks out on his face—equally as big as the grin that's on mine.

Megan almost stops in her tracks, but I run over to Larry and embrace him in a big hug.

"Penny! So good to see you."

"You too, Larry. This is my friend Megan," I say, gesturing to her even though she's gone completely quiet. "Larry is Noah's security on set."

"I'm glad I found you in this crazy crowd. Come on, I have strict instructions to make sure you don't get lost."

With Larry as our guide, I feel so much safer. He leads us round to a nondescript fence, where a man is slumped in a chair. It's an inconspicuous entrance to the backstage area, but then I guess if you put up a lit-up sign saying MUSICIANS HERE then you'd be asking for trouble.

Once we pass through the gate, Larry hands us our backstage passes, and Megan's face lights up when she sees hers.

"Will you be all right here on your own for a bit, Megan, while I go and see Noah?" It's a stupid question, as she's dashed off almost before I've finished the question.

"Noah will be free in about five minutes," Larry says.

I take a deep breath.

"Are you OK, Penny?" Larry looks at me, a concerned frown on his face.

"I'll be fine, Larry," I say, trying to sound braver than I feel. "I just have to get this over with."

He nods. "I'm glad I have a moment to talk to you. Is this yours?" He takes something out of his pocket, and I recognize it immediately: it's my phone. It still has the bright pink cover on it, with the stars that Noah drew in Sharpie round the edges.

"Oh my god, where did you find this?" I turn it over and over in my hand, staring at it like it's a foreign object.

"I found it in Dean's room."

"In Dean's room? Why would Dean have it?"

Larry nods. His face is more serious than I have ever seen it; he looks more like a bodyguard than ever before. This is not the fun, happy Larry that I'm used to.

"Do you think someone could have put it there? A . . . crazy fan or something? My photos were stolen from this phone—the ones that someone used to threaten me and my friends."

"I know, Penny. I think Dean has had this the entire time."

"Oh," I say, my voice sounding small. If that's true then that means . . .

I don't have time to dwell on it, as I hear Noah shout my name. I want to tell him my theory about the phone straightaway. But the last time I saw him all I did was accuse and argue; and I know I need to hear him out first. I slip it into my handbag, knowing I will come back to it later.

My heart is pounding at a million beats per minute. This is it: everything I've been imagining and building up in my head is about to be played out in real life. I need to keep calm and stay cool.

He walks over to us, and I want to run up to him, the same way I did to Larry, and give him a hug, but my feet are rooted to the floor. His are too, and he stops a few steps away from me.

"Well, I'll leave you kids to it," says Larry. "But, Penny, when you're done, come find me and I'll make sure you get home safely."

"Thanks, Larry. You're the best," I say.

Noah smiles at me, but there's something tentative in it. "Hey. Should we go somewhere a little more private to talk? There's nobody on the tour bus right now so we could go there."

I nod. Noah seems like a dulled-down version of himself. He is smiling, but I feel like there isn't a lot of life behind his eyes, which are normally so bright and sparkly. We walk in a strange, uncomfortable silence over to the bus. I don't like this. I don't like that we're not able to talk. It's not us at all. I hope that once we get onto the bus the atmosphere will change.

Noah asks me to take a seat on the sofa—it's the same place I sat down with Blake at the start of the tour. Noah sits next to me and places his outstretched hands on the small coffee table. He looks out of the window, where it's just about possible to make out a small gap in the fence and see the festival happening outside.

He smiles. "So . . ."

"So . . ." I smile back. "How have you been?"

Noah shakes his head. "I can't go through all this small talk. I just wanna cut to the chase."

I nod.

"So, I guess my first question is: Why did you leave like that? Why didn't you come and say goodbye properly?"

I feel a tightness grip my throat as I realize this conversation has very quickly become serious. I curse inwardly at his American straightforwardness, but this is what I came for, after all. "It was too hard to say goodbye to you face-to-face. When I'm with you, it's hard to be annoyed or frustrated or sad. I thought we were over. Accusing me of lying about Blake was so wrong, Noah. The fact that you would even think I could make something like that up, just for your attention . . . I was devastated."

I look at his face, but I can't quite look him in the eye. *Keep it together, Penny. Keep it together.*

"You're right, Penny: it *was* wrong of me. I should have spoken to you properly and I should have listened to you. That's one of the reasons I asked you to come here when you got in touch. And why I've asked for someone to join us . . ." He looks up above my shoulder and nods to someone standing behind me. I whip my head round and my breath catches as I see Blake standing at the top of the bus stairs.

"Hey, Penny," he says, and his voice has lost some of its normal snarky edge.

"Oh, um . . . hi, Blake," I say, crossing my arms over my chest.

"Look, when Noah said you were coming here, I asked him if I could see you because I wanted to apologize for that night in Paris. Honestly, I know it was wrong, and I know it won't make any difference to you what I say or change what I did, but I mean it: I was drunk and out of line."

"Blake—"

"Wait—that's not all. Afterwards, I panicked. Even though I knew I was in the wrong, I didn't want Noah to kick me off the tour. I didn't want to lose my job or my friend, so I told him you'd come on to me. I thought you guys would work it out—I just . . . I wasn't thinking."

I am completely speechless, and my throat feels numb. "Seriously?"

"I know; it was so stupid."

I've never been able to trust Blake, but I feel like maybe this time he's telling the truth. Still, I can't forgive him that easily.

Noah catches my eye. "He told me the truth when he was drunk in Stockholm. Honestly, Penny, I was so angry . . . but when he was sober we talked, a lot. Blake recognizes he has a real problem. So he's going home to deal with it."

"It's true," Blake says. "I'm not going on the World Tour with Noah. Tour life isn't good for me."

Blake stares at me for a few moments, his eyes pleading. I know he wants me to give some sign that I'm accepting his apology, but I can't give it to him. I swallow hard before replying. "Wow. Well, I hope you get the help you need."

Blake nods. "I know I'm a long way from forgiveness from both of you but . . . maybe one day?" He looks so hopeful, but deep down I know it's not enough yet. The hurt is just too raw.

"To be honest, I'm not sure. What you did really upset me, Blake. But I do appreciate your apology."

"You've said your piece now. You can go," says Noah, his voice cold and hard.

"See you around."

When he's gone from the bus, I turn back to Noah. "Wow . . . I wasn't expecting that. Thank you." My heart aches for him. I know that Noah will miss his best friend— even despite what he did—and I hope that Blake really does get the help he needs so that he can repair the relationships he's damaged.

"And now it's my turn again. When Blake told me that, I wanted to get in touch straightaway—"

"Why didn't you?" I look him in the eyes, and I feel a huge thud in my chest.

"Because you asked to be left alone . . . and I knew it was more than just the Blake stuff." Noah flicks his wavy brown hair back from his face and rests his head in his hands. "I didn't want to make you even angrier, or to make the situation worse. The minute you texted me, I had to reply. It was so hard for me not to contact you, but I also wanted to respect what you asked for. I've hated not having you on the tour."

Noah's words are like music to my ears. All the questions that have been circling in my mind—*Did he miss me? Did he believe me? Was he refusing to call because he hated me?*—I now have the answers to. I feel a sense of reassurance and calm come over me.

"Thank you for respecting my wishes, but it still hurt not to hear from you. I guess I thought you would try anyway. But, in the end, I wasn't ready until now."

"Do you . . . do you think there's any way for us to make this work?" Noah looks up at me, and my heart reaches out to him. But my head stays in charge. "I don't know, Noah. What happened with Blake was the last straw, but there were other things too. I just don't think I'm cut out to be on the road either. I still need to figure out what I want to do with *my* life, and I don't think I can do that if I'm just tagging along with you." It's one of the hardest things I've ever said, but I feel completely relieved.

Noah sighs. "You're the best thing that's ever happened to me, Penny. But my music is my passion and my life. I don't want to have to choose between you."

I reach out and grab his hand. "No, you absolutely do not have to choose between us. I've seen you onstage, Noah— it is where you're in your element. You should never give that up. But you have to give me time. Time to just . . . figure out who I am."

There's a long pause that seems to stretch out into eternity, but he doesn't let go of my hand. "I'm going to miss you, Penny. Every day."

"Me too," I say.

He lifts my hand and kisses my knuckles. It takes every ounce of my willpower not to throw my arms round him and tell him that we can be together no matter what. But I know that I would still be miserable on tour, that Noah needs this time to cement his success, and that I need this time to figure my life out.

"What made you change your mind?" he asks.

"What do you mean?"

"Why did you get in touch now? Was it just because I was coming to the UK? I would have flown back from wherever I was to see you—you should have known that."

I shake my head. "No, it wasn't that. It was Alex. I didn't tell you this, but Elliot and Alex broke up too."

"No way!" Noah's jaw drops. "You've got to be kidding me. Those two were perfect."

"I thought so too. But TheRealTruth's message really shook Alex up, and he ran away from the relationship. Now, though, he's come out to his whole family and it's so great for him—he wants to share that with Elliot and win him back. We've got this whole surprise set up for Thursday night at the bandstand in Brighton. We're even going to play one of your songs—you know how much they love 'Elements.'"

Noah squeezes my hand, and I feel a spark of electricity between us. But, before anything can catch light, he gets up from the sofa. "I've really got to go, Penny. My set is about to start. But, please, feel free to stay on the bus for a bit if you don't need to leave yet . . . I'd love to see you after the show too."

I shake my head. "I'm going to go. I'm meeting my friends."

"So this is goodbye?" Noah says.

"I . . . I guess so."

We hug each other like we should have done in Paris. His arms envelop me, and I throw my hands round his waist, burying my face into the side of his neck, breathing in his scent. The hug lasts longer than it should, neither of us wanting to let go. Then he pulls away. For a moment, our lips are so close that, with just the tiniest movement, we could kiss and this whole breakup would be forgotten.

Instead we break apart even further, and I watch as he disappears down the stairs and out through the front door of the bus.

Chapter Fifty-Four

I can't face heading back outside just yet, so I take Noah's suggestion and sit on the bus for a while, staring at everything around me. I need to drink it in because this is likely to be the last time I will ever get to experience it.

The musky scent of boys' aftershave hangs in the air, and there's a row of small stickers from apples underneath one of the windows—leftovers from the hungry crew. Xbox games are sprawled across the table in front of me, reminding me of Blake—but I'm glad to note that the twinge of disgust that previously accompanied any thoughts of him is a little bit less prominent than before. I look down towards the back of the bus—past lines of empty beer bottles and the beginnings of a mosaic someone's started to make with the empty bottle caps—and I spot Noah's old hoodie. It's hanging limply on a hook, the white strings looking frayed and slightly grey. It is the very hoodie that he draped over me when we had our picnic up on the roof of the Waldorf Astoria back in December. The same one he left for me in the care package in Rome.

I suddenly remember how that felt, having him place it over my arms to keep me warm. I felt protected, safe—a feeling I haven't felt for so long, not since the car accident that triggered my anxiety in the first place. I walk over to the hoodie and hold it up close to my chest, breathing in the faded scent of Noah's aftershave.

I don't know whether I feel happy or sad. All I can think about is how badly I want Noah to wrap the hoodie round me again, to hold my hand and tell me everything will be OK, that the World Tour is cancelled and that he's just going to spend the rest of his life with me in Brighton, where we'll walk our puppy on the beach on a Wednesday evening and do yoga together on the lawn every morning.

But that's just a dream.

While my emotions battle with each other, I realize that standing alone in Noah's tour bus, sniffing his hoodie, might look very bizarre if someone were to walk in, so I throw it back on the hook and walk towards the door. I stop in my tracks when I hear voices just outside the bus door. One is a very loud, commanding voice that I recognize as Dean's.

I tiptoe towards the front of the bus and peer out over the stairs. Dean's leaning casually against the door, talking to two men in blazers and coloured chinos with lanyards round their necks. There is an equally loud voice in my head telling me that eavesdropping is a silly idea—especially as the last time I did this it ended in tears. But then I hear Dean mention my name and I can't help but listen.

"Noah and Penny are finished, donezo. Look, all I'm saying is that Ella Parish would be amazing for Noah's career.

She's up-and-coming; she looks great. The pair of them would cause a media frenzy."

If someone had taken a picture of me at that very moment, I would have looked like one of those cartoon characters where steam starts billowing out of their ears and nose and their faces turn red in anger.

"I mean, if that's what Noah wants, then we can certainly start the wheels in motion with Ella. Can we get on to Lorraine about that ASAP, Collin?" One of the blazers turns to the other and then smiles back at Dean. It takes absolutely every ounce of self-control in my body to remain calm and not leave this bus kicking and screaming about what an awful plan that is.

"Good, then it's settled." Dean extends his hand, and the men shake on it. "We can arrange some paps to catch them in Australia. Maybe holding hands on the beach?"

I can't listen any more. Another fake relationship? How could Dean think that is a good idea? Noah would never want Dean to do this, especially not after what happened with Leah.

Then I remember the phone, now in my bag, and my red-hot rage boils over. Suddenly things begin clicking together. Has Dean been responsible for this all along? Noah was told that it was Leah Brown's management who insisted on their fake relationship, but, thinking about it now, what would she have ever gained from that? It's Noah who needed the boost. It's Noah whose career needed the lift. And it's Dean who is making *all* the decisions about Noah's career.

The talking stops and I hear footsteps coming up the tour-bus stairs. My heart leaps in my chest and I look around for somewhere to hide, but it's too late. Dean comes bounding onto the tour bus, a huge grin on his face.

The grin fades and he curses loudly and clutches at his chest when he sees me standing there. "Penny, what are you doing in here? You nearly gave me a heart attack." He laughs weakly. We both stand there, staring at each other, until he realizes I'm not smiling back.

I can see the understanding dawn on his face and he turns a slight shade of grey. Anger is rising up inside me like lava in a volcano, but the calm voice of Ocean Strong comes out instead.

"Have you always been this much of an idiot, Dean?"

"So, you heard me outside? You're not going to mess this up for Noah, are you, Penny?"

"*I'll* mess things up? It seems like you're doing that perfectly well for him on your own! I mean, what exactly do you think you're doing? Do you want to see Noah succeed because he's so incredibly talented, or do you want to ruin everything he has that isn't his music career by staging fake relationships and destroying his real ones?"

Suddenly I feel like the most powerful person on this planet. I feel tall, confident, and in control. I'm loud, concise, and clear, and I stare at Dean as his face warps and his confidence shrinks. He mutters something and I don't quite hear him so I raise an eyebrow and he repeats himself.

"I don't know what you mean—you're crazy. I think you need to run home, back to Mummy and Daddy." He shrugs, trying to move past me to get whatever it was he came in for.

I move in front of him so he can't. He looks at me and then abruptly his face changes. He doesn't look weak and scared anymore; he looks angry. I keep my confident posture and continue to stare at him, but inside I'm freaking out.

"Get out of my way, Penny."

"Not before you answer my questions." I dig around in my bag and bring out my old phone. "You've had this the whole time, haven't you? Larry gave it to me earlier—he found it in *your* room."

"And so what if I did?"

I swallow hard, trying to hold my nerve. "Tell me honestly: are you TheRealTruth?" My voice is shaking now. He laughs and, at first, I think he's going to deny that he has anything to do with it, but he doesn't. Instead, he starts clapping.

"You got it. Someone handed your phone in to security and it made its way to me. I thought all my Christmases had come at once. I thought that with a couple of messages you'd be scared off straightaway, but I'll give you credit—you had more guts than I anticipated."

Everything is still so confused in my brain; I can't make sense of it all. "But . . . why? Why did you visit my house and convince my parents to let me come on the tour if you didn't even want me there? Why not just refuse?"

"What, and just make Noah want you even more? Come on, Penny." He rolls his eyes. "This way I could *show* him just how unsuited you are for this life. It was bad enough when Noah went rogue at Christmas—I thought this whole tour would be off, all our hard work down the drain. But then he went and met you: sweet, adorable, *normal* girl Penny Porter. For a while, it worked for Noah's story. Made the girls love him. But now you've run your course." He walks past me and sits down on the sofa and leans over to open the mini fridge.

He cracks open a beer and leans back, now brimming with self-confidence. I turn and watch him, but edge slightly closer to the door as I do.

"So you thought the best solution was to blackmail me?" I say, trying hard to control my anger. "How old are you, *twelve*? You don't see Noah—you see dollar signs. And why did you have to drag my friends into it? They had nothing to do with me and Noah."

He takes a sip of beer and smacks his lips together, before grinning wide like the Joker from *Batman*. "Finally made you leave, though, didn't it? When the text message and emails didn't work, I thought taking Noah away might. It was so easy to add in meetings, make him busy, unable to have your silly mystery days—and, even though he treated you badly, you *still* stuck around. Then we had that conversation on the bus and it clicked with the pictures I'd downloaded from your phone. I finally knew how to get rid of you. *Poor friends all broken up, so Penny has to go back home to save the day.* It was perfect.

"Look, you're a sweet girl, but what else do you have to offer? You're a kid. You need to go back to playing with your dolls, or I dunno . . . making daisy chains in the field with your friends. Just leave Noah to do what he does best: play his music, make his millions, and become the global superstar he's destined to be. He doesn't need you for a distraction. You're not good for his brand. I'm just being a good manager.

"Let's face it: the only good thing to come from him meeting you was his bestselling song 'Autumn Girl.' And I'm afraid that's where this fairy tale ends."

Chapter Fifty-Five

It feels like I've forgotten how to breathe. I feel the anger swirling around inside me like a tornado as I watch Dean sipping from his beer, smirking. But, before I can think of something to say to him, there's a noise from behind me and I see Dean jump to his feet, knocking his beer over on the table.

"So, *this* is what a good manager does, is it, Dean?" I turn and see Noah standing behind me, his eyes narrowed.

As he strides past me towards Dean, he brushes his hand over my lower back and I know that Noah is going to fight in my corner.

"Noah, I don't know what you heard but—" Dean stands with his arms in the air as Noah approaches him.

My feet are rooted to the floor—I couldn't move even if I wanted to.

"I heard everything, Dean. The whole conversation. What the hell is wrong with you? I trusted you." He looks away, his nose wrinkled in disgust. "I can't even bear to look at you. The way you just spoke to Penny made me feel physically sick."

Noah looks over at me, and then back at Dean. I can see the muscles in his arms and neck tensing, his breath heavy. I don't think I've ever seen Noah this angry before, but it isn't just anger; it's hurt. He's been through so much—from dealing with the death of his parents, to being away from Sadie Lee and Bella—and all the while trusting Dean with his career and to do what is best for him.

"Noah, please, let me explain." Dean grabs his arm, but Noah shakes him off.

"Just get out. I don't want to work with you or see your face ever again. You're fired." Noah looks at the floor now, as the spilt beer drips on Dean's suit trousers and shiny leather shoes.

Dean opens his mouth to say something but nothing comes out. Instead, he barges past Noah, knocking him off balance slightly. He then walks past me and gives me a hateful glare.

We both watch in silence, through the window, as Dean marches out of the VIP area and into the crowds of festival-goers. Suddenly he doesn't look so important; he looks like a selfish man with nothing going for him.

Noah stands and stares. I reach forward and hold his hand. Without saying anything, he clutches it tightly. We stand for a moment until he lets go and flops down on the sofa. He deflates like a balloon, letting out a long sigh. He drops his head into his hands, his hair cascading through his fingers.

"What do I do now? Dean is the only manager I've ever had. Clearly he was terrible, but he organized all this. The tour . . . everything." Noah looks around the bus with a worried expression, and I can tell he's picturing everything crumbling in front of his eyes.

I sit down next to him and place my hand on his knee, which is poking out through a rip in his jeans.

"It's not Dean who got you here—it's you. Everything he did was a step in the wrong direction anyway. You need new management, someone who's going to *actually* have your best interests at heart and help you to grow as both a recording artist *and* a person." He turns to me and smiles, his dimples appearing like magic.

"How is it that you always know what to say, Penny? You're very wise, you know."

My stomach flips as his eyes meet mine. Like a magnet, I feel completely connected to Noah. It's like the tension that was left over after our latest goodbye has been carried off with Dean and his beer-stained shoes. I suddenly get the urge to kiss Noah, but I don't. Instead, I think about how I can actually help this situation that he's in.

"Wait—Leah gave me the number for someone in her management team a while back. She said that if I ever needed her urgently I'd be able to get to her through this woman. I think her name was Fenella. Maybe give her a call? If they can't sign you, they can maybe at least give you advice?"

I whip out my phone and transfer the number across to his.

"Thanks, Penny," Noah says. "I seriously don't know what I am going to do without you." He jumps up. "I'm due onstage! I only came back to grab some posters that I'd signed for these competition winners. I'm going to have to go, but, even if you still don't want to stick around, can I call you?"

"Sure," I say.

I watch Noah hurry off the bus, and I feel happy that things might have finally worked out for the best. I grab my bag and head off to find Megan, smiling to myself as I wonder exactly how much trouble she's got herself into.

Chapter Fifty-Six

The pop-up gallery for our school showcase looks amazing.

The school has taken over one of the small, cute stores tucked away in the Lanes for the exhibition. With the sun streaming through the big windows onto the whitewashed walls and blue tiles, it almost feels like we've been transported to some far-off Greek island. Our photography-exam work is displayed on the walls, hung off rustic wooden planks, and it looks gorgeous.

To my surprise, when I arrive the tiny place is absolutely packed. There is even someone handing out drinks and canapés. In the midst of planning the surprise for Elliot, I had *almost* forgotten that tonight also meant my photography was going to be on display. I'd always been dead against the idea of showing off my work, thinking it would be an awful trigger for my anxiety. However, Leah helping me to believe that my photography could turn into something more than a hobby—a real profession—was an eye-opener, but it's also something that could never happen if I didn't show any of my work in public.

"I'm really proud of you, Pen-face. These are incredible." Elliot and I stand side by side. As he sips his sparkling orange juice, he wraps an arm round me. I feel my face blush crimson as he studies the photos. Elliot has always been my biggest cheerleader, and for that I love him very much.

"Thanks, Wiki." I squeeze him into my side by pulling on his waist and we just stand together, connected by a sideways hug, looking at all my photographs displayed on a wall alongside the work of my other talented classmates.

"I have to say, I *especially* like this one," Elliot says with a wink.

Of course he does, because it features him. It's a silhouette of him standing outside the Royal Pavilion in Brighton, the domes lit up orange in front of a darkening sky. It was for a series of pictures I called *Local*, about special areas of Brighton that are close to my heart.

"How is everything with Noah? Have you spoken since the weekend?" He lowers his voice and draws me into a quieter corner. "I'm sorry I couldn't come with you to the festival, but it was good for me to have some time with my parents. Now *there's* a sentence I never thought I'd say."

I shake my head. "No, we haven't spoken, but we've texted. He's busy sorting out everything to do with Dean. I don't know what's going to happen with us. There are no hard feelings there and we both seem happy. I'm a bit scared that if we really make a go of this again—properly—it will hurt more than ever and I'll turn into one of those crazy, jealous stalker girlfriends while my famous boyfriend goes on tour. It takes up a lot of headspace . . ." I bite my nails and let out a huge sigh.

"I know what you mean. His life is about to get a lot crazier. But you know, Penny, he was very lucky to have you. I can't believe his manager was the creepy stalker after all!"

"I know," I say—I'm still stunned by the revelation.

"Maybe it's like murderers—you should always look at the people closest to the victim first."

"Well, he's in good hands now." Leah's manager had been all too happy to help when Noah called. "I'm so glad that it's working out for him."

"It's not just all about him, you know, Penny. Yes, he is extremely cute and plays the guitar like an absolute god and sings like an angel, but you are really very special too"—he raises an eyebrow—"in your own weird way."

We laugh together and I notice Miss Mills approaching us. She's made a real effort today, tying her hair up in a really chic chignon and wearing a stunning LBD. I'm always impressed at how normal teachers look outside of school. It's easy to forget that they have lives beyond the hallways and the classrooms.

"Penny, I was worried you wouldn't show! Don't your photos just look so stunning like this? I'm so proud of all my students. And you must be Elliot—or should I say Wiki?" She extends a hand to Elliot and he holds it and curtseys.

"A pleasure to meet you," he says as he dips on his heel, smiling in the cheeky way he does. Miss Mills giggles and Elliot slides off to look at other people's work and to follow the tray of pizza canapés that are rapidly disappearing.

"How has your summer been?" asks Miss Mills. "Have you been OK, anxiety-wise?"

I can imagine so many students would reel with

embarrassment at the thought of their teacher knowing so much about their personal lives, but when Miss Mills talks to me it's like we're best friends and I instantly feel at ease.

"It's been the most challenging summer I think I've ever had—a total emotional roller coaster! But now I feel the most *me* I've felt in a really long time. I feel like I've discovered a lot about myself—maybe in the hardest way possible, but it's definitely been an experience and I wouldn't change it."

She gives me one of those smiles that is both warm and a little sympathetic. "They say everything happens for a reason."

"And for the first time I am starting to think that might actually be true. I know that anxiety is a part of my life, and maybe in time I can change that, but for now I want to live a full life. I have anxiety, but it's not who I am."

"This is the best thing I've ever heard you say, Penny. I want to see you succeed in everything you do, and I don't want you to feel like there is anything in your way. There are people out there who could learn a lot from the things you write about, and even the photos you take." She points at my photography display and gives me a huge, beaming smile.

"I think I might make my blog public again . . ." The words slip out of my mouth before I've even thought about them. This must be what it's like to be Elliot—always speaking without thinking first.

I watch as Miss Mills's face fills with excitement, and she starts jumping up and down, clapping her hands with glee. I try to shush her so that everyone else enjoying the gallery doesn't turn and stare, but Elliot has already noticed and scuttles over.

"What's going on here? Give me the good news." He sidles up and looks between the two of us, trying to read our faces.

"Penny is going to blog again, publicly!" She claps her hands together.

"That's *awesome* news, Pen!" he says, giving me a huge hug. "I bet *Girl Online*'s fans have missed reading your posts."

I smile before I sneak a quick look at my watch and realize we still have an hour before Alex will be ready for us, and we can't stay here much longer as the party is starting to wind down.

"You know what—I could write a blog now. I know somewhere with free Wi-Fi *and* that's open late for coffee and cake."

"Seriously?"

"Yeah!" I say. "I have my laptop in my bag. I'll buy you a slice of cake if you come?"

"Well, you know I never say no to good cake! Come on then, you eager little writer."

We say goodbye to Miss Mills and head towards a little café in the Lanes that is still open and serving sparkling elderflower (Elliot's favourite on a summer evening) and delicious thick slabs of carrot cake covered in cream-cheese frosting. We sit outside since it's such a warm evening, choosing a bench underneath a canopy of coloured fairy lights. I pull my laptop out of my bag and start typing a blog post that's been brewing for some time.

Elliot is scrolling through his phone as I type. He lets out a long sigh and I look up at him sharply. "Are you OK, E?"

"Oh, don't mind me. I'm just looking at pictures of Alex. Look at this—have you ever seen anyone more adorable?"

He turns the phone round and shows me a picture of Alex sitting on a fallen log in the New Forest. He's smiling up at the camera, clearly looking at Elliot with so much love and affection. It's a look I know well, because it's the way Noah used to look at me.

"Maybe I should call him? Seeing how you and Noah managed to patch things up and be friends again makes me feel like I owe it to Alex to do the same. You know, I still love him, Penny."

"Oh, uh . . . maybe wait for me to finish this post? Then I'm all ears. You need my full attention for a decision like that!"

Elliot frowns at me, but then nods. I don't want to be dismissive of his feelings but the last thing I want to do is ruin Alex's surprise. It warms my heart to hear Elliot say these things and gives me a good feeling for tonight.

"Why don't you read it to me?" Elliot says, putting his phone facedown on the table.

I nod. "OK, here we go . . ."

23 July

A Whole New Start

Hello, World!

I feel like I'm writing to a long-lost friend, one who's been missing from my life for far too long.

To be honest, I feel a little apprehensive about typing this, but here goes.

For a while now, I've been blogging as **Girl Offline . . . never going online**. I've still been writing and posting here, even though I knew full well that nobody (except a handful of people) would be able to read the things I had to say.

I felt like I'd lost my voice, and this blog wasn't a happy place for me anymore.

I'm going to change that now. I've decided that, from today onwards, there is no more offline. It's a big decision for me to make, and a lot of things have had to change in my life for me to realize this isn't just something I *want* to do; it's something I *need* to do.

One of the last posts you may have read from me told you to make the right choices when posting online, to focus on being nice and spreading positivity.

So, this time, I want to start off by talking about not letting negativity into your life.

We all have one life, and we can choose how we want to live it. It's important to realize that, no matter what anyone else says or how people may try to influence the way you do things, it's ultimately down to you. Whether that's a bully, an online troll, an authority figure, a parent, a friend or a partner that you feel is oppressing you, only YOU can live for you. You can't live in someone else's shadow, or permanently try to please someone else, because then what do you have to show for it? You won't have any of your own accomplishments, you won't reach your personal goals, and you'll only be ticking someone else's boxes for them. If there is something in life you really want to do, then do it. You'll only ever live this day once in your lifetime, so start now.

Sometimes the hero of the fairy tale isn't a handsome prince. Sometimes it's you.

Girl Online . . . going offline xxx

As Elliot bursts into a round of applause, I hit publish. It feels so strange but so amazing to be making my blog posts live again.

I refresh the page a few times to watch the comments come in. One of the first ones is from Pegasus Girl.

HIGH-FIVE AND ALL THE HUGS AND EXCITED DANCES xxx

And that's when I know that *Girl Online* is officially back.

✶ ✶ Chapter Fifty-Seven ✶ ✶

Before I know it, it's time to take Elliot to the bandstand. I have butterflies in my stomach and I'm so excited for Elliot to see Alex, but I'm nervous for Alex as well. Sure enough, I look down and notice that Alex has texted me.

> Ready when you are :) I'M SO NERVOUS, PENNY. WHAT IF THIS ALL GOES HORRIBLY WRONG? A x

I quickly text back.

> Alex, he is pining for you right now. This won't go wrong. P x

I almost immediately get a reply from what I can only imagine is the most nervous and fidgety Alex ever.

OH DEAR GOD, THE PRESSURE.
See you soon x

I pop my phone back into my bag before Elliot can ask who I'm texting, then go to stand up.

"C'mon, Elliot. I have a surprise for you." I grab him by the hand as he looks at me in horror.

"Oh god, no, Penny. I'm not playing that stupid game in the park again where you made me pretend to forage for nuts like a squirrel. That was a one-off."

He takes his hand out of mine and glares at me as I laugh out loud. The vivid memory of Elliot scrambling around under an oak tree with his hands up by his mouth and chattering his teeth is just hilarious.

"No, silly. Follow me."

I drag Elliot up from the table and refuse to answer any of his questions, much to his frustration.

We walk down towards the sea, our arms linked. It's quiet, and the crash of the waves and the squawk of the seagulls fill our ears as we stroll along the promenade. It's such a beautiful evening and already delicate strands of pink and purple are staining the sky. It's going to be a stunning sunset, and I'm so glad that it's all working out exactly to plan for Alex.

Elliot leans his head on my shoulder as we walk. "I used to

do this with Alex in the evening. Just stroll along, listening to the sea. It was the only time he wasn't worried about us being seen together. It was our favourite thing to do. It felt all secret and romantic."

We pause for a moment and lean on the railings. Elliot picks at a bit of white paint that is crumbling off and stares out at the sea with sad eyes. I've never seen him look so upset, and a tear rolls down his cheek. "Do you think I've messed it all up, Penny? Do you think I'll never get to see him . . . or kiss him . . . or touch him ever again?"

I give his arm a squeeze. "Don't worry, Els. Everything will work out in the end."

"But how do you know?"

"I just have a feeling about these things," I say. "Come on, you can't show up to your surprise looking all puffy-eyed." I pass him a tissue, then pull him into a giant hug.

"Thanks, Penny." He wipes his eyes and sniffs dramatically. "OK, onwards! Where is this surprise of yours?"

"Just a little bit further," I say.

"You're being so mysterious, Princess P! I like it. Hey, what's going on at the bandstand?"

I look up, and my jaw drops: the bandstand looks incredible. Alex has clearly been hard at work, decking it out with fairy lights on the outside.

"I don't know," I say, feigning ignorance. "Maybe someone is having a wedding?"

"Wow, I've never seen it look like that before. You should take a picture!"

I oblige, taking out my camera and snapping away. The sun is going down, and the warm light is making the beautiful cast-iron structure and its copper roof glow. It looks amazing—especially with the ruins of the old West Pier in the background.

"Did you know that the bandstand opened in 1884?" Elliot says.

"I had no idea it was that old!" I exclaim.

"Yep, but it was restored a few years ago to its original condition. I think it would be the most romantic place to get married, don't you?"

"Why don't we go take a closer look?"

"Ooh, can we?" Elliot's face lights up. "It won't make us late for this surprise?"

I grin. "I don't think so," I say.

When we get closer to the bandstand, I can see that Alex has decorated all along the gangway that we need to cross to reach the bandstand itself, where a heavy velvet curtain is draped over the entrance. I assume Alex is hiding behind it.

There's a sign hanging on the front that says: CLOSED FOR A PRIVATE PARTY.

"Oh, that's a shame," says Elliot.

I nudge him in the ribs. "Maybe look a little closer?"

Right underneath the sign is the picture I took of Alex and Elliot at The Sketch's concert, blown up for everyone to see.

"What . . . what is this?" Elliot says, backing up a few paces.

His face is white as a sheet, and he looks on edge—like he is about to bolt. And suddenly I worry that everything is about to go terribly wrong.

Chapter Fifty-Eight

"Is this a joke?" Elliot asks.

I shake my head. "I think you need to go in." I smile at him and point to a chalkboard sign that reads: ELLIOT, FOLLOW ME.

He swallows, searching my face for any sign that this is fake, then takes a slow step forward. I hang back, letting him experience it for himself, but he reaches out and grabs my hand, pulling me along with him. There is a beautiful spiral path made from rose petals set out on the floor of the narrow gangway. Around the path and hanging from the railings are lots of Alexiot memories: photos of Elliot that I've never seen before, ticket stubs from the movies and gigs they've been to together, even the label from the first scarf that Elliot bought Alex as a present.

Elliot delicately treads the path, reading little notes and laughing at photos that Alex had secretly taken of him. There is one where Elliot must have fallen asleep in Alex's car, his mouth wide open. Alex has taken a selfie with Elliot behind him, giving a thumbs-up. Elliot smiles and chuckles at all the memories, and already I can see new tears in his eyes—but they're tears of happiness this time, not sadness.

It seems to take forever but we finally reach the velvet curtain covering the entrance to the bandstand itself. I stand up on my tiptoes and kiss Elliot on the cheek, then I nudge him to go through. He lets go of my hand, takes a deep breath, and steps beneath the curtain.

Standing at the back of the bandstand, silhouetted by the setting sun, is Alex—looking extremely dapper in a smart suit. There are lanterns and tea lights hanging from the ornate iron curlicues decorating the edge of the roof, and the ceiling itself is filled with white fairy lights. Paper pom-poms and bunting stretch between the pillars. It really is like something from a movie. This is definitely the most romantic thing I've ever witnessed and I'm not even the slightest bit bitter that it isn't for me. It's taking all that I have not to dissolve into a puddle of happy tears.

Elliot steps forward until he is face-to-face with Alex. Alex takes up both his hands and looks at him with big, wide eyes.

"Elliot Wentworth. I can never take back the hurt I caused you, but I want to do everything I can to try to make us right again."

Elliot looks at Alex's lips and then back up to his eyes, and I feel electricity spark between them. I'm grateful that this structure is iron, not wood—the chemistry between them is so intense it feels like it could set the bandstand on fire.

"I'm speechless, Alex. Nobody has ever done *anything* like this for me before." Elliot looks as though he might burst into tears or self-combust into a cloud of confetti with sheer happiness.

"Will you dance with me?" Alex extends his arm and Elliot places his hand in Alex's.

I hear the first few guitar chords of "Elements" start to play, but I'm confused. I haven't seen Alex hit a play button, and I can't see where the music is coming from. Then I hear footsteps coming down the gangway and my heart leaps into my throat. The curtain twitches, and Noah steps through.

His hair is scraped back off his face, but it is still slightly curly. His ripped jeans have been replaced with suit trousers and he is wearing a tight white shirt with the sleeves rolled up, emphasizing his muscular body underneath. All this and—of course—he has his beautiful guitar, on which he is playing "Elements." My stomach flips as he shoots a little sideways smile at me.

He starts singing Alexiot's song, his husky, soft voice layering beautifully over the chords on his guitar. Elliot and Alex dance together as the sun disappears beneath the horizon. The lights look even twinklier now it's dark, and I watch with tears in my eyes. This really is something from a dream—I can only imagine how Elliot must be feeling right now.

Noah is here.

I can't quite believe it.

After Noah has finished singing, Alex, Elliot, and I clap furiously. But then Elliot steps away from Alex, just far enough that I worry he's going to say that he's still not going to take him back. I can't bear to watch if Elliot is not going to forgive Alex.

"Alex, this is amazing . . . but I still don't know if I can be with you. Not if it's like before."

"It's not going to be like before, Elliot. I promise."

"How can I know?"

"Come with me," Alex says. "There's one more *element* to this surprise."

"There's more? Holy jeepers, Alex—this is too much."

"No, Elliot," Alex says. "It's hopefully just enough."

He leads Elliot over to the edge of the bandstand. Then he raises his voice and says loudly, "Ready? Three . . . two . . . one!"

Chapter Fifty-Nine

On cue, people start to pour out of the bandstand café and onto the beach below us. They look up at Alex, Elliot, Noah, and me standing up on the bandstand's main stage and they all begin to shout and cheer, big smiles on their faces. Immediately I spot Alex's parents along with Elliot's and mine.

Noah pulls out a microphone, seemingly from nowhere, and plays one of his more upbeat songs. Everyone down on the beach starts dancing. Alex turns to Elliot and says, "I want to show the world that you're mine. But, until it can be the world, how about just our friends and family?"

Elliot throws his arms round Alex's neck and they kiss, to the raucous applause of everyone down below on the beach. I try to clap the loudest, adding in an extra-loud wolf whistle for good luck.

After Noah finishes his live set, music comes on over a sound system, and Alex and Elliot walk hand in hand down the gangway to join the revellers on the beach.

I linger behind, watching as Noah puts his guitar away. He keeps on smiling up at me, and each time he does I feel the butterflies in my stomach take over. Those dimples get me every time.

"Hey, Penny. You don't mind that I texted Alex to ask if I could join the surprise, do you?" he asks.

I shake my head, unable to trust myself to speak.

"Good. I wanted to do something special for him and Elliot. And I thought it might give us a chance to talk again. Is that OK?"

I nod. He places his hand on my lower back and guides me down towards the beach without saying another word. I'm suddenly very aware of the fact that I am wearing a crop top as his hand caresses the skin on my back. When we reach the end of the gangway, I catch sight of Larry, who is leaning up against the metal railings that separate the promenade from the beach.

"Hi, Larry!" I say. I walk over to him and give him a big hug. He has a tear in his eye.

"Oh, Penny, it's good to see you. I'm sorry for the tears— I'm just such a sucker for a happy ending." He wipes his cheeks and gestures over to Elliot and Alex. "I hope you get one too," he adds, winking.

"Thank you," I say with a small smile.

Noah patiently waits for me to return, then we move away from the party. He offers his hand to help me down a steep slope of stones. The beach is blissfully empty and the warm glow of the sun lingers even as the moon is rising in the sky. I turn and look at Noah. His eyes are dark but so inviting and he has a bit of stubble along his chiselled jaw. I look over my shoulder at Alex and Elliot's party and spot them with their arms wrapped round each other. They look so happy.

Noah and I sit down on the beach, settling in among the pebbles. Noah reaches up and brushes a loose curl off my face, his fingertips lingering on my cheek.

"I want to stay here with you, Penny. I want this. I want us." He places his hand down on the warm stones and I put my hand on top of his. We sit in silence as I breathe in the fresh sea air and the seagulls dive and swoop above us. We sit and watch, hand on top of hand, as the waves roll in. It reminds me so much of the beginning of the year, when he turned up and surprised me with Princess Autumn on the beach. It's funny how things come full circle.

My heart drops as reality hits. "You can't stay here—I can't let you give up on your dream. You're doing what you've always wanted to do. What you were born to do." I look at him now and he's looking back at me, biting his lip.

"And I can't ask you to give up your life for me either," he says with a sigh. "I don't want to have to drag you along with me. It's not fair. You have your own life to live. Imagine all the things you'd be doing if you'd never met me."

I feel a sense of sadness roll over me like the waves. If I'd never met Noah, we wouldn't be sitting here now. I wouldn't have all these exciting memories, and my anxiety would be so much worse. Noah has helped me to come to terms with myself, and everything I've experienced with him has contributed to the way I live my life in this very moment.

"You're so talented, Penny, and one of the things I love about you is that you are so brave. Sure, you have your clumsy moments, but I love those too." He chuckles, and I join in. There's no tension between us, and everything feels relaxed and easygoing—just like when we first met.

"What do we do, then?" I say, with slight hesitation. Normally I'd be scared of Noah's answer. Is he going to tell me we'll never see each other again? Is this the last moment we'll share together? But something inside me feels like it's the right thing to ask. We can't carry on the way we are, constantly battling to make our lives head in the same direction.

"I don't know. All I know is that I just want to stay in this very moment, with you."

"Me too."

Noah picks up my hand and kisses my fingers lightly, then clutches them in both his hands as he looks back out over the sea.

"You'll always be my Inciting Incident," I say, as he grips my hand tighter in his.

"I guess now it's kinda like the end of the film . . . but it's not the closing credits. I told you before, Penny. You're my forever girl. I mean that." Tears are building up in his eyes as he smiles at me. Then he pulls me into a hug. We hold each other, eyes shut, listening to the sounds of the waves and the faint cheers rising from Alex and Elliot's party in the background.

I can feel his heart beating on my chest as his finger traces an ant line on my back and I let myself melt into him. As we break apart, we both smile at each other and turn back to watch the sea crashing on the stones. I feel a lump in my throat as a wave of understanding and serenity crashes over me.

Two tears escape down my face. I wipe them away and sigh as Noah stands up and extends his hand to me to help me. Our moment is over.

I put my hand in his and they fit together perfectly, like a jigsaw. As he lifts me to my feet, I feel my heart lift at the same time.

Our eyes connect as I take a step towards him, the decision made in my mind. It might be the end of this chapter. But, for us, our story is only just beginning.

⋆⭒ *Acknowledgments* ⋆⭒

After the success of my first novel, starting on book two was a daunting prospect—especially with so many of you eagerly awaiting the return of Penny and Noah. I wouldn't have been able to do it without my editor and now friend, Amy Alward. Our "Writing Wednesdays" were filled with plenty of snacks, reams of notes, the constant sound of tapping at the keyboard, and lots of laughter. Amy has helped me grow as an author but also as a person; she encouraged my crazy ideas and always knew the right things to say when things got a bit hard. Wednesdays just won't be the same from now on!

To the rest of the amazing team at Penguin who have helped bring the *Girl Online* books to life: thank you to Shannon Cullen, Laura Squire, Kimberley Davis, and Wendy Shakespeare for their editorial support; Tania Vian-Smith, Gemma Rostill, Clare Kelly, and Natasha Collie for their amazing marketing and publicity skills; Zosia Knopp and the rights team for getting *Girl Online* translated into so many different languages around the world; and the entire sales team for their continued belief and enthusiasm.

My managers, Dom Smales and Maddie Chester, are two of my biggest cheerleaders. (I'll give you a moment to imagine Dom in a tiny skirt with pom-poms.) Their continued support and endless encouragement meant I was able to stay focused. Thank you, Maddie, for being a constant positive influence and a best friend. I'm very happy that you are by my side, giving my hand an excited squeeze when all these crazy things happen.

Thanks to my amazing family for always being my biggest supporters, especially Mum and Dad for constantly allowing me to do whatever my heart desires and being by my side through both success and failure. Knowing you are always proud of me means I don't fear any outcome. Joe, thank you for always being that one person that brings out the absolute best in me, and for challenging me to push harder when I feel like I can't. My Brighton family, Nick, Amanda, Poppy, and Sean, thank you for your continued support, constant stream of laughter, and always being there for me with open arms.

My amazing friends who inspire and encourage me with their creativity and share in my excitement. There is nothing more heartwarming than a group of people who are supportive of everything you do. Thank you for the laughter and the hugs.

Lastly, to my boyfriend, Alfie, for being a calming influence and keeping my head above water. I would not be able to function half as well without you. I'm very happy that I get to share this whirlwind life with you (even though you fell asleep when I read you the first chapter).

Zoe Sugg

ON TOUR

Zoe Sugg, aka Zoella, is a vlogger from Brighton, UK. Her beauty, fashion, and lifestyle vlogs have gained her millions of YouTube subscribers, with even more viewing the vlogs every month. She won the 2011 Cosmopolitan Blog Award for Best Established Beauty Blog and went on to win the Best Beauty Vlogger Award the following year. Zoe has also twice received the Best British Vlogger Award at the 2013 and 2014 Radio 1 Teen Awards and the 2014 and 2015 Nickelodeon Kids' Choice Award for UK's Favourite Vlogger, and she was named Web Star for Fashion and Beauty at the 2014 Teen Choice Awards.